"No-holds-barred?"

"I've heard all about you, over the years. They say you're one of the brightest young hostesses in politics. I might have recognized you in one of those designer gowns you wear. Insiders say you're the brains and drive behind your brother. But you don't look so tough to me."

"Pneumonia will make the toughest of us mellow, just briefly," Nikki said, inclining her head. "So it's war, is it?"

"That's how I fight," Kane returned, ramming his hands deep into his pockets.

"Fair enough. But there's one condition. No mudslinging."

He lifted an eyebrow. "You know better."

She felt her face color with bad temper and her own hands clenched together. "No mudslinging about what we did together," she said, forcing the words out.

He wanted to hit her where it hurt most. She'd made a fool of him.

"We had a one-night stand," he said. "And I'm not running for public office. If I were, you might actually worry me."

Nikki had once been warned, "Men love in the darkness and are indifferent in the dawn." Now that phrase came back to her with vivid force....

"Diana Palmer is a mesmerizing storyteller who captures the essence of what a romance should be."

–Affaire de Coeur

Also available from MIRA Books and
DIANA PALMER

LAWLESS
DESPERADO
THE TEXAS RANGER
LORD OF THE DESERT
THE COWBOY AND THE LADY
MOST WANTED
FIT FOR A KING
PAPER ROSE
RAGE OF PASSION
ONCE IN PARIS
AFTER THE MUSIC
ROOMFUL OF ROSES
CHAMPAGNE GIRL
PASSION FLOWER
DIAMOND GIRL
FRIENDS AND LOVERS
CATTLEMAN'S CHOICE
LADY LOVE
THE RAWHIDE MAN

Watch for DIANA PALMER's newest novel
RENEGADE
Avalable in hardcover
August 2004
from HQN Books

DIANA PALMER

After Midnight

ISBN 1-55166-742-8

AFTER MIDNIGHT

Visit us at www.mirabooks.com

Printed in U.S.A.

After Midnight

Chapter One

Seabrook had been the Seymour family's vacation spot for twenty years. It was a beautiful small community island offering a marina, golf course, a private club and a welcome break from the hectic pace of the resorts.

This particular stretch of it was connected with some of the wealthiest Charleston families. Nicole Seymour didn't have a million dollars, but the Seymour name granted her entry into the wealthiest circles of society as only the oldest South Carolinian names could. This beach property had originally been purchased by her father on speculation. But when the planned community started taking shape in 1992, he held on to his acreage and built a cottage on it for family vacations. At his death, it had gone to Nicole and her brother, Republican

Congressman Clayton Myers Seymour, Representative of the First Congressional District of South Carolina.

The Seymours of Charleston were one of the most respected families in the state and it wasn't surprising that when Nikki's brother had first announced his candidacy for the House of Representatives seat from his district three years ago, he was immediately supported by the local Republican vanguard. He was elected without even a runoff in the general election two years ago, to Clayton's surprise and Nikki's delight.

Nikki's social standing made her the perfect hostess for Clayton. During his three years in Washington, D.C., her brother had done a good job. So had Nikki, helping to curry favor for him, because she had a knack for presenting unpopular points of view. She was in the process of organizing dinner parties and reelection fund-raising galas for Clayton. He'd just announced his candidacy for reelection, and it promised to be a tough race. Clayton not only had Republican opposition from his own party, but the field of Democratic candidates included Sam Hewett, a well-known and liked businessman who had a virtual empire behind him, not to mention the clout of a very dangerous tabloid paper out of New York. In fact, Sam's campaign administrative assistant was one of the sons of the tabloid owner.

Nikki had just put the finishing touches on the organization of another gala for Clayton in Washington, D.C., in September, after the general primary election. She hoped with all her heart that it would also serve as a celebration of Clayton's hoped-for victory in the primary. Those preparations, coupled with her participation in the world-famous Spoleto Festival in Charleston had exhausted her. She was weak from a bout of pneumonia that she'd just recovered from. Now that the festival was almost over, Nikki was recuperating at the family retreat. Clayton wouldn't need her for a few days and she relished the peace and quiet of the beach house. This particular section of the island was fairly isolated, dotted with only a few houses, most of which were very old and belonged to families with old money. The two surrounding the Seymour cottage were owned by families from other areas of the state, and were usually unoccupied until late June.

She stretched as the sun beat down on the deck where she was comfortably sprawled on a padded lounger. She was tall and slender, perfectly proportioned. Her body was as sensual as her slanted pure green eyes and the bow curve of her pretty mouth. She sparkled when she was happy, an enchanted columnist had said by way of description—and despite her height, she had the mischievous disposition of a pixie. With her thick black hair cut in a wedge around her soft oval face, she even had the look of one. But behind the beauty was a quick mind and an impeccable reputation. If others thought her a bit too wary and cautious, Nikki knew these qualities had helped thwart political enemies when they laid traps for her brother.

Her small breasts lifted and fell slowly as she lay breathing in the delicious sea air. It was early June, and unseasonably cool. A lot of renovation had been done since Hurricane Hugo passed through Charleston and the coastal areas in September of 1989, and Nikki and Clayton's beach house had been one of the ones damaged by high winds. Although they had made the most necessary repairs, many decorative accents had yet to be restored. Unlike many of their neighbors, the Seymours didn't have unlimited funds from which to renovate. Nikki and Clayton were working on a five-year plan to restore the beach house to its former glory.

The sound of a float-plane caught her attention. She shaded her eyes and watched its silvery glitter as it landed not far from her house. This area had no shortage of tycoons. In fact, Kane Lombard had recently bought the old Settles place a few houses down the beach from Nikki and Clayton's, not far from where the plane had landed. Lombard was a Houston oilman who headed a conglomerate which included Charleston's newest automobile manufacturing company. Nikki had heard that personal tragedy seemed to follow the man, culminating months ago in the violent death of his wife and son in Lebanon during a business trip.

Three weeks ago, he'd moved into the beach house property and his yacht had a slip at the marina. Nikki had seen a photograph of it in the Charleston paper's society section.

Nikki had never met him, and there were no full-face or close-up photos of him in newspapers, except for one that Nikki had seen in *Forbes Magazine.* Even the tabloids couldn't catch him on film. Of course, his family did own one of the biggest tabloids in the country. The Lombards of Houston, like the Seymours of Charleston, came from old money. The difference was, the Lombards still had their money. They lived in New York now, not Texas, where they maintained their exclusive tabloid.

The sound of the plane faded and Nikki stretched again. She felt restless. She knew all the right people and she had a comfortable income from the sculptures she did for local galleries. But she was empty inside. Sometimes it bothered her that she was so completely alone except for her brother.

She had been married, briefly; a marriage that destroyed all her illusions and made her question her own sexuality. Her father needed a favor from a U.S. senator by the name of Mosby Torrance, a South Carolinian. Mosby had been under siege because of, among other things, his long-standing bachelor standing. Mosby had agreed to the favor, which would save Nikki's father from certain bankruptcy, but only in return for Nikki's hand in marriage.

Nikki shivered, remembering her delight. Mosby was fourteen years her senior, an Adonis of a man, with blond hair and blue eyes and a trim, athletic figure. She'd been swept off her feet, and nothing would have stopped her from agreeing to the union. She'd only been eighteen years old. Naive. Innocent. Stupid.

Her father might have suspected, but he never really knew about Mosby until it was much too late. Nikki had emerged from the marriage six months later, so shaken that the divorce was final before she was completely rational again.

She never could admit what she'd endured to her father or brother, but afterward, Clayton was especially kind to her. They grew very close, and when their father died, she and her brother continued to share the huge Charleston house near the Battery. As he entered politics, Nikki was his greatest support. She learned to organize, to be a hostess, to charm and coax money from prospective supporters. She did whatever Clayton needed her to do to help him, both at his Charleston office and in Washington, D.C., where she had gained some repute as a hostess. She always created just the right mix of people at banquets and cocktail parties, with motifs and themes that radiated excitement and interest. She was very successful at her endeavors. But the old fears and lack of self-confidence kept her free of relationships of any sort. She couldn't trust her judgment ever again. She could live without a man in her life, she'd decided. But she was twenty-five and lonely. So lonely.

The sun was getting too warm. She stood up and slipped a silky blue caftan over her green-and-gold bathing suit, loving the feel of it against her soft, tanned skin. A movement on the beach caught her eye and she went to the railing to look out over the ocean. Something black was there, bobbing, in the surf. She frowned and leaned over to get a better look, shading her eyes from the sunlight. A head! It was a person!

Without even thinking, she darted down the steps and ran across the beach, stumbling as the thick sand made her path unwieldy. Her heart raced madly as she began to think of the possibilities. Suppose it was a body washing up on the beach? What if she found herself in the wake of a murder? Or worse, what if it were a drowning victim? She had no lifesaving training, a stupid thing to admit to when she had a holiday home on the beach! She made a mental note even in her panic to sign up for lifesaving courses at the Red Cross.

As she reached the surf, she realized that the body in the water was a man's. It was muscular and husky and very tall-looking with darkly tanned skin and dark hair. She knelt quickly beside it and felt for a pulse. She found it. Her breath sighed out and she realized only then that she'd been holding it.

She managed to roll the man over onto his belly, just out of the surf. Turning his face to one side, she began to push in the center of his back, a maneuver she'd seen on one of the real-life rescue series on TV. The man began to cough and retch, and she kept pumping. Seconds later, he jerked away from her and sat up, holding his forehead. He was a big man for all his leanness. Thank God, she wasn't going to have to try and drag him any farther out of the surf!

"Are you all right?" she asked worriedly.

"My head...hurts," he choked, still coughing.

She hesitated for a second before she began to look through his thick wet hair. She found a gash just above his temple. The blood had congealed and it didn't look very deep, but he'd been unconscious.

"I think I'd better call an ambulance," she began. "You could have a concussion."

"I don't need an ambulance," he said firmly.

He coughed again. "I fell off a Jet Ski and hit my head. I remember that." He scowled. "Funny. I can't remember anything else!"

Nikki sat very still. The hem of her caftan was soaked from the rising surf. She gnawed on her lower lip, a habit from childhood, while she struggled with the question of what to do next.

"Would you like to come up to my beach house and rest for a bit?" she asked in her softly accented voice.

He lifted his head and looked at her, and she felt a shock all the way through her. He seemed very familiar. She couldn't quite place him, but he looked like someone she knew. Could she have met him at the Spoleto Festival?

"I must be visiting someone around here," he began slowly. "I couldn't have come far."

"You're disoriented," she said. "When you've rested, perhaps you'll remember who you are. I believe amnesia of this kind is very temporary."

"Are you a nurse?"

Her eyebrows lifted. "Why not a doctor?" she asked.

"Why not a nurse?" he asked, his eyes and his tone challenging.

She threw up her hands. "You're going to be one of those sharp, difficult people, I can tell. Here, let's see if we can get you underway. Oh, for a wheelbarrow...'' She eyed him. ''Make that a front-end loader.''

''If you're trying out for stand-up comedy,'' he murmured, ''don't give up your day job.''

His deep voice was unaccented. If anything it sounded midwestern. He was wearing a waterproof Rolex watch and the swimming trunks he had on were designer marked. He was no transient. And he was much too old to be a college student on summer vacation, she thought wickedly as she noted the streaks of gray at his temples. He had to be almost forty. Certainly he was older than her brother.

She felt uncomfortable with the close physical contact that was necessary now, but she forced herself to yield to the situation. He couldn't very well stay down here on the beach all day.

She eased under his arm and slid her hand around his back. His skin was olive tan and silky, rippling with muscle. He was fit for a man of his age, she thought, her eyes dropping involuntarily to the broad chest with an incredibly thick mass of curling black hair that ran in a wedge from his collarbone all the way down into the low-slung swimming trunks around his lean hips. Most men, since her marriage, repelled Nikki. This man, strangely, didn't. She already felt comfortable with him, as if the sight of his almost nude body was familiar to her.

Of course, he had the kind of body that even a disinterested woman couldn't help but admire right down to long, tanned, powerful legs with just enough hair to be masculine and not offensive. She drew his arm over her shoulder, holding it by the hand. He had nice hands, too, she thought. Very lean and big, with oval nails immaculately kept. No jewelry at all. She wondered if that was deliberate. Where his watch had shifted, there was no white line, so his tan must be of the year-round variety.

"Easy does it," she said gently. The feel of all the muscle so close was really disturbing. She hadn't been so close to a man since her tragic marriage. He attracted her and she immediately forced her mind to stop thinking in that direction. He needed her. That was all she must consider now.

"I can walk by myself," he said gruffly, and then stumbled as he tried to prove it.

Nikki managed not to smile. "One step at a time," she repeated. "You're injured, that's all. It's bound to affect your balance."

"Are you sure you first name isn't Florence?" he muttered. "Maybe it's Polyanna."

"You're very offensive for a man the ocean spit out," she remarked. "Obviously you left a bad taste in its mouth."

He didn't smile, but his chest tightened a little.

Nikki guessed he was repressing a laugh. "Maybe so."

"Do you feel sleepy or nauseous?" she persisted.

"No. Dizzy, though."

She nodded, her mind running quickly through possibilities. She needed to get a look at his eyes to tell if the pupils were equal or overly dilated, but that could wait.

"Are you a nurse?" he asked again.

"Not really. I've had some first-aid training, and," she added with a mischievous glance upward, "a little experience with beached whales. Speaking of which..."

"Stop right there while you're ahead," he advised. "God, what a headache!" His big hand went to his head and he groaned.

Nikki was getting more nervous by the minute. Head injuries could be quickly fatal. She didn't have the expertise to deal with something this serious, and she had no telephone. What if he died?

He glanced sideways and saw the troubled look on her face. He glowered even more. "I'm not going to drop dead on the beach," he said irritably. "Are you always this transparent?"

"In fact, I've been told I have a poker face," she said without thinking. She looked up into his dark eyes and found herself staring into them with something approaching recognition. How frightening, she thought dimly, to be like that with a stranger, and especially such an unfriendly one!

"You have green eyes, 'Florence Nightingale,'" he said. "Green like a cat's."

"I scratch like one, too, so watch out," she murmured with far more bravado than courage.

"Point taken." He eased the pressure of his arm around her and went the last few steps up to the deck under his own power. He stopped, holding his head and breathing deliberately, for a few seconds.

"I could do with a cup of coffee," he said after a minute.

"So could I." She eased him through the sliding glass doors and into the kitchen, watching him lower his huge frame into a chair at the kitchen table. "Are you going to be all right?"

"I'm sure that I'm tough as nails normally." He rested his elbows on the clean surface of the oak table and held his head in his hands. "Do you often find strange men washed up on your beach?"

"You're my first," she replied. "But considering the size of you, I'm hoping for an ocean liner tomorrow."

He lifted an eyebrow at her as she busied herself filling the drip coffeemaker.

"Have you lived here long?" he asked, making conversation.

"We've had the place a few years."

"We?"

"The, um...man who lives here and I," she replied noncommittally. It wouldn't do to tell him she was single and on her own. "He normally drives down on Friday evenings," she lied.

He didn't seem to register the information. Perhaps he didn't know what day it was.

"Today is Friday," she said, just in case. "My friend is very nice, you'll like him." She glanced over her shoulder at him. "Any nausea yet? Drowsiness?"

"I haven't got concussion," he replied tersely. "I'm not sure how I know that I'd recognize the symptoms. Perhaps I've had it before."

"Perhaps you haven't." She picked up the telephone and dialed.

"What are you doing?" he asked curtly.

"Phoning a friend. He's a doctor. I want to... Hello, Chad?" she said when the person answered. "I've just rescued a swimmer who was suffering from a bang on the head. He's conscious and very lucid," she added with a meaningful glare at her houseguest. "But he won't let me call an ambulance. Could you stop by here when you get back from the golf course and just reassure me that he isn't going to drop dead on my floor."

Chad Holman laughed. "Sure. No sweat. Let me ask you a couple of questions."

He did and she fielded them to her guest, who replied reluctantly.

"I think he'll do until I get there," Chad reassured her. "But if he drops off and you can't wake him or if he has any violent vomiting, call the ambulance anyway."

"Will do. Thanks."

"Any time."

She hung up, feeling relieved now that she had a professional opinion on her guest's condition. "Well, I don't want any dead bodies in my living room, especially not one I can't even drag!" she informed him mischievously.

He scowled at her. "Dead bodies. Dead..." He shook his head irritably. "I keep getting flashes, but I can't grasp anything! Damn it!"

"The coffee's almost ready. Maybe a jolt of caffeine will start your brain working again," she suggested.

She perched on a stool at the counter, her long bare legs drawing his eyes. She glared at him.

"Don't get any ideas about why you're here, if you please," she said, her voice soft but vaguely menacing just the same.

"Don't worry. I'm absolutely sure that I don't like green-eyed women," he returned shortly. He sat back in the chair with a rough sigh and shifted, one big hand idly rubbing the thick hair on his chest. He made her very self-conscious and nervous. He looked aggressively masculine, whether he was or not. She fidgeted.

"I can find you something to put on, if you like," she said after a minute.

"That would be nice. Your male friend leaves things here, I suppose? To remind you that you cohabit with him?"

She didn't like the sarcasm, but she didn't rise to it. She slipped easily off the stool. "The shirt may be a bit tight, but he's got some baggy shorts with an elastic waist that probably will fit you. I won't be a minute."

She darted into Clayton's bedroom and borrowed the biggest oversize shirt he owned, a three-colored one, and a pair of big tan shorts. They hung on her brother, but they were probably going to be a tight fit on the giant she'd found washed up on the beach.

She carried the clothes back in to him. "The bathroom is through there," she said, nodding down the hall. "Third door on the right. You'll find a razor and soap and towels if you'd like to clean up. Are you hungry?"

"I think I could eat," he said.

"I'll make an omelet and toast."

He got to his feet very slowly, the clothes in one large hand. He hesitated as he turned to leave the room, looking very big and threatening to Nikki.

"I don't remember anything. But I'm not a cruel man, if it helps. I do know that."

"It helps." She managed a smile.

"I'm not used to accepting help from strangers," he added.

"Good thing. I'm not used to offering it to strangers. Of course, there's a first time..."

"...for everything," he finished for her. "Thanks."

He left the room and Nikki got out eggs and condiments, proceeding to make an omelet.

He showered and shaved before he changed into the dry clothes and joined her in the kitchen. He was still barefoot, but the shorts did fit. The shirt showed off muscles that had obviously not been obtained by any lengthy inactivity. He was fit and rippled, very athletic. Nikki had to remind herself not to look at him too hard.

"What do you like in your coffee?" she asked as she poured it into thick white mugs and set them on the spotless green-and-white checked tablecloth.

He frowned as he sat down. "I think I like cream."

"I'd have thought you were a man who never added anything to his coffee," she murmured with amusement.

"Why?"

"I don't know. You seem oddly familiar to me,

as if I know you. But I don't believe that I've ever seen you before,'' she said quietly.

He shrugged. ''Maybe I have that kind of face.''

Her eyebrows arched. ''You?''

He smiled, just faintly. ''Thanks.'' He sipped his coffee and pursed his lips. ''Very nice. Just strong enough.''

''I make good coffee. It's my only real accomplishment, except for omelets. I'm much too busy to learn how to cook.''

''What does your poor friend eat?'' he asked.

''He lives on fast food and restaurant chow, but he isn't home much.''

''What does he do?''

She studied him. ''He's in energy,'' she said, which was the truth. He sat on the Energy and Commerce Committee that dealt with it.

''Oh. He works for a power plant?''

''That's pretty close,'' she agreed, hiding the amusement in her eyes as she thought about the power that particular committee wielded nationally.

''And what do you do?''

''Moi?'' she laughed. ''Oh, I sculpt.''

''What?''

''People.''

He looked around at the furniture, but the only artwork of any kind that was visible were some prints she'd purchased.

"I sell my work in galleries," she told him.

He decided to reserve judgment on that reply. The house was a dump, and she had to know it. She obviously had little money and lived with a man who had even less. He knew that he couldn't afford to trust her. He wished he knew why he was certain of that. "Do you have any of your work here?"

"A bust or two," she said. "I'll show you later, if you like."

He sampled the omelet. "You're good."

"Thanks." She studied his face. It was pale, and he seemed to be having a hard time keeping his eyes open. "You're drowsy."

"Yes. I don't know how I know it, but I'm pretty sure that I haven't been sleeping well lately."

"Woman trouble?" she asked with a knowing smile.

He frowned. "I'm not sure. Perhaps." He looked up. "I can't possibly stay here..."

"Where would you go?" she asked reasonably. "You can't wander up and down the beach here, the police will pick you up for vagrancy. Do you remember where you live?"

"I don't even know my name," he confessed heavily. "You can't imagine how intimidating that is."

"You're right." She searched his tanned face,

his dark eyes. He looked incredibly tired. "Why don't you have an early night? I'll send Chad in to check you out when he swings by. He's a friend," she added. "He'll do it as a favor, so you don't have to worry about his fee. Things will look so much better in the morning. You might remember who you are."

"God, I hope so," he said gruffly. "The man…who lives here. You said he'd be here later?"

She nodded, her eyes as steady as if she'd been telling the truth, and he was fooled.

"Then it will be all right, I suppose. I appreciate your trust. I could be anybody."

"So could I," she said in a menacing tone, grinning.

He got the point. When she showed him to the guest bedroom, he fell on the bed without bothering to turn back the covers. Within seconds, he was sound asleep.

He was still sleeping when Chad stopped by to check him. Nikki waited in the living room until the doctor came out, bag in hand, gently closing the door.

"He's all right," he assured her with a grin, his blond good looks fairly intimidating to her because he still reminded her a little of her ex-husband. "A little disorientation, but that will pass quickly. There's been no real damage. By morning he should remember his name and after he gets past the very terrible headache he's going to have, he should be all right. I'm leaving some tablets for him when he wakes up groaning.'' He produced them from his bag and handed them to Nikki. ''Otherwise, you know what to look for. If you get in trouble all you have to do is call me. Okay?''

''Okay. Thanks, Chad.''

He shrugged. ''What are friends for?'' he asked with a big grin. He left, closing the door gently behind him.

Later, when Nikki went back to check on her houseguest, he was lying on his back, completely nude in the soft glow from the night-light on the wall.

Nikki stood and just stared at him helplessly, feeling her body tingle and burn with old familiar longings that she desperately tried to bank down. This man attracted her as even Mosby hadn't—in the beginning. She looked at the long, muscular lines of his tanned body with aching need.

He must sunbathe nude, she thought idly. He was magnificent. Even that part of him that was most male didn't offend or repel her. She was surprised at her own lack of inhibitions as she stared at him, feeling vaguely like a Peeping Tom. He did look vaguely familiar as well. That bothered her. Not as much, of course, as his body did in stark nudity.

Oddly, she found men revolting for the most part. This one was special. She loved the way his big body looked without clothes. She wondered how that hand, almost the size of a plate, would feel smoothing over her soft skin in the darkness.

The thought pulled her up short. She turned and went out of the bedroom, closing the door gently behind her.

Chapter Two

Nicole slept fitfully that night, haunted by images of her houseguest sprawled in magnificent abandon on the bed in the guest room. She woke up earlier than usual. She slipped into a neat blue patterned sundress before she went to the kitchen, barefoot, to make breakfast. It was a good thing that she had plenty of provisions, she thought. Judging by his size and build, the man in the guest room was a man with a more than ample appetite.

She'd just dished up scrambled eggs to go with the sweet rolls and sausages when the man came into the living room from Clayton's bedroom. He was wearing the shorts she'd found for him, an old pair that Clay had worn, with the shirt whose edges didn't quite meet in front. He looked out of sorts, and vaguely confused.

"Are you all right?" she asked immediately.

He glowered at her. "I feel like an overdrawn account. Otherwise, I suppose I'll do." He spoke without any particular accent, although there was a faint residual drawl there. His was not a Charleston accent, though, she mused; and she ought to know, because her own was fairly thick.

"I do have some aspirin, if you need them," she said.

"I could use a couple, thanks."

She went to get them while he sat down at the table and poured coffee into his cup and hers. He shook out a couple of aspirin tablets into his big hand and swallowed them with coffee.

"You've remembered, haven't you?" she persisted.

"I've remembered a few things," he confessed. "Not a lot." He felt for his watch and frowned. Hadn't he had one when he went into the water? A diver's watch?

"Oh, I almost forgot!" She jumped up and reached onto the counter by the stove, producing the missing wristwatch. "Here. This was still on your wrist and almost unfastened when I found you. I stuck it in my robe pocket and didn't notice it until this morning when I started to put the robe in the laundry. Good thing I didn't wash it," she laughed. "However do you tell time with something so complicated?"

She didn't recognize a diver's watch. Did that mean she didn't realize how expensive it was?

He took it from her. "Thanks," he said slowly.

"It still works, doesn't it?" she asked idly as she ate her eggs. "I didn't know they made waterproof watches."

"It's a diver's watch," he informed her, and then waited for her reaction.

"I see. Do you skin-dive?" she asked brightly.

He did, occasionally, when he wasn't sailing his yacht. He didn't want to mention that. "Sometimes," he said.

"I wanted to learn, but I'm too afraid of water," she told him. "I can't even swim properly."

"Then why have a beach house?" he asked curiously. "Or isn't it yours?"

She saw the way he was looking at her and interpreted it correctly. That watch wasn't cheap, and he'd apparently remembered more than he wanted her to know. So he thought she was a gold digger, did he? She was going to enjoy this.

"Well, no, it belongs to..." She stopped suddenly, not wanting to give too much away. His face was all too familiar, more so this morning. "It belongs to the man who owns this place. He lets me stay here when I like."

He glanced around and his expression spoke volumes.

"The hurricane got it," she said quickly. "He

hasn't had time to do many repairs.'' That, at least, was true. But it didn't sound that way to her guest. In fact, he looked even more suspicious.

He didn't say anything else. He concentrated on the meal Nikki had prepared. His dark eyes slid over her pretty face and narrowed.

''What's your name?'' he asked curiously.

''Nikki,'' she replied. Even if he knew of her family, he wouldn't know of the nickname, which was used only by family and very close friends. ''Do you remember yours?''

He studied her thoughtfully while he wavered between the truth and a lie. She was obviously a transient here, in her boyfriend's house. He was new to the area. It was highly unlikely that she'd even know who he was if he introduced himself honestly. He kept a low profile. In his income bracket, it paid to do that.

He laughed at his own caution. This woman probably didn't even know what the CEO of a corporation was. ''It's McKane,'' he said offhandedly. ''But I'm usually called Kane.''

Fortunately, Nikki had her eyes on her coffee cup. She didn't show it, but inside she panicked. The familiar face she couldn't place before now leaped into her consciousness vividly. She knew that name all too well, and now she remembered where she'd seen the face, in a business magazine of Clayton's. Kane Lombard was reclusive to the point of being a hermit, and the photograph of him had been a rarity for such a successful businessman.

Her brother had just had a very disturbing run-in with Kane Lombard over an environmental issue in Charleston. Lombard, she knew, was backing the leading Democratic contender for Clayton's House seat.

Her mind worked rapidly. She didn't dare let Lombard know who she was, now. They'd spent the night together, albeit innocently. Wouldn't that tidbit do Clayton a lot of good in a national election? In some parts of the country, especially this one, morality was still enough to make or break a politician; even his sister's morality. And Lombard was helping the opposition.

Her fingers closed around her coffee cup and she lifted her eyes with a schooled expression on her face. Everything would be all right. All she had to do was ease him out of here without letting on that she knew him. Since he didn't travel in the same circles as Clayton and herself, chances were good that she'd never see him up close again anyway.

"It's a nice name. I like it." She smiled as if she genuinely didn't recognize him.

He relaxed visibly. His firm mouth tugged into a smile. "Thanks for taking care of me," he added. "It's been a long time since anyone had to do that."

"Nobody's invulnerable," she reminded him. "But next time, you might check that there aren't any rocks around when you decide to use the Jet Ski."

"I'll do that."

He finished his coffee and reluctantly, she thought, got to his feet. "I'll return your friend's clothes. Thanks for the loan."

"I can run you home, if you like," she offered, knowing full well that he wouldn't risk letting her see where he lived. He thought she was an opportunist. She could have laughed out loud at the very idea.

"No, thanks," he said quickly, smiling to soften the rejection. "I need the exercise. You've been very kind." His eyes were shrewd. "I hope I can repay you one day."

"Oh, that's not necessary," she assured him as she stood. "Don't we all have a moral duty to help each other out when we're in need?" She looked at her slender, well-kept hands. "I'm sure you'd do the same for me."

That last bit was meant to rattle him, but it didn't work. She looked up, impishly, and he was just watching her with a lifted eyebrow and a faintly indulgent smile.

"Of course I would," he assured her. But he was wary again, looking for traps, even while his eyes were quietly bold on her soft curves.

"It was nice meeting you," she added.

"Same here." He gave her a last wistful appraisal and went with long, determined strides toward the front door. He walked as if he'd go right over anything in his path, and Nikki envied him that self-confidence. She had it, to a degree, but in a standing fight, he was going to be a hard man to beat. She'd have to remember and warn Clayton not to underestimate Lombard; and do it without revealing that the source of her information was the man himself.

The rambling beach house where Kane lived was in the same immaculate shape he'd left it. His housekeeper had been in, apparently unconcerned that he was missing. That shouldn't surprise him. Unless he paid people, no one seemed to notice if he lived or died.

He chided himself for that cynical thought. Women did agonize over him from time to time. He had a mistress who pretended to care in return for the expensive presents he gave her with careless affection. But no one cared as much as his son had. He closed his eyes and tried not to remember the horror of his last sight of the young boy.

There was a portrait of his son with his late wife on the side table. He looked at that, instead, remembering David as a bright young man with his mother's light hair and eyes and her smile. Although he and Evelyn had grown apart over their years together, David had been loved and cherished by both of them. See what you get for sticking your nose in where it doesn't belong, he thought. Just a routine business trip, you said, and they could go with you. Then all hell broke loose the day they arrived, and he and his family were caught innocently in the cross fire.

He'd blamed himself bitterly for all of it, but time was taking away some of the sting. He had to go on, after all.

The new automotive plant in an industrial Charleston suburb had certainly been a step in the right direction. Planned long before the death of his family, it had just begun operation about the time they were buried. Now it was the lynchpin of his sanity.

He changed into a knit shirt and shorts, idly placing his borrowed clothing to be washed before he returned it. Nikki's sparkling green eyes came to mind and made him smile. She was so young, he mused, and probably a madcap when she set her mind to it. For a moment he allowed himself to envy her lover. She had a pretty body, slender and winsome. But he had Chris when he needed a woman desperately, and there was no place for a permanent woman in his life. He made sure that Chris knew it, so that she wouldn't expect too much. Marriage was out.

He picked up the telephone and dialed the offices of the Charleston plant. What he needed, he told himself, was something to occupy his mind again.

"Get Will Jurkins on the line," he replied to his secretary's polite greeting.

"Yes, sir," she said at once.

A minute later, a slow voice came on the line. "How's the vacation going, Mr. Lombard?"

"So far, so good," Kane said carelessly. "I want to know why you've terminated that contract with the Coastal Waste Company?"

There was a pause. Jurkins should have realized that his superior would fax that information up to Kane Lombard. Sick or not, Ed Nelson was on the ball, as many plant managers were not. "Well... uh, I had to."

"Why?"

The word almost struck him. Jurkins wiped his sweaty brow, glancing around from his desk to the warehouse facility where dangerous materials were kept before they were picked up by waste disposal companies. It was considered less expensive to hire that done rather than provide trucks and men to do it. The city could handle toxic substances at its landfill, but Lombard International had contracted CWC to do it since its opening.

"I believe I mentioned to you, Mr. Lombard, that I noticed discrepancies in their invoices."

"I don't remember any such conversation."

Jurkins kept his head, barely. "Listen, Mr. Lombard," he began in a conciliatory tone, "you're a busy man. You can't keep up with all the little details of a plant this size. You sit on the board of directors of three other corporations and the board of trustees of two colleges, you belong to business organizations where you hold office. I mean, how would you have the time to sift through all the day-to-day stuff here?"

Kane took a breath to stem his rush of temper. The man was new, after all, as chief of the waste disposal unit. And he made sense. "That's true. I haven't time to oversee every facet of every operation. Normally, this would be Ed Nelson's problem."

"I know that. Yes, I do, sir. But Mr. Nelson's had kidney stones and he had to have surgery for them last week. He's sort of low. Not that he doesn't keep up with things," he added quickly. "He's still on top of the situation here." That wasn't quite true, but the wording gave Lombard the impression that Nelson had agreed with Jurkins's decision to replace CWC.

Kane relaxed. Jurkins was a native of Charleston. He'd know the ins and outs of sanitation, and surely he'd already have a handle on the proper people to do a good job. "All right," he said.

"Who have you contracted with to replace CWC?"

"I found a very reputable company, Mr. Lombard," he assured his boss. "Very reputable, indeed. In fact, two of the local automotive parts companies use them. It's Burke's."

"Burke's?"

"They're not as well-known as CWC, sir," Jurkins said. "They're a young company, but very energetic. They don't cost an arm and a leg, either."

Kane's head was hurting. He didn't have time for this infernal runaround. He'd ask Nelson when he got back to the office the following week.

"All right, Jurkins. Go ahead and make the switch. I'll approve it, if there's any flak," he said. "Just make sure they do what they're supposed to. Put Jenny back on the line."

"Yes, sir! Have a good vacation, sir, and don't you worry, everything's going along just fine!"

Kane made a grunting sound and waited for his secretary to come back on the line. When she did, he began shooting orders at her, for faxes to be sent up to his machine, for contract estimates, for correspondence. He hadn't a secretary here and he hesitated to ask for Jenny to join him, because she had a huge crush on him which he didn't want to encourage. He could scribble notes on the letters for answers and fax them back to her. Yes, that would work.

While Kane was debating his next move, a relieved Will Jurkins pushed back his sweaty red hair and breathed a long sigh, grinning cagily at the man standing beside him.

"That was a close one," he told the man. "Lombard wanted to know why I made the switch."

"You're getting enough out of this deal to make it worth the risk," came the laconic reply. "And you're in too deep to back out."

"Don't I know it," Jurkins said uneasily. "Are you sure about this? I don't want to go to jail."

"Will you stop worrying? I know what I'm doing." He slipped the man a wad of large bills, careful not to let himself be seen.

Jurkins grimaced as he counted the money and quickly slipped it into his pocket. He had a child with leukemia and his medical insurance had run out. He was out of choices and this cigar-smoking magician had offered him a small fortune just to switch sanitation firms. On the surface, there was nothing wrong with it. But he was uneasy, because Burke's sanitation outfit had already been in trouble with the environmental people for some illegal dumping.

"Burke's is not very reliable," he began, trying again. "And I already made one major mistake here, letting that raw sewage get dumped accidentally into the river. If they catch Burke putting anything toxic in a bad place, it will look pretty bad for Lombard International."

"Burke's needs the business," the raspy-voiced man said. "Trust me. It's just to help him out. There's no way it will be traced back to you. You need the money don't you?" When Jurkins nodded, the man patted him on the shoulder and smiled, waving the cigar around. "Nobody will know. And I was never here. Right?"

"Right."

Jurkins watched the man leave by the side door. He went into the parking lot and climbed into a sedate gray BMW. A car like that would cost Jurkins a year's salary. He wondered what his benefactor did for a living.

Clayton Seymour had gone down the roster of Republican representatives over a new bill which affected cable television rates. He and his legislative committee—not to mention part of his personal staff—were helping his friend, the minority whip, gather enough representatives together for a decisive vote on the issue. But he was going blind in the process. He looked out his window at the distant Washington, D.C., skyline and wished he was back home in Charleston and going fishing. He maintained only two district offices, whereas most of the other House members had anywhere from two to eight.

Each of those offices back home in South Carolina had full-time and part-time staffers who could handle requests from constituents. In addition, he'd appointed a constituent staff at his Washington office, along with his legislative, institutional, and personal staff. It sounded like a lot of people on the payroll, but there were actually only a handful involved and they were eminently qualified. Most had master's degrees. His district director had a Ph.D. and his executive legislative counsel was a Harvard graduate.

He was ultimately satisfied with the job he'd done. During his term in office, he'd remained within his budget. It was one of many feathers in his political cap. In addition, he had seats on the Energy and Commerce Committee and the Ways and Means Committee, among others. He worked from twelve to fourteen hours a day and occasionally took offense at remarks that members of Congress were overpaid layabouts. He didn't have time to layabout. In the next congress, over eleven thousand new pieces of legislation were predicted for introduction. If he was reelected—*when* he was reelected—he was going to have to work even harder.

His executive administrative assistant in charge of his personal and constituent staff, Derrie Keller, knocked on the door and opened it all in the same motion. She was tall and pretty, with light blond hair and green eyes and a nice smile. Everybody was kind to her because she had such a sweet nature. But she also had a bachelor's degree in political science, and was keen-minded, efficient, and tough when the situation called for it. She headed the personal staff, and when she went to Charleston with Clayton, that position also applied to whichever of the two district offices she visited.

"Ah, Derrie," he said on a long-suffering sigh. "Are you going to bury me in paperwork again?"

She grinned. "Want to lie down, first, so we can do it properly?"

"If I lie down, three senators and a newspaperman will come in and stand on me," he assured her. He sat upright in his chair. He was good-looking—tall, dark-haired and blue-eyed, with a charismatic personality and a perfect smile.

Women loved him, Derrie thought; particularly a highly paid Washington lobbyist who practiced law named Bett Watts. The woman was forever in and out of the office, tossing out orders to anyone stupid enough to take them. Derrie wasn't. She was simply biding her time until her tunnel-visioned boss eventually noticed that she was a ripe fruit hanging low on the limb, waiting for him to reach up and…

"Are you going to stand there all day?" he prompted impatiently.

"Sorry." She put the letters on his desk. "Want coffee?"

"You can't bring me coffee," he said absently. "You're an overpaid public official with administrative duties. If you bring me coffee, secretarial unions will storm the office and sacrifice me on the White House lawn."

She knew this speech by heart. She just smiled. "Cream and sugar?"

"Yes, please," he replied with a grin.

She went out to get it, laughing at his irrepressible overreaction. He always made her laugh. She couldn't resist going with him to political rallies where he was scheduled to speak, because she enjoyed him so much. He was in constant demand as an after-dinner speaker.

"Here you go," she said a minute later, reappearing with two steaming cups. She put hers down and sat in the chair beside his desk with her pad and pen in hand.

"Thanks." He was studying another piece of legislation on which a vote would shortly be taken. "New stuff on the agenda today, Derrie. I'll need you to direct one of the interns to do some legwork for me."

"Is that the lumbering bill?" she asked, eyeing the paper in his lean hands.

"Yes," he said, mildly surprised. "Why?"

"You're not going to vote for it, are you?"

He scowled as he lifted his cup of coffee, fixed with cream just as he liked it, and looked at her while he sipped it gingerly. "Yes, I am," he replied slowly.

She glared at him. "It will set the environment back ten years."

"It will open up jobs for people who can't get any work."

"It's an old forest," she persisted. "One of the oldest untouched forests in the world."

"We can't afford to leave it in its pristine condition," he said, exasperated. "Listen, why don't you meet with all those lobbyists who represent the starving mothers and children of lumbermen out west? Maybe you can explain your position to them better than I could. Hungry kids really get to me."

"How do you know they were really starving and not just short a hot lunch?"

"You cynic!" he exclaimed. He sat forward in his chair. "Hasn't anybody ever explained basic economics to you? Ecology is wonderful, I'm all for it. In fact, I have a very enviable record in South Carolina for my stand against toxic waste dumps and industrial polluters. However, this is another issue entirely. People are asking us to set aside thousands of acres of viable timber to save an owl, when people are jobless and homeless and facing the prospect of going on the welfare rolls—which is, by the way, going to impact taxpayers all the way from Oregon to D.C."

"I know all that," she grumbled. "But we're cutting down all the trees we have and we're not replacing them fast enough. In fact, how can you replace something that old?"

"You can't replace it," he agreed. "You can't replace people, either, Derrie."

"There are things you're overlooking," she persisted. "Have you read all the background literature on that bill?"

"When I have time?" he exploded. "My God, you of all people should know how fast they throw legislation at me! If I read every word of every bill..."

"I can read it for you. If you'll listen I'll tell you why the bill is a bad idea."

"I have legislative counsel to advise me," he said tersely, glaring at her. "My executive legislative counsel is a Harvard graduate."

Derrie knew that. She also liked Mary Tanner, an elegant African American woman whose Harvard law degree often surprised people who mistook her for a model. Mary was beautiful.

"And Mary is very good," she agreed. "But you don't always listen to your advisors."

"The people elected me, not my staff," he reminded her with a cold stare.

She almost challenged that look. But he'd been under a lot of pressure, and she had a little time left before the vote to work on him. She backed down. "All right. I'll work my fingers to the bone for you, but I won't quit harping on the lumber bill," she warned. "I don't believe in profit at the expense of the environment."

"Then you aren't living in the real world."

She gave him a killing glare and walked out of the room. It was to her credit that she didn't slam the door behind her.

Clayton watched her retreat with mixed emotions. Usually, Derrie agreed with him on issues. This time, she was fighting tooth and nail. It amused him, to see his little homebody of an assistant ready to scratch and claw.

The telephone rang and a minute later, Derrie's arctic voice informed him that Ms. Watts was on the line.

"Hello, Bett," he told the caller. "How are you?"

"Worn," came the mocking reply. "I can't see you tonight. I've got a board meeting, followed by a cocktail party, followed by a brief meeting with one of the senior senators, all of which I really must get through."

"Don't you ever get tired of lobbying and long for something different?" he probed.

"Something like giving fancy parties and placating political adversaries?" Bett asked sarcastically.

Clayton felt himself going tense. "I know you don't like my sister," he said curtly. "But a remark like that is catty and frankly intolerable. Call me back when you feel like rejoining the human race."

He put the phone down and buzzed Derrie. "If Ms. Watts calls back, tell her I'm indisposed indefinitely!" he said icily.

"Does she like virgin forests, too?"

He slammed the phone down and took the receiver off the hook.

Clayton phoned Nikki that evening. He didn't mention Bett's nasty remark or his fight with Derrie, which had resulted in her giving him an icy good-night and leaving him alone with cold coffee and hot bills. He had to depend on his district director for coffee, and Stan couldn't make it strong enough.

"I'm not going to be able to turn loose for at least two weeks," he said sadly. "I'd love to spend some time with you before we get our feet good and wet in this campaign, but I've got too much on my plate."

"Take some time off. Congress won't be in session much longer."

"I know that. I am a U.S. Representative," he reminded her dryly. "Which is all the more reason for me to push these so-and-so's into getting down here to vote when our bill comes up. I can't leave."

"In that case, don't expect me to wail for you."

"Would I? Anyway, you need the rest more than I do," he said on a laugh. "How's everything going?"

"Fine," she said. "Nothing exciting. A big fish washed up on the beach..."

"I hope you didn't try to save it," he muttered. "You're hell to take on a fishing trip, with your overstimulated protective instincts."

"I let this one go," she said, feeling vaguely guilty that she was keeping a secret from him. It was the first time, too. "It wasn't hurt very badly. It swam away and I'll never see it again." That much was probably true.

"Well, stay out of trouble, can't you?"

"Clay, I'll do my very best," she promised.

"Get some rest. You'll need it when autumn comes and the campaigning begins in earnest."

"Don't I know it," she chuckled. "Good night."

"Good night."

She hung up the phone and went to lounge on

the deck, watching the whitecaps curl rhythmically in to the white beach. The moon shone on them and as she sipped white wine, she thought that she'd never felt quite so alone. She wondered what Mr. Lombard was doing.

Chapter Three

Kane Lombard was sitting on his own deck with a highball, thinking about Nikki. It had been a productive day. Most days were, because the job was everything to him. But now, as he contemplated the moonlight sparkle on the ocean, he felt unfulfilled.

He was thirty-eight years old. He'd had a wife, and a son. There had been a twelve-year marriage which, while not perfect, at least gave him a sense of security. At least he'd been in love when he married, even if things had gone sour a few years later. Now he was among the ranks of the single men again, but without the youth and idealism that made marriage a viable prospect. He was jaded and somewhere along the way, he'd lost all his illusions about people. About life. He was like those waves, he thought, being aimlessly thrown onto the beach and then forgotten. When he died, there would be nothing to leave behind, nothing to show that Kane Lombard had lived on this planet.

That wasn't totally true, he chided himself as he swallowed a sip of the stinging highball. He had the company to leave behind. The name would probably be changed somewhere down the line, though. Names didn't last long.

He leaned back on the chaise lounge and closed his eyes. Nikki. Her name was Nikki, and she had black hair and green eyes and the face of an angel. He liked the way she looked, the way she laughed, as if life still had wonderful things to offer. He knew better, but she made him optimistic. He needed someone like that.

Not permanently, of course, he told himself. He needed an affair. Just an affair. Would she be willing? She seemed to find him attractive enough. If he took her out and bided his time, would she be receptive? He sloshed the liquid in the glass, listening to the soft chink of the ice cubes against the watery roar of the ocean. Perhaps she was lonely, too. God knew, there was no monopoly on loneliness. Like the air itself, it permeated everything. His eyelids felt heavy. He closed them, just for a minute…

It was dawn when he woke, still lying on the chaise lounge, with the chill morning air in his face. The glass, long since forgotten, had fallen gently to the deck and was dry now, the ice and whiskey melted and evaporated on the wood floor. He got up, stretching with faint soreness. His head was much better, but there were still vestiges of a headache. He stared out over the ocean, and was jarred from his thoughts when the telephone rang.

His housekeeper was apparently in residence, because the ringing stopped, to be replaced by her loud, stringent voice.

"Telephone, Mr. Lombard!" she called.

"I'll take it out here," he returned gruffly.

She handed him the phone and he nodded curtly as he took it, waving her away. "Yes?" he asked.

"I'm Todd Lawson, Mr. Lombard," a deep voice replied. "I work for your father and brothers in New York at the *Weekly Voice,*" he prompted when there was a long pause on the other end of the line.

Kane recognized the name. Lawson was his father's star reporter, if a man who was better at creating news than gathering it could be called a journalist.

"Yes, I know you," Kane said. "What do you want?"

"Your father sent me to Charleston to do a little prospecting. He wants me to see what I can find on the Republican U.S. Representative incumbent, Seymour. I've just checked into a hotel here. Any ideas about a good place to start looking for skeletons?"

"I can't help you. I haven't lived in Charleston long enough to know many people. I only know Seymour through the mails and the telephone," he added curtly. "If I put a step wrong, he'll be over me like tarpaper, I know that. We had a sewage leak a couple of weeks ago, accidental, and he's been after my neck ever since. He went on television to point fingers at me as a perfect example of a money-hungry anticonservationist." He shook his head. "He's gungho on this industrial pollution issue. It's his number one priority, they say."

"Interesting that he's fighting for the lumber bill out west," Lawson murmured, tongue in cheek.

"The habitat of an owl out west apparently doesn't do him as much political good as digging out industrial polluters on his doorstep."

"You said it."

"Keep me posted, will you?"

"You bet."

He put down the receiver. Seymour was an odd bird, he thought. The man had little material wealth, but his old Charleston heritage had helped put him in office. The backing of Senator Mosby Torrance hadn't hurt, either. The junior U.S. senator from South Carolina was a personable man with an equally impeccable reputation, even if he had a failed marriage behind him. Mosby's marriage had been very brief, Kane understood, and rather secretive, but that had been because of his bride's tender age, his sources told him. He couldn't quite remember, but it seemed that there had been some connection with the Seymours before that. He'd have to remember and tell Lawson. It wasn't important enough to try to reach the reporter, even if he knew where to look. No matter. Lawson would call back.

In the campaign headquarters of Sam Hewett, candidate for the Democratic nomination to the U.S. House of Representatives for the district that included Charleston, South Carolina, a heated discussion was taking place between Hewett and his advisers.

"You can't risk a personal attack on Seymour at this point," Norman Lombard muttered through a cloud of cigar smoke. His dark eyes lanced the candidate, who was tall and thin and rather nervous. "Let us take care of anything in that line. My father owns the biggest tabloid in America and my brothers and I are solidly behind you, financially and every other way. You just shake hands and make friends. For now, worry about nothing more than the Democratic nomination. When the time comes, we'll have enough to slide you past Seymour at the polls."

"What if I can't gather enough support?" Hewett asked uneasily. "I'm not that well-known. I don't have the background that Seymour does!"

"You'll have the name identification when we get through with you," Norman said, chuckling. "My dad knows how to get the publicity. You'll get the votes. We guarantee it."

"You won't do anything illegal?" the candidate asked.

The question seemed to be perennial in Hewett's mind. Lombard sighed angrily and puffed on his cigar. "We won't have to," he assured the other man for the tenth time. "A little mud here, a little doubt there, and we'll have the seat in our grasp. Just relax, Sam. You're a shoo-in. Enjoy the ride."

"I want to win honestly."

"The last person who won honestly was George Washington," Lombard joked cynically. "But never mind, we'll do our best to keep your conscience quiet. Now, get out there and campaign, Sam. And stop worrying, will you? I promise you, it will all work out for the best."

Hewett wasn't as certain as his advisor appeared, but he was a newcomer to politics. He was learning more than he wanted to about the election process every day. He'd been idealistic and enthusiastic at the outset. Now, he was losing his illusions by the minute. He couldn't help but wonder if this was what the founding fathers had in mind when they outlined the electoral process. It seemed a real shame that qualifications meant nothing at all in the race; it was a contest of personalities and high-tech advertising and money, not issues. But on that foundation, the election rested. He did want to win, he told himself. But for the first time, he wasn't sure why.

It had thrilled him when the Lombards backed him as a candidate. It had been Kane Lombard's idea initially. Kane liked Sam because they were both yachtsmen, and because Sam supported tax cuts and other incentives that would help his fledgling automobile manufacturing industry in Charleston. Mainly, Sam thought, it was because Clayton Seymour had taken an instant dislike to Kane and had done everything possible to put obstacles in his path when the auto manufacturing firm first located in Charleston. The antagonism had been mutual. Now, with Kane's latest bad luck in having a sewage spill into the river, Seymour had attacked him from every angle.

Sam didn't like dirty politics. He wanted to win the election, but not if it meant stooping to the sort of tactics Seymour and his mentor Mosby Torrance were using against Kane. The double-dealing at city hall had been shocking to Sam, with both politicians using unfair influence to delay building permits and regulatory requirements.

Privately, Sam thought a lot of their resentment was due to the national reputation of the tabloid

Kane's father and brothers owned in New York. It was increasingly focusing on politics and it had done some nasty exposes on pet projects of Senator Torrance. It had also made some veiled threats about going on a witch-hunt to drag out scandals in Congress, beginning with southern senators and representatives. That had been about the time Kane announced the building of his plant. It had also coincided with Seymour's bid for reelection.

Having Kane so close to home was making Seymour and Torrance nervous. Sam began to wonder what they had to hide.

Nicole had driven her small used red sports car into the village market near the medical center to get milk and bread—the eternal necessities—and fresh fruit. She'd just walked onto her porch when she heard the sound of a car pulling to a stop behind her.

She turned, and found Kane Lombard climbing out of a ramshackle old Jeep. She wondered just for an instant where he'd borrowed such a dilapidated vehicle before the sight of him in jeans and a white knit shirt made her heart start beating faster.

He smiled at the picture she made in cutoff denim shorts and a pink tank top. That dark tan gave her an almost continental look.

"You tan well," he remarked.

"Our ancestors were French Huguenots, who came to Charleston early in the seventeenth century to escape religious persecution in Europe," she told him. "I'm told that our olive complexion comes from them."

"I brought back the things you loaned me." He handed her a bundle. "Washed and pressed," he added.

"With your own two hands?" she teased.

He liked the way her eyes sparkled when she smiled. She made him feel young again. "Not quite." He stuck his hands in his pockets and studied her closely, with pursed lips. "Come for a ride."

Her heart skipped. She couldn't really afford to get mixed up with her brother's enemy, she told herself firmly. Really she couldn't.

"Just let me put these things away," she said.

He followed her inside and wandered around the living room while she put the perishable things into the refrigerator and the bread in the bread box.

"I should change..." she began.

"Why?" He turned, smiling at her. "You look fine to me."

"In that case, I'm ready."

She locked the door, grateful that she hadn't any photographs setting around that might clue him in to her relationship with Clayton. Nor was there anything expensive or antique in the beach house.

She and Clayton didn't keep valuables here, and the beach house remained in the name of their cousin who also had access to it. That kept nosey parkers from finding Clayton when he was up here on holiday. Records on land ownership were not hard to obtain, especially for someone like Kane Lombard.

He unlocked the passenger door and helped her inside. "It's not very neat in here," he said, apologizing. "I use this old rattletrap for fishing trips, mostly. I like to angle for bass down on the Santee-Cooper River."

"You don't look like a fisherman," she remarked. She clipped her seat belt into place, idly watching his hard, dark face and wondering at the lines in it, the silvery hair at his temples. He was older than she'd first thought.

"I hate fishing, as a rule," he replied. He started the Jeep and reversed it neatly, wheeling around before he sped off down the beach highway. The sun was shining. It was a glorious morning, with seagulls and pelicans scrounging for fish in the surf while a handful of residents walked in the surf and watched the ocean.

"Then, why do it?" she asked absently.

"My father loves it. He and I have very little in common, otherwise. I go fishing with him because it gives me an excuse to see him occasionally—and my younger brothers."

"How many do you have?"

"Two. No sisters. There are just the three of us. We drove my mother crazy when we were kids." He glanced at her. "Do you have family?"

"Not many, not anymore," she said, her voice very quiet and distant.

"I'm sorry. It must be lonely for you."

"It's not bad," she replied. "I have friends."

"Like the one who lets you share the beach house with him?" he asked pointedly.

She smiled at him, unconcerned. "Yes. Like him."

Kane made a mental note to find out who owned that beach house. He wanted to know the name of the man with whom Nikki was involved. It didn't occur to him then that his very curiosity betrayed his growing involvement with her.

All along the beach, people were beginning to set up lawn chairs and spread towels in the sun. It was a warm spring day, with nothing but a sprinkling of clouds overhead.

"I love the ocean," Nikki said softly, smiling as her wide green eyes took in her surroundings. "I could never live inland. Even the freighters and fishing boats fascinate me."

"I know what you mean," he agreed. "I've lived in port cities all my life. You get addicted to the sight and sound of big ships."

He must mean Houston, but she couldn't admit

that she knew where he was from. "Do you live here?" she asked.

"I'm on holiday," he said, which was true enough. "Do you stay here, all the time?"

"No," she confessed. "I live farther down the coast."

"In Charleston?" he probed.

"Sort of."

"What does sort of mean?"

"I live on the beach itself." She did. She lived in one of the graceful old homes on the Battery, which was listed in the National Register of Historic Places and which was open to tourists two weeks a year.

He could imagine in what kind of house she normally lived. He hadn't seen her in anything so far that didn't look as if she'd found it in a yard sale. He felt vaguely sorry for her. She had no one of her own except her indifferent lover, and her material possessions were obviously very few. He'd noticed that she drove a very dilapidated red MG Midget, the model that was popular back in the 60s.

"Feel like a cup of coffee?" he asked, nodding toward a small fast-food joint near the beach, with tables outside covered by faded yellow umbrellas.

"Yes, I do, thanks," she told him.

He parked the jeep and they got out. Nikki strolled to the beachside table and sat down while

Kane ordered coffee. He hadn't needed to be told how Nikki took hers. He brought it with cream and sugar, smiling mischievously at her surprise.

"I have a more or less photographic memory," he told her as he slid onto the seat across from her.

"I'll remember that," she said with a grin.

He lifted his head and closed his eyes, letting the sea breeze drift over his darkly tanned face. It had a faintly leonine look, broad and definite, with a straight nose that was just short of oversized, a jutting brow with thick eyebrows, and a wide, thin-lipped mouth that managed to be sexy and masculine all at once. His eyes were large and brown, his pupils edged in black. They were staring at her with faint amusement.

"You look Spanish," she blurted out, embarrassed at having been caught looking at him.

He frowned slightly, smiling. "My great-grandmother was a highborn Spanish lady," he replied. "She was visiting relatives near San Antonio, where my great-grandfather was a ranch foreman. As the story goes, they were married five days after they met, leaving a raging scandal behind them when they moved to Houston to prospect for oil."

"How interesting! And did they find any?"

"My great-grandfather was prospecting up around Beaumont when Spindletop blew its stack in 1901," he told her. "He made and lost a fortune in two months' time.'' He didn't add that his great-grandfather had quickly recouped his losses and went on to found an oil company.

''Poor man.'' She looked up from the coffee she was sipping. ''His wife didn't leave him because he lost everything, did she?''

''She wasn't the type. She stuck by him, all the way.''

''That doesn't happen very often anymore, does it? Women sticking by men, I mean,'' she added wistfully. ''Now, marriages are expendable. Nobody does it for keeps.''

He scowled. ''You're very cynical for someone so young.''

''I'm twenty-five,'' she told him. ''Not young at all for this day and age.'' She studied her brightly polished fingernails, curled around the foam cup. ''For the rest, it's a cynical world. Profit even takes precedence over human life. I'm told that in the Amazon jungles, they kill the natives without compunction to get them off land the government wants to let big international corporations develop.''

He stared at her. ''Do you really think that with all the people this planet has to support, we can afford to allow primitive cultures to sit on that much arable land?''

Her green eyes began to glitter. ''I think that if we develop all the arable land, we're going to have to eat concrete and steel a few years down the line.''

He was delighted. Absolutely delighted. For all her beauty, there was a brain under that black hair. He moved his coffee cup around on the scarred surface of the table and smiled at her. ''Progress costs,'' he countered.

''It's going to cost us the planet at the rate we're destroying our natural resources,'' she said sweetly. ''Or aren't you aware that about one percent of us is feeding the other ninety-nine percent? You have to have flat, rich land to plant on. Unfortunately the same sort of land that is best suited to agriculture is also best suited to building sites.''

''On the other hand,'' he pointed out, ''without jobs, people won't be able to afford seed to plant. A new business means new jobs, a better standard of living for the people in the community. Better nutrition for nursing mothers, for young children.''

''That's all true,'' she agreed, leaning forward earnestly. ''But what about the price people pay for that better standard of living? When farm mechanization came along, farmers had to grow more food in order to afford the equipment to make planting and harvesting less time-consuming. That raised the price of food. The pesticides and fertilizers they had to use, to increase production, caused the toxic byproducts to leach into the ground, and pollute the water table. We produced more food, surely, but the more food you raise, the more the population grows. That increases the amount of food you *have* to raise to feed the increasing numbers of people! It's a vicious circle."

"My God, you talk like an economist," he said.

"Why not? I studied it in college."

"Well, well." He grinned at her. "What did you take your degree in?"

"I didn't finish," she said sadly. "I dropped out after three and a half years, totally burned out. I'll go back and finish one day, though. I only lack two semesters having enough units to graduate, with a major in history and a minor in sociology."

"God help the world when you get out," he murmured. "You could go into politics with a brain like yours."

She was flattered and amused, but she didn't let him see the latter. He mustn't know how wrapped up she already was in politics.

"You're not bad yourself."

"I took my degree in business administration," he said. "I did a double minor in economics and marketing."

"Do you work in business?" she asked with deliberate innocence.

"You might say so," he said carelessly. "I'm in marketing."

"It must be exciting."

"Sometimes," he dodged. He finished his coffee. "Do you like to walk on the beach?" he asked. "I enjoy it early in the morning and late in the afternoon. It helps me clear my mind so that I can think."

"Me, too," she said.

"Kindred spirits," he said almost to himself, and she smiled.

He put the garbage in the receptacle and impulsively slid his hand into Nikki's.

It was the first deliberate physical contact between them, and sparks flew as his big, strong fingers linked sensuously between her slender ones. She felt their warm touch and tingles worked all the way down her body. She hadn't felt that way in years. Not since Mosby…

She caught her breath and looked up at him with something like panic in her green eyes.

"What is it, Nikki?" he asked gently.

His deep voice stirred her even more than the touch of his hand. She felt him, as if they were standing locked together. Her eyes looked into his and she could almost taste him.

"Nothing," she choked after a minute. She pulled her fingers from his grasp firmly, but hesitantly. "Shall we go?"

He watched her move off ahead of him, her hands suddenly in her pockets, the small fanny pack around her waist drooping over one rounded hip. She looked frightened. That was an odd sort of behavior from a woman who'd let him share her home for a night, he thought idly. She hadn't been afraid of him then.

She paused when he caught up with her, feeling guilty and not quite herself. She looked up at him with a rueful, embarrassed smile.

"I don't trust men, as a rule," she confessed. "Most of them have one major objective when they start paying attention to a woman. I've never been accused of misleading anyone. That's why I'm going to tell you right now, and up front, that I don't sleep around, ever."

"At least you're honest," he said as they continued to walk toward the beach.

"Always," she assured him. "I find it's the best policy."

"Do you sleep with the man who owns the beach house?"

"What I do with him is none of your business," she said simply.

"Fair enough." He put his hands in his pockets and looked down at her while they strolled along the white sand. Whitecaps rolled, foaming onto the nearby shore, and above head the seagulls danced on the wind with black-tipped white wings spread to the sun.

"You're very big," she remarked.

He chuckled. "Tall. Not big."

"You are," she argued. "I'm five foot five and you tower over me."

"I'm barely six foot two," he told her. "You're a shrimp, that's why I seem big to you."

"Watch your mouth, buster, I'm not through growing yet," she said pertly, cutting her sparkling eyes up at him.

He chuckled. "Smart mouth."

"Smart, period, thank you so much."

"Now that we both know you won't sleep with me, can we hold hands? Mine are cold."

"I might have suspected there would be an ulterior motive," she mentioned. But all the same, she took her left hand out of her pocket and let him fold it under his warm fingers.

"You aren't cold," she protested.

"Sure I am. You just can't tell." His fingers tightened, and he smiled at the faint flush on her cheeks as the exercise began to tell on her. "You ninety-seven-pound-weakling," he chided. "Can't you keep up with me?"

"Normally I could run rings around you," she said heavily. "But I'm getting over a bout of pneumonia."

He stopped abruptly, scowling. "Idiot! You don't need to be out in this early morning chill! Why didn't you say something?"

His concern made her heart lift. "It's been a week since I got out of bed," she assured him.

"And I haven't been sitting home idle all that time."

"You haven't done much exercising, either, have you?"

"Not really," she admitted. The help she'd given with the Spoleto Festival had involved a lot of telephone calls and assistance that she could give sitting down. Her strength was still lagging behind her will.

"What a waif and stray it is, and it hasn't much of a mind at times, either," he murmured softly.

She started to take offense when he moved suddenly and swept her into his warm, strong arms. He turned and started walking back the way they'd come.

Nikki was totally breathless with surprised delight. It was the first time in her life that she'd experienced a man's strength in this way. She wasn't sure she liked the feeling of vulnerability it gave her, and that doubt was in her eyes when they met his at close range.

"I can see the words right there on the tip of your tongue," he said softly, his deep voice faintly accented and very tender as he smiled at her. "But don't say them. Put your arms around me and lie close to my chest while I carry you."

Shades of a romantic movie, she thought wildly. But the odd thing was that she obeyed him without question, without hesitation. There was a breathy little sigh escaping from her. She dropped her eyes to his throat, where thick hair showed in the opening, and she felt a sweet swelling in her body as he drew her relentlessly closer. Her face ended up in the hot curve of his throat, her arms close around his neck.

"Nikki," he said in a rough, husky voice, and his arms suddenly contracted, crushing her soft breasts against the wall of his chest as he turned toward the car.

It was no longer a teasing or tender embrace. Her nails were biting into his shoulders as he walked, and she felt the closeness in every single pore of her body. Her breasts had gone hard-tipped, her heart was throbbing. Low in her stomach, she felt a heat and hunger that was totally without precedent.

"Oh, baby," he whispered suddenly, and she felt his open mouth quite suddenly on the softness of her throat where her tank top left it bare to her collarbone.

She closed her eyes with a shaky gasp. The wind blew her hair around her face and cooled the heat in her cheeks. He was warm and strong and he smelled of spices. She wanted him to strip her out of her clothes and put his warm, hard mouth on her breasts and her belly and the inside of her thighs. She wanted him to put her down on the beach and make love to her under the sky.

With a total disregard for safety and sanity, her hand tangled in the thick, wavy hair at the back of his head and she pulled his mouth down to the soft curve under her collarbone.

Chapter Four

Kane's head was spinning, but when Nikki coaxed his mouth down, he came to his senses with a jolt. It was a public beach, for God's sake, and he was a man who didn't need this sort of complication!

He jerked his face up and put her down abruptly. He stepped back, trying not to show how shaken he was. It had been a long time since he'd felt anything so powerful. He looked into her dazed, misty, half-closed green eyes.

She was shaken, too, and unable to hide it. His lips had almost been touching her bare skin when he'd withdrawn them. She felt as if she'd been left in limbo, but she had to keep her head.

"Thank you," she said. "I knew that you could

save me from myself,'' she managed with irrepressible spirit.

He smiled in spite of himself. ''I suppose I did. But I'd never have believed it of myself. I'm not one to throw away opportunities, and you have a mouth like a ripe apple.''

''I'm thrilled that you think so.''

He burst out laughing, absolutely delighted. ''In that case, don't you want to come with me to a quiet, deserted place?''

''Of course I do.'' She pushed back her disheveled hair. ''But we've already agreed that it wouldn't be sensible.''

''You agreed. I didn't.''

She was having trouble with her legs. They didn't want to move. And the throbbing need in her body was getting worse, not better. How ironic of her to suddenly explode with passion for a man after all this time, and the man had to be her brother's worst enemy in the world!

''Stop tempting me to do sordid things,'' she told him firmly. She pushed back her disheveled hair. ''I'll have you know that I'm a virtuous woman.''

''That may not last if you spend much time around me. How about going sailing with me?''

Her hand poised above her hair. ''Sailing?''

''Your eyes lit up. Do you like sailing?'' he asked.

"I love it!"

He chuckled. "I'll pick you up early tomorrow." He paused. "If you're free?"

She knew what he was asking. He meant, would her "live-in lover" mind?

"He isn't jealous," she said with a slow smile.

"Isn't he?"

His dark eyes sketched her face and he began to worry. He knew he was losing his grasp on reality, to take this sort of chance. She appealed to him physically. That was all. There was an added threat. What if she found out who he was?

His own apprehension amused him. What if she did, for God's sake? What could she do, blackmail him because they'd spend an innocent night together?

"The man I live with and I...we have an...open relationship," she assured him.

"I hope you aren't entertaining ideas that I might be willing to take his place," he said slowly. "I enjoy your company, and I find you very attractive. But I'm not in the market for a lover. I already have one."

Why should that shock her? She shifted a little and averted her eyes to the beach. She wasn't shopping for a lover, either. Not with her past. So wasn't it just as well that he didn't want one?

"That suits me," she replied absently. "I don't care for purely physical relationships. I wouldn't mind a friend, though,'' she added suddenly, her green eyes linking with his as she smiled. ''I have very few of those.''

''I doubt if anyone can boast more than one true friend,'' he said cynically. ''Okay. Friends it is.''

''And no funny stuff on the sailboat,'' she said, returning to her former mood with mercurial rapidity. ''You can't lash me to the mast and ravish me, or strip me naked and use me to troll for sharks. You have to promise.''

He grinned. ''Fair enough.''

''Then I'll see you tomorrow.''

''I don't think we can avoid it,'' he agreed. ''Come on. I'll take you home.''

That evening, sitting alone on the deck, her conscience nagged at her. It didn't help that Clayton telephoned to tell her about the progress he was making.

''I've won over a new ally,'' he told her, and mentioned the congressman's name. ''How's that for a day's work?!''

''Great!'' she said, laughing. ''Uh, how's the owl controversy?''

''It's a real hoot,'' he muttered. ''Derrie and I aren't speaking because of it. Here I am a conservation candidate, voting against a little owl and a bunch of old trees just because it will mean new jobs and economic prosperity. She thinks I'm a lunatic."

"Was the moon full?"

"Cut it out. You're my sister. Blood is thicker than water."

"Probably it is, but what does that have to do with anything?"

He scowled. "I can't think of a single thing. How are you? Getting some rest?"

"Enough." She hesitated. "I...met someone."

"Someone? A man? A real, honest to God man?"

"He looks like one. He's taking me sailing."

"Nikki, I'm delighted! Who is he?"

She crossed her fingers on her lap. "Just an ordinary man," she lied. "He's into...cars."

"Oh. A mechanic? Well, there's nothing wrong with being a mechanic, I guess. Can he sail well enough not to drown you?"

"I think he could do anything he set his mind to," she murmured dreamily.

"Is this really you?" he teased. "You were off men for life, the last time we spoke."

"Oh, I am," she agreed readily. "It's just that this one is so different." She added, "I haven't ever met anyone quite like him."

"Is he a ladies' man?"

"I don't know. Perhaps."

"Nikki," he began, hesitating. She'd had a

rough experience at an early age. She was vulnerable. "Listen, suppose I come up for a few days?"

"No!" She cleared her throat and lowered her voice. "I mean, there's no need to do that."

"You're worrying me," he said.

"You can't protect me from the world, you know. I have to stand on my own two feet sometime."

"I guess you do," he said, sounding resigned and not too happy. "Okay, sis. Have it your way. But I'm as close as the telephone if you need me. Will you remember that?"

"You can bet on it."

"Then I'll speak to you soon."

When he hung up, Nikki let out the breath she'd been holding. That was all she needed now, to have Clayton come wandering up to the house and run head-on into his worst enemy. Things were getting complicated and she was certain that she needed to cut off the impossible relationship before it began. But she couldn't quite manage it. Already, Kane had gotten close to her heart. She hoped that it wouldn't break completely in the end.

She wondered how Kane was going to keep her in the dark about his wealth. If he took her sailing in a yacht, even a moron would notice that it meant he had money.

The next day he solved the problem adroitly by mentioning that he couldn't rent the sailboat he'd planned to take her out in, so they were going riding in a motorboat instead. It was a very nice motorboat, but nothing like the yacht he usually took onto the ocean.

Nikki smiled to herself and accepted the change of conveyance without noticeable effect.

"I know I said I'd take you out on a sailboat," he explained as he helped her into the boat, "but they're not very safe in high winds. It's pretty windy today."

It was, but she hardly thought a yacht would be very much affected. On the other hand, it wouldn't do for her "ordinary" houseguest to turn up in a million-dollar-plus sailing ship, and he must have realized that.

"Oh, I like motorboats," she said honestly, her eyes lighting up with excitement as Kane eased into the driver's seat and turned the key. The motor started right up and ran like a purring cat.

He glanced at her with a wry smile. "Are you a good sailor?"

"I guess we'll find out together," she returned.

He chuckled and pulled away from the pier.

The boat had a smooth glide on the water's surface, and the engine wasn't overly loud. Nikki put up a hand to her windblown hair, laughing as the faint spray of water teased her nose.

"Aren't you ever gloomy?" he asked with genuine curiosity.

"Oh, why bother being pessimistic?" she replied. "Life is so short. It's a crime to waste it, when every day is like Christmas, bringing something new."

She loved life. He'd forgotten how. His dark eyes turned toward the distant horizon and he tried not to think about how short life really was, or how tragically he'd learned the lesson.

"Where are we going?" Nikki asked.

"No place in particular," he said. He glanced at her with faint amusement. "Unless," he added, "you like to fish."

"I don't mind it. But you hate it!" she laughed.

"Of course I do. But I have to keep my hand in," he added. "So that I don't disgrace the rest of my family. The gear and tackle are under that tarp. I thought we'd ease up the river a bit and settle in a likely spot. I brought an ice chest and lunch."

"You really are full of surprises," she commented.

His dark eyes twinkled. "You don't know the half of it," he murmured, turning his concentration back to navigation.

He found a leafy glade and tied the boat up next to shore. He and Nikki sat lazily on the bank and watched their corks rise and fall and occasionally bob. They ate cold cut sandwiches and potato chips and sipped soft drinks, and Nikki marveled at the tycoon who was a great fishing companion. Not since her childhood, when she'd gone fishing with her late grandfather, had she enjoyed anything so much. She'd forgotten how much fun it was to sit on the river with a fishing pole.

"Do you do this often?" she wanted to know.

"With my brothers and my father. Not ever with a woman." His broad shoulders lifted and fell. "Most of them that I know don't care for worms and hooks," he mused. "You're not squeamish, are you?"

"Not really. About some things, maybe," she added quietly. "But unless you're shooting the fish in a barrel, they have a sporting chance. And I do love fried bass!"

"Can you clean a fish?"

"You bet!"

He chuckled with delight. "In that case, if we catch anything, I'm inviting myself to supper." His eyes narrowed. "If you have no other plans."

"Not for two weeks, I haven't," she said.

He seemed to relax. His powerful legs stretched out in front of him and he tugged on the fishing pole to test the hook. "Nothing's striking at my bait," he grumbled. "I haven't had a bite yet. We'll give it ten more minutes and then we're moving to a better spot."

"The minute we move, a hundred big fish will feel safe to vacation here," she pointed out.

"You're probably right. Some days aren't good ones to fish."

"That depends on what you're fishing for," she said, concentrating on the sudden bob of her cork. "Watch this...!"

She pulled suddenly on the pole, snaring something at the end of the line, and scrambled to her feet. Whatever she'd hooked was giving her a run for her money. She pulled and released, pulled and released, worked the pole, moved up the bank, muttered and clicked her tongue until finally her prey began to tire. She watched Kane watching her and laughed at his dismal expression.

"You're hoping I'll drop him, aren't you?" she challenged. "Well, I won't. Supper, here you come!"

She gave a hard jerk on the line and the fish, a large bass, flipped up onto the bank. While Kane dealt with it, she baited her hook again. "I've got mine," she told him. "I don't know what you'll eat, of course."

He sat down beside her and picked up his own pole. "We'll just see about that," he returned.

Two hours later, they had three large bass. Nikki had caught two of them. Kane lifted the garbage and then the cooler with the fish into the boat.

Nikki forgave herself for feeling vaguely superior, just for a few minutes.

Kane had forgotten his tragedies, his business dealings, his worries in the carefree morning he was sharing with Nikki. Her company had liberated his one-track mind from the rigors that plagued men of his echelon. He was used to being by himself, to letting business occupy every waking hour. Since the death of his family, he'd substituted making money for everything else. Food tasted like cardboard to him. Sleep was infrequent and an irritating necessity. He hadn't taken a vacation or even a day off since the trip he'd taken with his wife and son that had ended so tragically.

Perhaps that very weariness had made him careless and caused his head injury. But looking at Nikki, so relaxed and happy beside him, he couldn't be sorry about it. She was an experience he knew he'd never forget. But, like all the others, he'd taste her delights and put her aside. And in two weeks after he left her, he wouldn't be able to recall her name. The thought made him restless.

Nikki noticed his unease. She wondered if he was as attracted to her emotionally as he seemed to be physically. It had worried her when he'd admitted that he had a lover. Of course, he thought she did, too, and it couldn't have been further from the truth. But it could be, she was forced to admit, remembering the feel of his big arms around her. He could be her lover. She trembled inside at the size and power of his body. Mosby had never been able to bring himself to make love to her at all. He'd only been able to touch her lightly and without passion. She hadn't known what it was to be kissed breathless, to be a slave to her body's needs, until this stranger had come along. There were many reasons that would keep her from becoming intimate with him. And the first was the faceless lover who clung to him in the darkness. She didn't know how to compete with another woman, because she'd never had to.

She forced her wandering mind back to the fishing. This had been one of the most carefree days of her life. She was sad to see it end. Kane had agreed to come to supper, but she was losing him now to other concerns. His mind wasn't on the fish, or her. She wondered what errant thought had made him so preoccupied.

"I have to make a telephone call, or I'd help you clean the fish," he said when he left her at the front door of her beach house with the cooler.

"Business?" she asked.

His face showed nothing. "You might call it that." He didn't say anything else. He smiled at her distractedly and left with a careless wave of his hand.

Nikki went in to clean the fish, disturbed by his sudden remoteness. What kind of business could he have meant?

Kane listened patiently while the angry voice at the other end of the telephone ranted and railed at him.

"You promised that we could go to the Waltons' party tonight!" Chris fumed. "How can you do this to me? What sort of deal are you working on that demands a whole evening of your time?"

"That's hardly your concern," he said in a very quiet voice. Her rudeness and lack of compassion were beginning to irritate him. She was a competent psychologist, and he couldn't fault her intellect. But their mutual need for safe intimacy had been their only common bond. Chris wanted a man she could lead around by the nose in any emotional relationship. Kane wasn't the type to let anyone, man or woman, dictate to him. He'd tired of Chris. Tonight, she was an absolute nuisance.

"When will you phone me, then?" she asked stiffly.

"When I have time. It might be as well if we don't see as much of each other in the future."

There was a hesitation, then a stiff, "Perhaps you're right. You're a wonderful lover, Kane, but I always have the feeling that you're going over cost overruns even when we're together."

"I'm a businessman," he reminded her.

"You're a business," she retorted. "A walking, talking industry, and I still say you should be in therapy. You haven't been the same since..."

He didn't want to hear any more. "I'll phone you. Good night."

He put the receiver down before she could say anything else. He'd had quite enough of her psychoanalysis. She did it all the time, even when she was in bed with him; especially when she was in bed with him, he amended. If he was aggressive, she labeled him a repressed masochist. If he was tender, he was pandering to her because he felt superior. Lately, she inhibited him so much that he lost interest very quickly when he was in bed with her, to the point of not being able to consummate lovemaking. That really infuriated her. She decided that his real problem was impotence.

If her barbs hadn't been so painful, they might have been amusing. He'd never been impotent in his life with anyone except Chris. Certainly he was more capable than ever when he just looked at Nikki. But, then, Nikki apparently didn't have any reason to hate and despise men. She was very feminine along with her intelligence, and she didn't tease viciously.

He got up and changed from jeans and jersey into dress slacks and a comfortable yellow knit shirt. Fried fish with Nikki was suddenly much more enticing than a prime rib and cocktails with Chris.

He selected a bottle of wine from the supply he'd imported and carried it along with him. He wondered if Nikki knew anything about fine white wine. She was an intelligent girl, but she hadn't the advantages of wealth. Probably she wouldn't know a Chardonnay from a Johannisberg Riesling. That was something he could teach her. He didn't dare think about tutoring her in anything else just yet. She could become even more addicting than alcohol if he let her. Chris was all the trouble he needed for the present.

Nikki had cleaned and fried the fish and was making a fruit salad and a poppyseed dressing to go with it when Kane knocked briefly and let himself into the cottage.

She glanced over her shoulder and smiled at him. "Come on in," she invited. She was wearing a frilly floral sundress that left most of her pretty, tanned back bare while it discreetly covered her breasts in front. She was barefoot at the kitchen table and Kane felt his body surge at the picture of feminine beauty she presented. How long had it been, he tried to recall, since he'd seen a woman in his own circle of friends wearing anything less masculine than a pin-striped business suit? Nikki dressed the way he liked to see a woman dress, not flaunting her curves but not denying it, either. She dressed as if she had enough confidence in her intellect not to have to hide her womanhood behind it.

"I've just finished the salad and dressing. Want to set the table?" she asked brightly.

He hesitated. He couldn't remember ever doing that in his life. Even as a child, there had always been maids who worked in the kitchen.

"The plates are there," she nodded toward a cupboard with her head. "You'll find utensils in the second drawer. Place mats and napkins are in the third drawer." She noticed his expression and his hesitation with faint amusement. "You do know how to set a table?"

"Not really," he admitted.

"Then it's high time you learned," she said. "Someday you may get married, and think how much more desirable you'll be if you know your way around a kitchen."

He didn't react to the teasing with a smile. He stared at her with a curious remoteness and she remembered belatedly the dead wife she wasn't supposed to know about.

"I don't want to marry anyone," he said unexpectedly. "Especially a woman I've only just met," he added without being unkind.

"Well, certainly you don't want to marry me right now," she agreed. "After all, you don't even know me. Sadly, once you discover my worthy traits and my earthy longings, you'll be clamoring to put a ring on my finger. But I'll have to turn you down, you know. I already have a commitment.''

His face went hard and his eyes glittered. He turned away from her and began searching in drawers. ''Some commitment,'' he muttered. ''The man doesn't even come to check on you. What if a hurricane hit? What if some criminal forced his way in here and raped you, or worse?''

''He phones occasionally,'' she said demurely.

''What a hell of a concession,'' he returned. ''How do you stand all that attention?''

''I really don't need your approval.''

''Good thing. You won't get it. Not that I have any plans other than supper,'' he added forcefully, glaring at her as he began to put things on the table in strange and mysterious order.

She didn't bother to answer the gibe. ''You really should take lessons in how to do a place setting,'' she remarked, noting that he had the forks in the middle of the plate and the knives lumped together.

''I don't want to make a career of it.''

''Suit yourself,'' she told him. ''Just don't blame me if you're never able to get a job as a busboy in one of the better hotels. Heaven knows, I tried to teach you the basics.''

He chuckled faintly. She turned and began to put

the food on the table. Afterward, she rearranged the place settings until they were as they should be.

"Show-off," he accused.

She curtsied, grinning at him. "Do sit down."

He held the chair out for her, watching when she hesitated. "I am prepared to stand here until winter," he observed.

With a long sigh, she allowed him to seat her. "Archaic custom."

"Courtesy is not archaic, and I have no plans to abandon it." He sat down across from her. "I also say grace before meals—another custom which I have no plans to abandon."

She obediently bowed her head. She liked him. He wasn't shy about standing up for what he believed in.

Halfway through the meal, they wound up in a discussion of politics and she didn't pull her punches.

"I think it's criminal to kill an old forest to save the timbering subsidy," she announced.

His thick eyebrows lifted. "So you should. It is criminal," he added.

She put down her fork. "You're a conservationist?"

"Not exclusively, but I do believe in preservation of natural resources. Why are you surprised?" he added suspiciously.

That was an answer she had to avoid at all costs. She forced a bright, innocent smile to her face. "Most men are in favor of progress."

He studied her very intently for a moment, before he let the idea pass. "I do favor it, but not above conservation, and it depends on what's being threatened. Some species are going to become extinct despite all our best efforts, you do realize that?"

"Yes," she said. "But it seems to me that we're paving everything these days. It's a travesty!"

"I've heard of development projects that were stopped because of the right sort of intervention by concerned parties. But it isn't a frequent occurrence," he remarked.

"I hate a world that equates might with right."

"Nevertheless, that's how the system works. The people with the most money and power make the rules. It's always been that way, Nikki. Since the beginning of civilization, one class leads and other classes serve."

"At the turn of the century, industrialists used to trot out Scientific Darwinism to excuse the injustices they practiced to further their interests," she observed.

"Scientific Darwinism," he said, surprised. "Yes, the theory of survival of the fittest extended from nature to business." He shook his head. "Incredible."

"It's still done," she pointed out. "Big fish eat little fish, companies which can't compete go under..."

"And now we can quote Adam Smith and a few tasty morsels from *The Wealth of Nations,* complete with all the dangers of interfering in business. Let the sinking sink. No government intervention."

She stared at him curiously. "Are you by any chance a closet history minor?" she queried with a smile.

"I took a few courses, back in the dark ages," he confessed. "History fascinates me. So does archaeology."

"Me, too," she enthused. "But I know so little about it."

"You could go back to school for those last two semesters," he suggested. "Or, failing that, you could take some extension courses."

She hesitated. "That would be nice."

But she didn't have the means. She didn't have to say it. He knew already. She'd ducked her head as she spoke, and she looked faintly embarrassed.

She had to stop spouting off, she told herself firmly. Her tongue would run too far one day and betray her brother to this man. She hadn't lied about college, though. Part of the terms of her settlement with Mosby Torrance at their divorce was that he would pay for her college education. And he had. She'd worked very hard for her degree. The pain she'd felt at her bad experience had spurred her to great heights, but she hadn't been able to finish. She'd had to drop out just after her junior year to help Clayton campaign. Kane didn't know that.

"What do you do for a living?" he asked suddenly.

She couldn't decide how to answer him. She couldn't very well say that she hostessed for her brother. On the other hand, she did keep house for him.

"I'm a housekeeper," she said brightly, and smiled.

He'd hoped she might have some secret skill that she hadn't shared with him. She seemed intelligent enough. But apparently she had no ambition past being her boyfriend's kept woman. That disappointed him. He liked ambitious, capable women. He was strong himself and he disliked women whom he could dominate too easily or overwhelm.

"I see," he said quietly.

He looked disappointed. Nikki didn't add anything to what she'd said. It was just as well that he lost interest in her before things got complicated, she told herself. After all, she could hardly tell him who she really was.

Chapter Five

Nikki put the dishes away while Kane wandered around the living room, looking at the meager stock of books in the shelves. She sounded like she was well-read, but the only books he noted were rather weathered ones on law.

"They were my father's," she told him. "He wanted to be a lawyer, but he couldn't afford the time."

Or the money, Kane thought silently. He glanced at her. "Don't you have books of your own?"

"Plenty. They're not here, though. The house tends to flood during storms and squalls, so we…I—" she caught herself "—don't leave anything really valuable here."

As if she probably had anything valuable. His dark eyes slid over her body quietly, enjoying its soft curves but without sending blatant sexual messages her way.

"You don't look at me as other men do," she said hesitantly. His eyebrows arched and she laughed self-consciously. "I mean," she amended, "that you don't make me feel inferior or cheap. Women are rather defensive when men wolf whistle and make catcalls. Perhaps they don't realize how threatening it can be to a woman when she's by herself. Or perhaps they do."

"You're very attractive. I suppose a man who lacks verbal skills uses the only weapons he has."

"Weapons." She tasted the word and made a face. "They are, aren't they? Weapons to demean and humiliate."

He moved closer. "You're destroying my illusions," he told her. "I was just thinking that you were unique—a woman comfortable in her femininity."

"Oh, I am," she said. "I enjoy being a woman. But there are looks and words that make me uncomfortable. I dislike harassment."

"Would you believe that men can be made just as uncomfortable by aggressive women?" he asked softly.

She laughed a little. "I suppose so. But one doesn't think of women making men uncomfortable."

"You'd be amazed," he confessed.

Her thin eyebrows drew slightly together. "Is she aggressive?"

He stilled. "She?"

"The woman you...your lover."

She was perceptive, he thought. Too perceptive. He smiled, but it wasn't a pleasant smile. "Yes," he said. "She's learned how to make me impotent, in fact, and she seems to enjoy it."

She flushed. "Sorry." She sat down on the sofa, busying herself with arranging the pillows.

"Oh, hell, I'm sorry, too," he said gruffly. He sat down in the armchair across from her, his arms crossed on his knees as he stared at her until she met his dark eyes. "You're remarkably inhibited for a woman your age."

"Am I?" She smiled vacantly.

It should have discouraged him. It didn't. His eyes narrowed as his mind started adding up discrepancies between her flirtatious nature and her reaction to blatant comments. "The man you're living with," he began. "You are lovers, aren't you?"

She stared at him while her mind struggled with answers that wouldn't give her completely away.

His lips parted and he let out a slow breath. "There's only one answer that fits this whole setup," he said quietly. "The man you share this beach house with...is he gay?"

She shifted uncomfortably. She couldn't let him

think that about the owner of the beach house, in case he found out somewhere down the road that it belonged to Clayton Seymour. On the other hand, her face had already given away the fact that she didn't sleep with the owner of the beach house.

"No," she said shortly. "He most certainly is not gay."

His eyes narrowed. "Then how can you be committed to him when he's never here? Or are you just a one-night stand he can't shake off?"

She got to her feet, her eyes blazing. "You make a great deal of assumptions for a man who knows nothing about my situation."

He got up, too. He shrugged, sticking his hands in his pockets as he studied her. "You don't add up. All I want is a straight answer. Do you have a lover or not?"

He'd put it in such a way that she could answer it if she wanted to, without implicating her brother. "I'm no maiden," she said—and it was true, because she'd been married to Mosby.

"I hardly supposed you were," he returned. His eyes slowly wandered over her. "I want you," he said bluntly.

She stared at him levelly. Well, what had she expected, professions of love eternal and a sparkly diamond? She drew in a slow breath. "For how long?"

"Until we get tired of each other," he said.

He was ruthless. She'd suspected that he was, but it was disconcerting to have proof. It was a good thing that she hadn't dashed in headfirst. She studied the floor at her feet, her eyes idly on her sandals and her pink-tipped toes. "I told you at the outset that I don't sleep around."

"Yes, you did. But I'm offering you more than that. I've given you the impression that I'm poor. I'm not." He moved closer, his powerful body intimidating as he stood just in front of her, so that the scent of his cologne teased her nostrils. "Nikki, I can pay for you to finish college. I can buy you a place of your own, one that you won't have to share."

She was almost shaking with indignation. Had he no idea what she was like. He knew that she was intelligent, but that counted for nothing. It was a body he wanted in bed, nothing more. She felt cheap, and she didn't like it.

She lifted cold green eyes to his, and he seemed taken aback by the hostility he saw in them. "I don't have a price tag," she told him very evenly.

A cynical smile brushed his hard mouth. "Don't you? Suppose I produced a wedding ring? Would that change your mind?"

At the mention of the words, nightmarish memories made her eyelids flicker. She turned away. "I have no interest in marriage," she said stiffly.

"Then you're a rarity in the world." He grew

more impatient and irritated by the second. She wasn't reacting as he'd expected. "Most women would trade themselves for the right offer."

Her hands clenched at her sides while she struggled for composure. She'd had years of practice at the polite, meaningless smile she used on overbearing people. She dredged it up now.

"Then perhaps you'd better fall back on the few you already know," she said. "I'd like for you to leave now."

"I thought I was doing you a favor by being honest," he replied, because he saw her clenched hands.

She was finding that out. "You're absolutely right, you did. It's marvelous to find out that my intelligence and my personality count for nothing with you, that as far as you're concerned, I'm just a slab of meat after all."

He scowled. "You weren't exactly a shrinking violet yesterday."

"One kiss and you think you're irresistible?" she asked, wide-eyed.

That did it. His eyes blazed with dark rage. "Who the hell do you think you are?" he demanded.

"Only a woman you've propositioned, don't let it worry you. I'm sure you'll trip over willing bodies on your way back to your own house. Do drive carefully. Thank you for the fishing trip. And goodbye,'' she added, smiling.

How he hated that damned plastic smile! He turned on his heel and strode angrily to the front door. He couldn't remember ever having felt such a violent hatred of a woman.

He went home in a stupor, uncertain why he'd made such a blatant proposition to someone for whom he was beginning to feel a rare tenderness. He didn't understand his own behavior.

It was worse when he remembered how she'd clung to him on the beach the day before, and how much he'd wanted to make love to her right there on the sand. He felt frankly threatened by his own confusion. His desire for her was growing by the second. He needed a woman tonight, badly, to get Nikki out of his thoughts.

But calling Chris was out of the question. He had two other women friends with whom he could satisfy these inconvenient longings. The problem was, they were halfway in love with him. He couldn't take one of them to bed without encouraging her. Damn the luck, he thought furiously. It was Nikki who'd aroused him, but she was the one woman in the world he didn't dare go to for satisfaction. What a joke fate had played on him!

Nikki cleaned up the house and went to sit on the deck. It was stormy-looking. There were dark clouds over the ocean, and she hoped the predictions of that tropical depression turning into a full fledged tropical storm were false. She had enough storms in her life.

She wondered if any other woman had ever rejected Kane Lombard after such a blatant proposition. Probably not, once they knew who he was. He had money all right, but what hurt the most was that he'd assumed that because he thought Nikki had none, he felt justified in using money as bait to get her into bed with him.

She dashed away angry tears. She doubted if he'd gone home to spend the night alone. He had a little black book. His photograph wasn't well-known, but he made the gossip columns, just the same. There had been stories in the media about his flings with women, after his wife's untimely death. He'd been almost a playboy, if the gossip columns could be believed. He wouldn't have to go far to find consolation, she knew, and she hated him for that, too.

Mosby had rejected her because he didn't like women. Kane had only wanted to have an affair with her. She seemed destined to spend her life alone.

She tried to tell herself that it was just as well. After all, she had no self-confidence. After her sad interlude with Mosby, she didn't trust her judgment anyway. But Kane wasn't like Mosby.

Well, it was for the best. She didn't want to

become addicted to a man her brother hated and that had already been in danger of happening. She was halfway in over her head and she might be grateful to him for calling it quits, she told herself. He might have just saved her heart from being completely broken. One day, Kane Lombard would have found out her real identity. But her depression lasted far into the night, and the next day, just the same.

Clayton had flown back to Charleston for the weekend, taking a sulky Derrie with him. She'd had a date with a promising Washington politician for a play and Clayton had deliberately conned her into this trip and out of D.C. For some reason that he didn't quite understand, he didn't want his executive assistant dating anyone.

It had needled him, that acerbic comment from Bett, the woman he'd been dating casually, about his sister. Bett didn't like Derrie, either. She considered Southern women too helpless and man-loving to be real, and she held them in contempt for what she felt was behavior demeaning to women. Derrie, on the other hand, held Bett in contempt for denying her womanhood while trying to become a man with breasts.

"Couldn't you stop glaring at me?" Clayton asked with a hopeful smile. "Your eyebrows are going to grow in that position and you'll look like a wrestler.''

Derrie tossed back her blond hair. ''Good! Then I can work for myself and make a lot of money.''

''You wouldn't enjoy a job that didn't let you spar with me,'' he said smugly. ''You'd be miserable.''

''I don't know. I might adopt one of those poor little spotted owls whose houses you're going to help cut down!''

Now he was glaring back. ''I'm not personally going to evict one single feathered resident of the northwest forest.''

''You're going to vote for a bill that does,'' she returned. She squared her shoulders, obviously setting down to fight.

''We have to provide jobs for the loggers,'' he began halfheartedly.

''Great idea. If you want to keep those men working, fund programs to retrain them. You'll have to do it eventually, when all the forests are gone.''

''Forests are being replanted,'' he said curtly. ''You're not listening.''

''I am. You're not. Forests are being cut down much faster than they can be replaced. Before you sit on that issue with your full weight, it wouldn't hurt to read a few contrary opinions on it.'' Her chin lifted. ''While we're on the subject, it might be just as well if you talked to a few people besides Ms. Watts about it. She is a lobbyist. They aren't paying her to tell you both sides of the issue—only theirs. And she's working for the timber industry."

"I hadn't forgotten," he said, his voice growing strained.

"Do remember when you vote," she added, getting out of her seat once the plane was down, "that the American taxpayers aren't getting the benefit of having Ms. Watts in bed with them. So they might not appreciate her position in the same way you do."

He got up in one lightning motion, more angry than he could ever remember being. "One day, so help me, Derrie...!" he burst out furiously.

"Oh, am I not supposed to know that you're sleeping with her?" she asked with feigned innocence. "Why, how could I not know, when she's advertised your relationship to everyone who works in the building!"

His jaw clenched. Derrie was exaggerating. She must be. "That's unfair."

"I wouldn't call it that, when she pulled a pair of her lacy pink panties out of your middle desk drawer in front of an aide and two administrative assistants," she said with fierce distaste. "Didn't she tell you she'd done it? My, my. How thoughtless."

While he was absorbing that blow, she turned

and walked down the aisle toward the exit. Still vibrating with rage and sudden uncertainty about his entire position, Clayton left the bags for his assistant and started toward the front of the plane. But he didn't hurry. He wasn't anxious to catch up with her until he cooled down.

Mark Davis, a junior member of Clayton Seymour's staff and a former investigative journalist, had uncovered an interesting little tidbit with some help from Senator Torrance's district director, John Haralson. He was savoring it in the privacy of his apartment while he poured the remains of a bottle of gin into a glass of ice and water. Haralson had all but given him the lowdown, swearing him to secrecy about how he'd obtained his information. Haralson had said that he didn't want to be directly connected with it, so he was giving the credit to Davis.

"Nice," he mused to himself. "Very, very nice." He'd connected with a representative from the biggest and best of the local waste disposal companies. The Coastal Waste Company man had told him that Kane Lombard had, without reason, suddenly dissolved his contract with the solid waste disposal group and replaced them with what was a little-known local company.

The CWC representative was still fuming about the incident, which had been inexplicable—his company had an impeccable reputation all over the southeast for its handling of dangerous waste disposal. CWC had drivers who were specially trained for the work. They used vehicles designated for only the purpose of handling toxic materials, and the vehicles were double insulated for safety. The drivers were trained in how to handle an accident, what to do in case of a leakage. The company had even been spotlighted on the national news for the excellence of its work. And now without reason, Kane Lombard had fired them. The damage to their reputation was at the head of their concern.

Had they tried to contact Lombard to find out his reason, Mark had asked. Of course they had, the CWC representative replied. But Lombard had refused to answer the call. That, too, was odd. He was a man known for not dodging controversy or argument.

What was very interesting was the name of the new solid waste contractor. Burke. There had been a local concern under that name which had been sued only a year back for dumping chemicals from an electroplating company directly into a vacant field instead of the small town's landfill. The contaminants had gotten into a stream on the property and some cattle on a neighboring piece of land had died. The farmer had seen something suspicious in the stream and had it chemically analyzed. His attorney had asked some questions and learned that a neighbor had seen Burke and his truck in the vicinity several times.

It hadn't been hard to connect the electroplating residue with Burke, since there was only one electroplating company in the county and none of its refuse was permitted at the landfill. The farmer had taken Burke to court and the city attorney had an inquiry underway. But the impending litigation hadn't stopped Burke. He was still hauling off waste in two dilapidated old trucks, and he wasn't seen taking any of his shipments into the city's landfills. Which raised the question of where he was taking it.

Mark smiled as he kicked off his shoes, put his glass on the bedside table, and sprawled on the bed. Lombard had already barely escaped a charge for letting sewage from the plant leak into the river. He was already on every environmentalist's list of prospective targets. Haralson had said that he had a hunch about a dumping site, but he'd have to have outside help to do any more digging.

If they could link Burke to Lombard's company and then to some illegal dumping site, the resulting explosion should be enough to knock the man's socks off. Lombard would be in over his head in no time, and the fact that Clayton would have brought the charges would help him in his reelection campaign. It might even turn attention away from the spotted-owl controversy. He and Derrie had tried their best to keep Clayton from getting involved in that debate. But perhaps this would smooth over the controversy.

Some days, Mark thought smugly, things just couldn't help going right. He picked up the telephone receiver and began to dial Clayton's house number. It was Friday night and Clayton Seymour was very predictable in one way: he was always home in Charleston by seven on a Friday evening.

He'd expected the candidate to sound tired, but Seymour actually snapped at him when he answered the telephone. "What is it that couldn't wait until Monday?" he added tersely.

Mark hesitated. "Perhaps this isn't a good time to talk about it," he said, faintly ruffled. "But I thought you'd like to know that Kane Lombard has contracted with a fly-by-night waste disposal company that's suspected of dumping toxic waste somewhere in the coastal marshes."

"What?!"

That did it. Mark grinned. "Can you believe it? He's been so careful in every other area not to antagonize anyone about conservation issues. Now here he goes and hires a local man with a really bad reputation to dump his toxic waste. And he fires a company with the best reputation in the business to do it!"

"Facts, Mark, facts."

"I've got them. Give me a few days and I'll prove it."

"Remind me to give you a raise. Several raises."

Mark laughed out loud. "In that case, you can have the videotapes in stereo with subtitles."

"Good man. I knew I made the best choice when I hired you. Don't cross the line, though," he cautioned. "Don't give him any ammunition to use against us."

"I'll make sure I don't."

"Thanks."

He hung up, his former bad humor gone in a flash of delight. Lombard had publicly announced his intention to fund the campaign of Clayton's Democratic opponent for his House seat and one of Lombard's brothers was Democratic candidate Sam Hewett's executive administrative aide. Not only that, Lombard had been making some nasty, snide comments about Seymour having the background but not the brains and know-how to do the job.

This might be a little on the shady side, to expose a potential adversary's chief supporter thwarting the environmental laws. But if it gave Clayton a wedge to use in the election, then he was going to use it. He'd been bested too many times by people without scruples.

At least he didn't take money under the table,

he thought, rationalizing his use of what Nikki would call gutter tactics. No doubt Nikki would disapprove, if she knew. But then, he added, he would be doing the city a service, wouldn't he? And perhaps it would make people stop hounding him about that infernal owl!

In the meanwhile, there was no reason for Nikki to know anything yet. She needed her vacation. He wasn't going to spoil it by calling her up to tell her how he was gaining on his rival. There would be plenty of time for that later.

He couldn't help but wonder how young Mark had managed to dig up such a tasty scandal for him. He really would have to watch that eager young man. He was an asset.

Derrie unpacked her bags in her small apartment and lamented about the nice dinner and play she could have been enjoying if Clayton hadn't dragged her back to Charleston with him. He never worked on Saturday, but he'd convinced her that tomorrow was going to be the exception and he couldn't work without her.

Not that she cared much about the D.C. official she'd been going to share the dinner and play with. In fact, he was something of a bore. But it had been an opportunity to show Clayton that he wasn't the only fish swimming within hook range.

Who am I kidding, she asked her reflection in

the mirror. She had two new gray hairs among the thick blonde ones. She also had wrinkles at the corners of her big dark blue eyes, and dark circles beneath them from lack of sleep. She'd worked for Clayton for three years in Washington and he never noticed her at all. He was too busy enjoying the companionship that his political standing gave him.

He was very discreet, but there were women in his life. Derrie stood on the sidelines handing him letters to sign and reminding him of appointments, and he never did more than tease her about her deprived social life. Which was his fault, of course, since she didn't want to go out with anyone except her stupid boss.

The newly-elected congressman who'd taken her with him to Washington three years ago was changing before her eyes, she asserted as she got ready for bed. He'd run for the office on a conservation platform, but it was eroding these days. His lack of defense for the spotted owl was just the latest in a line of uncharacteristic actions lately.

It was the first issue Derrie had braced him on, but not the first she'd opposed. He'd had angry letters from any number of constituents about his voting record during the present session of Congress. He'd voted against most environmental issues, ever since he'd been sleeping with Bett. He'd hired that investigative reporter right off the local news show, and was using him to find flaws in other peoples' characters that he could use for leverage to accrue votes for issues he championed. And he was suddenly associating a lot with his ex-brother-in-law, Senator Mosby Torrance, an active anticonservation and pro-liberal advocate. He was also voting the way Torrance wanted him to on major bills. In fact, he'd introduced a couple of bills for Torrance.

Derrie wondered if Nikki had noticed these changes in Clayton's personality. Nikki hadn't been well, and Clayton had spent more time in Washington than ever during the past six months. It was well-known that Bett and Senator Torrance were occasional companions. Perhaps he was using Bett to entice Clayton. Or perhaps there was some other connection. No one knew why Nikki and Mosby had broken up. Knowing Nikki as she did, Derrie blamed Torrance. Anyone who couldn't live with Nikki had to be a basket case.

She climbed into bed and pulled up the covers, heartsick and demoralized. She'd never argued so much with Clayton before. Now it seemed she was fated never to do anything else. She really must have a long talk with Nikki about him…

Bett Watts was going over accounts on her computer when the telephone rang stridently. She reached out a hand distractedly to pick it up.

"Bett?"

She turned away from the computer. "Yes. Hello, Mosby. What can I do for you?"

"You can tell me that you've convinced Clayton to let me handle this thing about Lombard."

"Don't worry," she said gently. "I can promise you that. I've got him right in my little fingers."

"My God, I hope so. Don't let him do anything on his own, do you understand? Nothing!"

She hesitated. "Well, certainly, I'll take care of it. But, why?"

"Never mind. I'll tell you what you need to know. Good night."

She hung up, curious, but not worried. Mosby was careful and discreet. But she did wonder what he had in mind.

Chapter Six

It had been so simple at first, Kane told himself as he piloted his sailboat out into the Atlantic. All he had to do was ignore Nikki and her influence would disappear like fog in the hot sun. But she hadn't. It had been three days and he was more consciously aware of his own loneliness than he could remember being since the death of his wife and son a year ago.

He lifted his dark face into the breeze and enjoyed the touch of it on his leonine features. One of his forebears has been Italian, another Spanish, and even another one Greek. He had the blood of the Mediterranean in his veins, so perhaps that explained why he loved sailing so much.

He glanced over his shoulder at his crew. They were working furiously to put up the spinnaker, and as it set, his heart skipped a beat. The wind slid in behind it, caressed it, then suddenly filled it like a passionate lover and the sailboat jerked and plowed ahead through the water.

The wind in his hair tore through it like mad fingers. Kane laughed at the sheer joy of being alive. It was always like this when he sailed. He loved the danger, the speed, the uncertainty of the winds and the channels. In colonial days, he was sure that he would have been a pirate. At the very least, he'd have been a sailing man. There was nothing else that gave him such a glorious high. Not even sex.

He spun the wheel and brought the sailboat about to avoid collision with a lunatic in a high-powered motorboat. He mumbled obscenities under his breath as he fought the wake of the other boat.

"Damned fools," he muttered.

Jake, his rigger, only laughed. "It's a big ocean. Plenty of room for all sorts of lunatics."

The older man was wiry and tough. He had red hair, going gray, and a weather-beaten sort of leathery skin. Jake had crewed for the yacht *Stars and Stripes* with Dennis Connor in the America's Cup trials the year she won the race. Like the other tough seamen who survived that grueling sport, Jake had a freeness of spirit that gave him a kinship with Kane. From the time Kane was a boy, he had looked to Jake for advice and support in hard times. The older man was in many ways more his father than the tabloid owner in New York who shared his name.

"You're troubled," Jake observed as they traveled seaward amid the creaking of the lines and the flap of the spinnaker as Kane tacked.

"Yes."

"Bad memories?" Jake probed.

Kane took a slow breath. "Complications. I seem to be acquiring them in bunches like bananas lately. Especially one slender brunette one."

"A woman. Not a professional woman...?"

Kane chuckled. "No. She's the pipe and slippers sort, to be avoided at all costs."

"Not like Chris, in other words."

Kane gave him a narrow look. "No. Definitely not like Chris. She isn't an opportunist."

"What is she?"

"Intelligent and proud," he muttered. "Possessive. Independent." He didn't want to talk about her. "I don't want another hard fall. One in a lifetime is enough."

"Oh, by all means, avoid entanglements," the older man agreed easily. He glanced up at the ballooned sail and smiled as he admired the set of it. "We're making good time. We really ought to enter this baby in the Cup trials."

"I don't want to sail in the Cup."

"Why not?"

"For one reason—because I don't have the time."

Jake shrugged philosophically. "I can't argue with that. But you're missing the thrill of a lifetime."

"No, I'm not. Look out there," he said, gesturing toward the horizon. "This is the thrill of a lifetime, every minute I spend on this deck. I don't have to prove anything to the world, least of all that I'm the best sailor in the water."

"Nice to feel that way. Most of us feel we have to live up to some invisible, indefinable goal."

"Why bother? You can't please most people. Please yourself instead."

Jake leaned against the rail and stared at him, hard. "That's selfish."

"I'm a selfish man. I don't know how to give." He met Jake's eyes, and his own were cold, leaden. "Like the rest of the minnows in this icy pond we call life, I'm just trying to stay alive in a society that rewards mediocrity and punishes accomplishment and intelligence."

"Cynic."

"Who wouldn't be? My God, man, look around you! How many people do you know who wouldn't cut your throat to get ahead or make a profit?"

"One. Me."

Kane smiled. ''Yeah. You.''

''You're restless. Isn't it about time we went back to Charleston and you did what you do best?''

''What do I do best,'' he asked absently, ''run the company or make waves for the local politicians?''

''Both. I don't run a major business, but I know one thing. It's damned risky to leave subordinates in charge, no matter how competent they are. Things go wrong.''

Kane turned to study his friend. ''Something you know from experience, right?''

Jake chuckled. ''Yeah. I sat out half a race and we lost the Cup.''

''Not your fault.''

''Tell me that every day. I might believe it.'' He glanced out over the sea toward the horizon. ''Storm blowing up. We're in for some weather. It might be a good idea to head back, before you get caught up in the joy of fighting the sea again,'' he added with a dark look.

Kane had cause to remember the last time he'd been in a battle with the ocean during a gale. He'd laughed and brought the boat in, but Jake hadn't enjoyed the ride. He'd been sick.

''Go ahead, laugh,'' Jake muttered.

''Sorry. I need a challenge now and again, that's all,'' he said apologetically. ''Something to fight, someone to fight. I guess the world sits on me sometimes and I have to get it out of my system."

"The world sits on us all, and you've more reason to chafe than most. It's just a year today, isn't it?"

"A year." Kane didn't like remembering the anniversary of the car bomb that had killed his family. He scowled and turned the wheel, tacking suddenly and sharply, so that the sailboat leaned precariously.

"Watch it!" Jake cautioned. "We could capsize, even as big as we are."

"I hate anniversaries," Kane said heatedly, hurt in his deep voice. "I hate them!"

Jake laid a heavy, warm hand on the broad, husky shoulder of his friend. "Peace, compadre," he said gently. "Peace. Give it time. You'll get through it."

Kane felt sick inside. The wounds opened from time to time, but today was the worst. The sea spray hit him in the face, and the wind chilled it where it was wettest. He stared ahead and tried not to notice that there were warm tracks in the chilled skin.

Chris was waiting for him in the beach house when he returned. He didn't like her assumption that she could walk in and boss his people around whenever she felt like it. She was giving Todd

Lawson hell because he was drinking up Kane's scotch whiskey. Ironically, she was sharing it with him.

What, he wondered, was Lawson doing here?

He walked in, interrupting the argument. They both turned toward him. Lawson was tall, just over six feet, very blond and craggy-faced. He was an ex-war correspondent and had the scars to prove it. He also had a real problem with career women, and his expression as he glowered at Chris punctuated it.

"I see you've met," Kane remarked. He went to the bar and poured himself two fingers of scotch, adding an ice cube to the mixture.

"Wouldn't collided be a better choice of words?" Chris asked testily. She glared back at Lawson. "Shall I leave, so that you *men* can discuss business?"

"Why?" Lawson asked innocently. "Don't you consider yourself one of us?"

Chris's face went an ugly color. From the severely drawn back hair to the pin-striped suit and bralessness under it, she felt the words like a blood-letting whip. She whirled on her heel and departed, so uncharacteristically shaken that she did it without even a word to Kane. Normally, Kane might have taken up for her. But today was a bad day. His grief was almost tangible.

"No purse, either," Lawson drawled, watching

her empty-handed departure. "Don't tell me. It's a sellout to carry something traditionally female."

Kane lifted an eyebrow. "What do you want?" he asked, irritation in the look he bent on his family's star reporter.

"To tell you what I've uncovered."

Kane's hand stilled with the glass of scotch held gingerly in it. "Well?"

"You take your scotch neat," Lawson remarked, moving closer. "I suppose you can take your bad news the same way. Seymour is after you. The rumor is that he's got something he can use to get you on environmental charges. Since that little incident last month, he's confident that he can find something."

"That incident was an accidental spill into the river," Kane said curtly. "We weren't charged."

"Not for that, no. But evidently Seymour thinks where there's one accident there are bound to be others."

Kane ran his hand through his windblown hair. He knew there were problems with his plant manager being absent so much, and there was a new man in charge of waste control. The new man had been responsible for the sewage leak. He was just new, that was all. He told Lawson so.

"New or not, he's clumsy. You can't afford to let this go without looking into it."

"Why is Seymour on my tail?"

"Because your family's tabloid is crucifying him over his support for the loggers, because your brother Norman is Sam Hewett's new executive administrative assistant for his campaign, and because your whole family is endorsing Hewett, Seymour's major Democratic opponent. But I think Seymour's ex-brother-in-law is behind this campaign to smear you."

"What ex-brother-in-law?"

"Senator Mosby Torrance."

Kane frowned. "Why would he be after me? He's a business advocate—notoriously a jobs-over-environment man. The Sierra Club would furnish the firewood to burn him at the stake. Like Seymour," he continued, "he's supporting the opponents of the spotted owl in the northwest."

"The spotted owl won't hurt Torrance very much right now because he doesn't have to run for reelection this year. But Seymour does, and the spotted owl bill has hurt him at home," Lawson said cynically. "However, a few well-placed and well-timed blows at industrial pollution in his home district could kindle a lot of public opinion in his favor and put him back in Washington. I don't know what he's found, but he's got something. You can bet if John Haralson is helping him—and he is—he's got something."

"Haralson."

"Senator Torrance's district director. Mr.

Sleaze,'' he added curtly. ''The original dirty tricks man.''

''Working for Seymour? That doesn't sound like Seymour. I'm a Democrat from the feet up, but even so, from what I've read about Seymour, he's never been a politician who tried to smear anybody for personal gain. He's an idealist.''

''Perhaps he's learned that idealism is a euphemism for naïveté in politics. You can't change the world.''

''That doesn't stop people from trying, does it?''

''Seymour is going to concentrate on you. Your family news tabloid has been his major embarrassment since this spotted owl thing began, and the press coverage he's been given has cost him points in the polls. If he can connect you with anything shady, the inference is that he can cost your family some credibility. That will also hurt Hewett—because your brother is his senior advisor. That's what your father thinks, anyway,'' he added.

''You're his star reporter,'' Kane said. ''What do you think?''

Lawson put his empty glass down. ''I think you'd better make sure there's nothing to connect your company with any more environmental damage.''

''I told you, that sewage leak was purely accidental. I don't have anything shady to worry about.''

"You sound very sure of yourself," Lawson said quietly. "But you've been away from work for a couple of weeks."

"I have competent managers," Kane said, getting more irritated by the minute.

"Do you?" Lawson straightened. He was almost Kane's own height. "Then why have you turned out a reputable company like CWC?"

"CWC." Kane nodded. "Oh, yes, I remember. I had a talk with the new solid waste manager. He said that CWC had done a sloppy job at enormous cost. He wanted permission to replace the company and get someone more efficient—and a little less expensive."

"That's very interesting. CWC has a very good reputation. One of the national news magazines recently did a piece on them. They're very efficient and high-tech."

Lombard pursed his lips and scowled. "Are they? Well, perhaps they've fallen down on the job. I'll look into it when I get back to Charleston. Meanwhile, what have you found out about Seymour?"

"Not much. But I've got a few rumors to check out about Seymour's connection with Mosby Torrance."

Kane laughed coldly. "Dig deep. I may need some leverage if he finds anything. Good God, I take a few days off and everything falls apart. I'd better telephone the plant and talk to that new man.''

''I wouldn't,'' the other man advised. ''Let me check around first.''

''Why?''

''If there's any under-the-table dealing going on, the fewer people who know we suspect, the better.''

''It won't do me any good to wait if Seymour's investigator finds anything illegal going on.''

''That's what worries us,'' Lawson said. ''Our sources think Seymour has found something. Worse, they think there may be some deliberate evidence.'' He stressed the words.

Kane rubbed the back of his neck, wincing as he touched a sunburned area. ''When it rains, it pours,'' he said to himself.

Lawson put down his glass. ''Well, all I have are suspicions right now, mainly because of Haralson's involvement. But I'll let you know if anything surfaces.''

Kane nodded, his mind already away from the small problem of waste disposal and back on Nikki.

John Haralson was sitting in Mosby Torrance's office, grinning from ear to ear.

''What do you know? Lombard's company just kicked out CWC in favor of old fly-by-night

Burke. Remember him? He was charged with dumping toxic waste in a swamp a year or more ago and he weaseled out of the charge."

"How do you know?" Mosby asked curiously.

Haralson pretended innocence. "Contacts. I have all sort of contacts."

Mosby studied the older man curiously. Haralson tended to work miracles, and usually Mosby didn't question how he accomplished them. But just lately, Haralson seemed to be getting a bit out of hand. He had to be more careful. His private life was precarious right now, he couldn't afford to have Haralson making anyone angry enough to start digging into Mosby's past.

"Go on."

"Well, Burke ordinarily charges about one-fifteenth of what Lombard was paying CWC for hauling off the waste. Now he gets what CWC used to get, and he doesn't have their overhead."

Mosby frowned. "That puts the onus on Lombard's hired man, not on Lombard himself. He's not getting anything out of it."

"We can make it look as if he is," Haralson said smugly. "We don't have to mention the kickbacks to his janitorial man. We can say that Lombard was cutting costs. It's a well-known fact that he's just recently laid off some employees because of the recession."

Mosby hesitated. ''You're talking about concealing facts.''

''Not permanently,'' Haralson said smoothly. ''Just long enough for the news media to pick up the story and run it a few times. They love dealing with industrial polluters. Save the planet, you know.''

''But...''

Haralson's eyes narrowed and he leaned forward intently. ''If you don't get Lombard's neck in a noose and squeeze, his man is going to eventually uncover the truth about you and Nikki and your marriage. Can you think what that will do to you, if the press get wind of it?''

''Oh, my God,'' Mosby said, shaken. ''It doesn't bear thinking about!''

''That's right. It could cost Seymour the election, and you your seat.''

Mosby was sweating. It wasn't the first time he'd compromised his ideals to save his career. And this time he had no choice. ''All right. Go ahead and do what you have to.'' He glanced up. ''But make sure that Clayton doesn't know how you're doing it. Do you have an investigator in mind?''

''You bet I do. He works for the Justice Department. He's FBI.''

''Hold it, what if we get charged with appropriating personnel...''

"It's all right. He's on vacation. They had to threaten to fire him to get him out of the office. He's been sitting around muttering for days about the inactivity. He jumped at the chance when I mentioned I had a small problem."

"Can he keep a confidence?"

"He's a Comanche Indian. You tell me."

"Does he have a name?"

"Sure. It's Cortez."

Mosby found himself grinning, the fear subsiding a little. Haralson always seemed to work magic. "You're kidding me."

"I'm not. One of his great-grandfathers was a Spaniard. He calls it the only bad blood in his family tree. His sense of irony is pretty keen, which is why he uses the anglicized name of the Spanish conquerer of Mexico. He spends his free time in Oklahoma with his parents. There, you couldn't pronounce his name."

"You say he's a good investigator."

"One of the best."

"There won't be a conflict of interest involved?"

"Only if we tell anyone he's helping us," Haralson said innocently.

He got a glare in return for his helpful comment.

"It was a joke! There's no problem," Haralson chuckled. "When he's on vacation, what he does with his free time is his own business. We're not asking him to do anything illegal, are we?''

Mosby wasn't so sure about that. ''No. I suppose not. In essence, we're asking him to look for a violation of the Environmental Protection Agency codes.''

''That's right. So just pretend I never said a word. I'll do what's necessary to save your bacon.''

Mosby's light eyes narrowed. ''Don't sweep anything under the carpet,'' he said.

''Not unless I have to,'' Haralson promised.

''You want me to save the hide of a *Texan?*''

''Not at all, Cortez...'' Haralson said quickly, trying to pacify the darker man. Cortez was powerfully muscled, scar-faced, with deep set large black eyes and a rawboned face that seemed to be all sharp, dark angles.

Cortez wasn't handsome, although the tall lean man seemed to draw women just the same. Anyway, his record since he'd joined the FBI was impressive and far outdistanced that of some of the handsomer agents.

''You know I hate Texans,'' Cortez was saying. He didn't blink. It was one of the more disconcerting things about him.

''If I remember my history, Texans weren't too fond of Comanches, either. But I'm not asking you to help a Texan. I'm asking you to help put one in front of a congressional subcommittee."

"Ah," Cortez said smoothly. "Is that so?"

"It is, indeed. I need a little help. A little detective work..."

"I'm on vacation. Do your own detective work."

"Cortez...?" Haralson held out an object on his palm.

The other man hesitated, his brow furrowing. "What is that?"

"You know what it is. You've been trying to beg, borrow, buy or steal it for the past five years. Help me out on this," he added, "and I'll sell it to you at the price you first offered."

Cortez's face hardened. "I don't want it at that price."

"Yes, you do." Haralson flipped it, emphasizing his possession of it.

Cortez groaned. "That's right, hit me in my weakest spot!"

"Always know a man's weaknesses when you plan to trade with him," Haralson chuckled. "Well?"

Cortez pushed back his raven-wing hair, his long fingers settling on the ponytail he wore it in when he was among whites. It seemed to draw more attention when he wore it down. "All right," he said bitterly. "But only because I'm a certifiable collector."

Haralson handed him the coin, a nineteenth-century two-and-a-half dollar gold piece.

"If you knew," Cortez murmured, handling the coin with something akin to reverence, "how many years I've been looking for one of these..."

"I do know. After all, I'm the one who bought it out from under you the day Harry in the code section put it on the market and I happened to be at FBI headquarters doing some research for Senator Torrance. I had a feeling it would come in handy one day."

Cortez gave him a skin-scorching glare. "So it did. All right, you'll get your pint of blood. I'll see if I can connect Lombard's larcenous employee to Burke's with something concrete. If I find anything illegal going on, I'll inform the appropriate people."

"Would I expect anything less from you?" Haralson asked with a wicked smile. "Trust me." He put his hand over his heart. "I have a soul."

"If you do, you keep it in your wallet," the Native American agreed. "I know you too well, Haralson. Just don't forget that you may have something on me, but I've got something on you, too. You had knowledge of a crime and didn't report it."

Haralson stared at him uncomfortably. He hadn't

thought things through that far. He and Cortez were acquaintances, not really friends, but they occasionally did each other some good.

Cortez didn't smile, he smirked. He didn't like Haralson, but the man could be useful at times. It wouldn't hurt to do him one small favor, so long as it didn't breach any legalities. Cortez followed the very letter of the law in most things. He turned away, coin in hand, and went to pick up his jacket. "I'll be in touch as soon as I've checked out a few people and places."

Nikki had waded out into the surf to watch the distant freighter sail out toward the horizon. She wondered how it had been during Charleston's early days as a port city, when great sailing ships came here, carrying their precious cargoes of spices and rum and, sadly, slaves.

Pirates had come from here, people like female pirate Anne Bonney and her cohort Stede Bonett. Descriptions of those early days had fascinated Nikki in college, so much so that she'd done three courses in colonial history. The somber and dignified George Washington came to life as her professor lectured about the way the old warhorse had put on his old Continental uniform in 1794 and led 15,000 volunteers off to put down the Whiskey Rebellion—and how the rebellious Pennsylvania distillers had quickly dispersed at little more than

Washington's threat of dire action. Far from the conventional image of George Washington with his little hatchet, the real man emerged from legend with stark clarity.

She wandered along with her toes catching in the damp sand and felt suddenly alone. Funny how a man she hadn't even known a week ago had made a place for him in her mind, in her heart. He didn't want Nikki in his, of course. He'd made that very plain. She supposed that, not knowing her, he'd classed her as a gold digger and decided to cut his losses before she found out who he was. How amusing that she did know, and had tried to subdue her own interest for equally good reasons.

She felt a chill and wrapped her arms around herself. Just as well that it was over, she told herself. The chill grew worse. She laughed, because her chest felt cloggy and she'd been sure she was completely cured. She'd make herself a hot cup of soup and see if that wouldn't help. Then she'd have an early night, and soon enough Kane Lombard would become a sad memory.

She woke in the middle of the night coughing uncontrollably. Her throat was sore and her chest hurt. This was going to need the services of a doctor, she realized. She dialed, but Chad Holman wasn't at home. She lay back down. He'd be back soon, she was sure. She'd just close her eyes and phone him later.

But it didn't quite work out that way. She slept and didn't waken until morning. When she did wake, she couldn't talk at all and she was coughing up colored mucus. It didn't take a high IQ to realize that meant an infection. She had bronchitis or a recurrence of pneumonia, and a fever to boot. She was too nauseated even to sit up. She couldn't talk, so how could she call anyone? She could tap on the receiver, but Chad was a doctor, not a communications specialist. She couldn't get word to him to come and see her, although he certainly would, just as he'd come to see Kane. The same would be true of Clayton.

But sailors knew Morse Code, she thought foggily. Certainly, they did! So if she could remember just the distress signal and how to spell her name in Morse, she could get Kane to come. He didn't want her, but in an emergency, that didn't even matter. Thank God she'd taken an interest in Morse Code when Clayton's senior legislative counsel Mary Tanner's boyfriend had bought his first shortwave. He and Mary had broken up years ago, but Nikki still remembered the code.

She had Kane's number. He'd given it to her to telephone him that last morning they'd gone out together. She painstakingly pushed the buttons. There was a pause and then a ringing sound. She waited. Waited. Three rings. Four. Five. Her heart began to sink when the phone was suddenly jerked up and an impatient male voice demanded. "Who's there?"

He was in a hurry. It didn't dawn on her that his housekeeper would normally have been answering the telephone, which was a good thing or she might not even have tried to get him. She tapped on the receiver.

"What the hell...?!"

She made a hoarse sound, afraid that he was going to slam the receiver down. She tried again. S...O...S...

The code caught his attention. "All right, I get the message, you're in trouble and you can't talk. Is it Chris?" he added, because he'd taught her Morse.

One tap. He frowned. "One for no, two for yes. Try again."

One tap.

He hesitated. Who could be doing this? Jake? "Can you give your name in Morse?" he asked.

There was a pause and a cough, and the cough made his breath catch. "*Nikki?* Nikki, is it you?"

Two taps. Two taps. "I'll be there in two minutes."

He put the receiver down and ran out the door.

Nikki lay back on the pillow, weak tears of gratitude rolling down her pale cheeks onto her dry, cracked lips. She hadn't thought he'd understand, but he had. And at least his voice had sounded concerned. That could have been an illusion. At the moment, she didn't care. She only wanted to sleep.

Chapter Seven

Nikki heard him at the door, but she was too weak and sick to know or care how he was going to get in. She only knew that he would. He was the sort who got things done even in an emergency. Nikki recognized that trait because she had it herself. She might go to pieces later, but she was always cool when it mattered most.

Kane discovered an unlocked window and went in through it. He found Nikki on the bed, feverish and sick, sounding as if she were breathing water in and out of her lungs.

"My God," he said quietly.

Her eyes opened, dark green with pain and illness in a face like rice paper. "Kane," she whispered, but her voice made no sound.

He didn't waste a minute. He wrapped her up in

the cover and carried her out the door to his waiting car. Ten incredibly fast minutes later, he walked into the nearest emergency room carrying her in his arms.

Time seemed to blur after that. She remembered voices and needles and the coldness of metal against her bare skin. Then she slept, very deeply, and the pain mercifully went away.

When she woke, it was dark and she was lying in an unfamiliar bed. It was king-size, with a white and brown and green color scheme that was repeated in the curtains and the bedclothes. The furniture was dark Mediterranean and as sturdy-looking as the man who obviously lived here.

She stirred, trying to raise herself, but it was just too much of an effort.

Kane opened the door and came in, wearing a black-and-white-toweling robe and nothing else. His dark hair was damp, if neat. He smelled of soap.

"Need something?" he asked quietly.

"I need to get to the bathroom," she whispered hoarsely.

"No problem there." He pulled back the covers, revealing Nikki in a pale blue silk gown, and lifted her gently free. "Silk. Does he buy them for you?" he asked as he carried her toward the bathroom.

"I buy them…for myself. Why am I here?" she croaked.

"Because I didn't fancy trying to sleep on that damned bed in your guest room again," he said bluntly. "How can I reach your lover to tell him where you are?"

"He's abroad," she lied shakily. "And I don't know where he is exactly."

He sighed. "Well, that solves one problem, at least. Here." He put her down. "If you need help, don't stand on modesty."

"I won't."

Several minutes later, her face washed, she opened the door and he returned her to bed.

He sat down beside her, disturbing the tie of his robe to reveal a portion of his broad, hairy chest. "Here, swallow this," he said, producing a pill from a small vial. "Doctor's orders," he added when she hesitated.

She took it from his big hand and managed to swallow it past her sore, tight throat. She grimaced as she handed back the glass of water he'd given her. Her eyes lingered on what she could see of his bare skin and as she dragged them away, he glanced down and chuckled at his state of undress.

"Was I giving you a floor show?" he mused. "Does it matter? You know what I look like. You stood in the doorway and stared at me that first morning after I washed up on your beach."

She flushed uncomfortably. "I didn't know you saw me."

''Oh, I was flattered,'' he remarked dryly, refastening the robe. ''But I've already got a lover.''

''Yes, so you've said.''

He reached down and touched her skin at the collarbone, feeling the heat and dampness of her skin, her involuntary withdrawal from his fingertips.

''I said some harsh things,'' he said quietly. ''You can't forget them. Probably it's a good thing. I have too many complications in my life right now.''

''So do I,'' she whispered. ''I only wanted to be friends. I never said I wanted to be your lover.''

''That's true,'' he said lazily. ''But your eyes say it all the time.'' He lifted his hand and softly traced around a taut nipple, watching her reaction to the blatant intimacy. Her body shivered and she caught her breath. ''What a fierce reaction for such an innocent little caress, Nikki,'' he said, his voice deep and seductive. His big hand flattened over her breast, feeling its firm, hot contour while his thumb and forefinger worked tenderly at the hard nub that crowned it. She was gasping now, even if her hand did raise to catch his wrist in a token protest.

His eyes were steady and speculative on her face. She wasn't accustomed to this kind of intimacy. Like a rank innocent, she was torn between the need to protest and the longing to submit. The pleasure she was feeling was all too evident. So was an odd fear.

"Doesn't he make love to you at all?" he asked quietly. "You're starved for a man's touch."

"Please...don't," she said, shaken.

His dark eyes slid down to the clinging fabric. Only spaghetti straps held the bodice in place, and he'd already dislodged one. His hand moved, slowly tugging it the rest of the way down until he bared her breast to the mauve rise of her nipple. Her eyes widened on his face, as if she couldn't believe what was happening.

"You let me touch it. Now, are you going to let me see it?" he whispered deeply.

Her nails bit into his wrist. This couldn't be happening! She was sick, she was helpless, perhaps it was the medicine...

"Yes," he murmured, completing the slow descent of the silk, and his eyes found her, enjoyed her, took pleasure from the exquisite creamy firmness of her breast in the sudden silence of the room.

No one had ever made her feel that she might die if he didn't do more than look. Not even in her younger days, before Mosby destroyed her confidence in her femininity, had she known such a primitive need.

"You have a little fever, still," he said, letting his fingertips touch her, trace her, worship her.

"Your skin is hot to the touch. Especially here, Nikki, where it's hardest. It makes you tremble when I caress it, doesn't it? It makes you want to pull me down and wrap your legs around my hips and pull me into you, because you know that's the only thing that's going to make the aching stop."

"Damn...you!" she choked.

"You don't want it any less than I do," he whispered. "Look, Nikki. Let me show you."

He stood up, his body vibrating with the same fever that held her captive. His hands loosened the single knot that held his robe in place. He pushed it aside and dropped it, and stood before her with magnificent pride in his aroused masculinity, in the perfection of his tall, hard-muscled body without a single white line to mar the even tan that covered it.

Nikki's face colored, but she couldn't look away. He was beautiful. Her eyes traced him with the same rapt fascination an artist would bend on a work of art. He was a work of art.

"You are utter perfection," she whispered.

"So are you." His legs held a faint tremor as he looked and wanted her just short of the point of madness.

"Oh, Kane," she bit off, too weak and shaky to do anything at all about the anguish of her need.

"It's been a very long time since I've been this

aroused,'' he said matter-of-factly. ''But you're hardly in any condition to satisfy me.''

With sheer force of will, he picked up his robe and shouldered back into it. Nikki lay watching him, helpless, submissive as she never would have been if she'd been completely well.

''That could become addictive,'' he mused, watching her pull up the loosened spaghetti strap to stay the confusion his dark eyes were causing.

''What?''

''Letting you look at me,'' he said, smiling faintly. ''I can never remember wanting the lights on before, when I was aroused like this. Have you ever made love in the light, Nikki?''

She couldn't stop shaking. ''I feel ill,'' she whispered.

''You are ill, little one,'' he said, contrite as he realized how ill she'd been. ''And I'm a brute for behaving like this. The sight of you in that gown has made me mindless, I suppose. You need rest, not sexual innuendoes.''

''Were they only that?'' she asked unguardedly, watching his face close up at the question.

''I wish I could tell you that they were,'' he replied curtly. ''But the fact remains that a relationship between you and me wouldn't work.''

''Are you sure?'' she asked hesitantly.

He sat down beside her, his expression one of reluctant resignation. ''Nikki, a year ago my wife and son were killed in an explosion,'' he said bluntly. ''I'm not coping very well, despite the lover I told you about. Sometimes nightmares keep me awake. I don't know how I feel, because I've tried so hard not to. It's too soon,'' he concluded roughly.

''I'm very sorry,'' she said gently. ''You must miss them terribly.''

''I do.'' He put his head in his hands and leaned his elbows on his knees. ''I miss them every day of my life. God, I'm so tired.''

''Am I contagious?'' she asked after a minute.

''I don't know. Some types of pneumonia are. Some aren't.''

''If you don't mind the risk, you might climb in here with me,'' she said, croaking with every word.

He looked down at her cold-eyed. ''Why?''

She managed a weak smile. ''Because you look very much as if you need someone to hold you.'' She pulled her arms free of the covers and held them up to him.

He was still wondering two hours later why he'd gone so eagerly into those outstretched arms. It hadn't been sex, because what he'd felt in her embrace was nothing if it wasn't tenderness. He'd rolled over with her, cradling the length of her overwarm body to his, holding her as he tried to cope with the nightmare his life had become.

She'd smoothed his dark hair, whispering soft

incoherences, and after a time, the edge of the pain had been dulled and he felt a sigh of peace ease out of his broad chest.

"It's all right to be alive, even if they can't be," she whispered at his ear. "They love you, too, and miss you, and know where you are. In some sense or other, they know."

His big hands flattened on her back, feeling the warmth of her seep into him, making him stronger. It was an incredible sensation, as if they were touching inside somehow, mind and heart and spirit. He wasn't sure he wanted to. On the other hand, the wonder of it overshadowed his doubts and fears, and suddenly all he could think about was how sweet it was to hold her. But it wasn't close enough.

"No," he whispered when she softly protested the sweep of his hands carrying away her gown. "No, let me. I want to be close to you all night. I won't take you. Let me hold you like this."

While he spoke, he shouldered out of his robe, and seconds later she was lying nude against his equally bare body. She shivered at the unfamiliar contact and tried to pull away, but he wouldn't permit it.

"You're afraid," he whispered, and his voice was both surprised and tender. "There's no reason to be. You're an invalid and I have too much conscience to take advantage of it."

"Are you sure?" she asked nervously.

His hands swept down her spine and he groaned pleasurably as he felt her silky skin in exquisite detail, her breasts on his chest, her belly against the helpless thrust of his body.

"No, I'm not sure, but I can't let you go," he murmured roughly. His hands pressed gently at the base of her spine and moved her, his long leg trespassing between her thighs.

"No," she said quickly, staying his hip. "No, don't."

He lifted his head and looked into her frightened eyes. None of this made sense. He moved back, but his hand slowly eased down and, containing her shocked jerk, he whispered her name softly and kissed her frightened eyes closed. The caresses weakened her resolve. He was touching her...!

She caught his arm, but it didn't stop him. He was slow and tender, but relentless. When she felt the sudden twinge of pain, she was unprepared for his shocked roar.

"My God!"

She swallowed. Her legs were trembling from the pleasure of his intimate testing of her, but her hand pulled at his invading one.

"You can't know," she said weakly. "A man can't know..."

He threw himself over onto his back, his eyes wide-open on the shadows that played against the ceiling. His body throbbed, his mind throbbed. He lay on top of the covers with moonlight streaming in the window and outlining him. He couldn't believe what he'd just found out.

"Kane?" she murmured. Her voice sounded rusty.

"Is he gay?"

She swallowed. "He doesn't want to sleep with me," she said, avoiding the implication.

"Why?" he persisted.

"It...isn't what you think."

He felt her move and his head turned. She was reaching for the cover, but he stayed her hand.

His eyes looked at her in a new way. The same boldness was there, but now there was curiosity and wonder.

"Haven't you ever wanted to, with someone?" he asked.

"Oh, yes," she replied honestly, remembering her unbearable pleasure when Mosby had asked her to marry him and she'd thought he felt the same raging desire she did.

"But you didn't?"

She met his eyes levelly. "He couldn't, Kane," she whispered. "He really wanted to, I think. But he...couldn't."

His breath felt suspended. "And you didn't want anyone else?"

She smiled sadly. "I'm afraid not."

He stared down at her without smiling back, without speaking. "I see."

"Your lover," she began. "You said she'd managed to make you impotent."

He lifted an eyebrow and faint humor stole into his eyes. "Yes. Well, obviously, you don't produce the same reaction."

She laughed through the weakness and pain. "No, I don't, do I?"

His eyes slid over her nudity with gentle appreciation. "You aren't in any condition now. But later, when you are..."

Her eyes fell to his chest. She couldn't tell him about her past, or her present. She'd lied to him all around. He would have to know eventually who she was.

"It isn't that easy," she said.

"I remember. You don't want to get pregnant." He let his eyes drift down to her flat stomach and he felt a jolt of pleasure at the thought of it growing large, round, as his wife's had years ago. His wife hadn't really wanted a child until Teddy was born, he recalled. She'd been viciously accusing and horrible, until they laid the tiny infant in her arms and she learned to love him.

"A baby is...a terrible responsibility," Nikki managed, without realizing what she was saying.

He wasn't listening. His big hand suddenly flattened on her stomach, so large that it covered most of her to the navel.

"Babies can be prevented," he said. "So can most diseases, with a very simple device." His eyes lifted back to hers. "I'll use one. There won't be a risk, of any kind, and you won't catch anything from me."

"You talk as if it's only the risk I don't want," she said. She was too weak to fight, and her illness had confused her. Surely that was the only reason she was lying here naked in a man's arms. "Kane, sex is more than a casual pastime to me," she added gently. "I want to be loved, not had."

"Do you think I won't know how to love you?" he asked quietly. His hand began to move, very tenderly. "How to please you? How to give you pleasure beyond your wildest dreams of intimacy?"

She pulled his hand away from her body with a shaky sigh. "What you want is a body to ease your physical need for sex," she whispered. "Presumably, you already have someone you can do that with. I want much, much more. I want total communion and total commitment. I want forever."

His face hardened and his eyes grew mocking. "Forever is an illusion. No one has forever."

"I will," she said stubbornly.

"You won't. You're living in dreams."

"Then I'll live in them. But I won't be taken in

a fit of screaming passion and then discarded like a morning paper that's just been read."

His dark brows arched in surprise.

"You know what I mean," she said stubbornly. "I won't be a sexual object to any man."

"You're naked," he pointed out. "So am I."

She dragged up the covers to her chin. "I'm sick," she said accusingly.

"So you are." He smiled at his own fallibility. "Do you want me to leave?"

She did. She didn't. Her eyes sought his and she vacillated.

He jerked the covers back, slid under them, pulled her close and replaced them. "Lay your cheek on my chest and go to sleep," he murmured.

There was no more argument left in her. She closed her eyes and her body seemed to melt into his. Only seconds passed before she was asleep.

In the morning, she woke in her gown and alone. She must have dreamed the whole thing, she thought dazedly. But it had seemed so real. She laughed at her own folly. She really did have to get her life back together.

When Kane stopped in the doorway later to check on her, she smiled warmly but without embarrassment and said that she was fine.

"I have to make a few telephone calls, but I'll

come back in time to have lunch with you. Can I have Mrs. Beale bring you anything?''

''No, thanks. I still have some of the juice she brought me at breakfast.''

''Okay.''

He smiled, letting his dark eyes slide over her pretty face. Even sick, she was lovely to look at.

''You've got a little more color than you had yesterday. How's the chest?''

''It's better,'' she assured him. ''Kane, thank you for bringing me here and taking care of me.''

''How could I let them put you in the hospital, when you have no one else to look out for you?'' he said quietly.

That wasn't true. She had a brother who loved her. But she couldn't admit it. ''Thank you anyway,'' she murmured while she wondered in a panic what would happen if Clayton should telephone late at night and not find her at the beach house. Would he rush up here looking for her, involve the police? She had to find a way to contact him.

Meanwhile, she looked at Kane with faint puzzlement and involuntarily, her eyes drifted to the pristine pillow beside her head.

He moved into the room and came to a stop beside the bed. ''Nikki, it wasn't a dream,'' he said soberly.

Her eyes dropped suddenly. On the covers, her nails looked like pink ice. "Then you know..."

"Yes. And so do you," he replied with a quizzical smile. "Everything there is to know about me, physically. Does it matter? I didn't seduce you, even if it was touch and go for a few minutes."

"I suppose not."

"Don't look so stricken. A few intimacies aren't going to stain that snow-white conscience too much. You're old enough to play with fire, aren't you?"

He was fire, she thought, studying him. He was a wildfire, and he caught her up every time he touched her. She'd never known what it was to be so helpless.

"You don't know anything about me, really," she said. "You might not like what you find out one day."

"What sort of dark secrets can a virgin have?" he asked, his voice soft as velvet.

"You might be surprised."

"And I might not." He reached down and brushed the unruly hair away from her oval face, his touch as tender as his voice. "I'm not going to love you, you know."

"I'm not going to love you, either," she whispered.

He bent and brushed his lips softly over her forehead, her closed eyes, her cheeks. He paused at her mouth, barely touching it.

"I'm contagious," she whispered, a plea in her voice.

"You won't be forever," he whispered back. He hesitated but after a heartbeat, he lifted his head.

He looked vibrantly alive, big and dark and dear. Nikki's eyes adored him hopelessly.

"Don't push your luck," he teased with black humor. "Last night is all too vivid in my mind."

"Don't you sleep with her like that?" she asked suddenly.

He chuckled at her fierce glare. "Not naked," he returned easily. "Usually it's in a feverish rush and then I get up and go home. Neither of us has much inclination toward tenderness. In fact, she doesn't really like sex. She likes controlling men. I tolerate the relationship because I don't want commitment and neither does she. I like it quick from time to time."

She was curious. She shifted a little against the pillow and studied him. "Was it like that with your wife, if you don't mind my asking...?"

"I felt very tender with my wife when we first married," he said, reading the question. "I was in love with her, and she with me. We reached heights that I've never found with anyone else. But it all went wrong when she got pregnant with Teddy. After he was born, she lived for him, I suppose I did, too. We lost each other in the act of becoming parents.'' At the mention of the little boy's name, something terrible flared in his eyes, in his face. The nightmare exploded, like the bomb that had wiped out the young life and all his hopes and dreams…

''Kane!''

She dragged herself up from the bed, shaky on her feet, but anguished at what she saw on his face. He was sweating and his eyes were wide, wild, dangerous.

''Darling, it's all right,'' she whispered, hugging him fiercely. ''It's all right, it's all right!''

He swallowed and his body jerked. His hands found her shoulders, resting heavily there while he fought the terror. He'd shut it out for a whole year. Now, with her, it was all coming back. The comfort she offered was making him vulnerable. He realized, shocked, that he felt safe to talk about it because Nikki was there to hold him when the nightmares came.

''Kane, don't look back,'' she said, nuzzling his chest with her cheek. ''You have to stop tormenting yourself.''

''They died,'' he said in a ghostly whisper. ''They were torn to pieces, lying there in the metal shards that had been a car.''

Her arms contracted. She could barely stand, but she couldn't leave him now. She smoothed her hands over his broad back through the soft knit shirt and heard his voice drone on, the painful memories spilling over from his mind to his tongue. Almost incoherently, he told her all of it, and his voice shook when he reached the end.

"I'm sorry," she whispered. "I'm so sorry, Kane."

The words were barely audible now as his voice and his strength gave out. He hadn't talked about it until now. He couldn't seem to stop. The fears and pain were dragged from him until he felt helpless.

"They never knew," she assured him. "It was quick. At least be grateful for that small mercy, that they didn't suffer."

"He was my son," he choked. "And what was left of him... God! God, I can't...think...can't bear to think of it...!"

She reached up and kissed his wet eyes, his face, gently comforting him while he relived the nightmare. Except that this time, he wasn't alone. He didn't have to face it by himself. His big arms pulled Nikki closer and for the first time in his life, he clung willingly to a woman for strength.

Nikki felt the moment when he came out of it, when his own will began to reassert itself.

His big hands contracted roughly on her shoulders. "I haven't spoken of it to anyone. Not even to my friend Jake."

"It's good to talk about the things that hurt most," she said quietly.

"So they say. So Chris says, constantly. She's a psychologist, she psychoanalyzes me when we aren't making love," he said, angry at himself for pouring out his pain and angry at Nikki for being here, for listening. He felt her stiffen as he continued, "She's very inventive in bed. She likes to get on top and..."

She jerked back out of his arms, savaged by the deliberate revelations as he'd known she would be.

"There's no need for this," she told him with cold pride. "I wanted to help, that's all. I wasn't asking for promises of forever or commitment."

He glared at her. "You wouldn't get them. Once was enough."

"You won't believe me, but I know exactly how that feels."

"Yes, I remember," he said with a mocking laugh. "He couldn't, could he?"

Her face paled. She turned and got shakily back into bed, pulling the covers up.

He hated himself for the look on her face. She'd been trying to help, but he couldn't accept his own vulnerability. He'd always thought he was invincible until Nikki came along.

"That was low," he said heavily. "I'm sorry."

She lifted her eyes but didn't say a word.

He jammed his hands in his pockets. It disturbed

him to see her in bed. ''If you need anything, just sing out.''

''I'm fine,'' she replied with involuntary formality. ''Thank you for taking care of me.''

''Who else did you have?'' he asked. He started out and then hesitated. ''Where did you learn Morse?'' he asked suddenly.

''I had a friend with a ham radio.''

He smiled. ''You thought I'd know the code. Why?''

''You're a sailor.''

Something changed slightly in his features. ''Because I can drive a motorboat?'' he asked.

She realized suddenly what she'd given away. A yachtsman could be expected to know Morse Code. But would an ordinary boater know it? Perhaps. Probably. She had to bluff.

''Well, you did, didn't you?'' she asked innocently. ''I thought anybody who was around boats would have to know the code. I mean, what if you had a communications breakdown or something and a lot of static?''

The suspicion slowly faded. ''I guess so,'' he said, and laughed dryly at his own sudden stupidity.

He shook his head as he turned and left the room. Nikki stared at the closed door for a long time. He wasn't the only one with unpleasant memories, and he'd brought some of her own back.

She had to get well quickly and get out of here. Charleston seemed very far away, and there was Clayton to inform about her illness. She only hoped that he didn't decide to telephone the beach house in her absence. Things could get very, very complicated if he did.

Chapter Eight

Cortez hated being stared at. In many big cities, he went unnoticed, but Charleston had a small town atmosphere and he looked alien with his dark bronze skin and long hair in its neat ponytail. Even the sunglasses he wore with his gray suit set him apart. The suit probably added to his uniqueness, he thought ruefully, he seemed to be the only person on the streets wearing one.

All the same, he was on the track of some interesting news for Clayton Seymour. It seemed that Kane Lombard had gone missing for a few days, and at the same time his plant manager had been out sick. It was during both absences that Burke's had been contracted to replace CWC. But the really damning thing was that Lombard had been contacted about the replacement. He'd given his approval, two of his employees had said so when they were questioned about it by Cortez, who had telephoned a state official to ask the questions.

He'd followed up that visit with one to Burke's, posing as a small businessman who might need to hire Burke. In the process he got an earful about Burke's latest deal with Lombard.

"Cherokee, aren't you?" his informant had asked. "I been up to Cherokee myself. Pretty impressive, seeing them chiefs stand out there in them pretty warbonnets. Must have had to kill a lot of eagles to get all them eagle feathers."

Cortez had almost bitten through his tongue while he tried to smile nonchalantly. He wanted to tell the man that Eastern Cherokees never wore warbonnets except for the tourists, that warbonnets were limited to the Plains Indians. He wanted to add that the Cherokees had been a very civilized people who had their own newspaper in their own language in the 1820s and that their capital of New Echota was in no way dissimilar to a white town of the same period. He could also have told the man that killing eagles was an offense for which a man could go to prison these days.

But he didn't. Over the years he'd learned that whites grouped Indians under one heading and stereotyped them, and that those old attitudes were as constant as the summer sun. It took more time than he was willing to spend to start spouting facts at a man who was already looking him over for a hidden tomahawk. It wasn't the first time he'd had to cope with the situation.

Laden with information that he could use, he was having a quick sandwich and coffee in a small café, and getting a frank appraisal from a pair of pale blue eyes. He turned his head and stared back. Usually that was intimidation enough to stop a curious person. It didn't stop this one. Her head tilted a little and the light caught her platinum-blond hair, making lights in it that held his attention. She couldn't be much more than a teen, he thought. She was slight and not especially pretty except for that hair. She was wrapped up in a huge denim jacket, odd because it was a hot day. Dirt stained it in random smudges. He frowned slightly. She looked like the fastidious sort. His eyes dropped. She was wearing Western boots, but not pretty city ones. Those were hard-used boots, with caked mud and scratches. She gained points.

His black eyes lifted back to hers. She smiled almost apologetically, as if she realized that he didn't want her attention, and went back to sipping her coffee.

His eyebrow jerked. She'd seen enough, had she? He laughed silently and finished his small meal, leaving a tip for the waitress before he went to the counter to pay his check. He had to find a local marsh. Burke's idiot employee had let something slip that he shouldn't have, and Cortez was going to take a quick look around the area. He'd have to buy a map and find out where to go.

He started to leave the café. On impulse, he walked to the young blond girl's table and stood next to her, his sunglasses dangling from one lean, dark hand.

She looked up and grinned. "I know. I was staring. I'm sorry if I made you uncomfortable."

Both eyebrows lifted. That was forthright enough. "Why were you staring?" he asked bluntly.

"You're a Native American, aren't you?" she asked, tilting her head a little more. He didn't reply. "There's something I've been dying to ask you, but I thought I'd already irritated you enough."

"What?" he asked curtly.

She hesitated. "Do you have shovel-shaped incisors?"

He let out a loud breath and one corner of his thin mouth drew up. Now it made sense. The mud-caked boots, the dirt-stained clothing. She'd been on a dig. "Good God, an archaeology student," he muttered.

"An anthropology major, doing my minor in archaeology," she corrected, and laughed. "How did you know?"

"You look as if you've been digging."

''Indeed we have,'' she said enthusiastically. ''We found part of a Woodland period pot with charred acorns in it. My professor says that it's over two thousand years old.''

''Along a river bottom, no doubt?''

She grinned. ''Why, yes!''

''Find anything else?''

''No. It wasn't a burial site, thank God,'' she said heavily. ''I wouldn't like to dig up somebody's great-grandfather. I think you get haunted for things like that.''

He smiled approvingly and checked his watch. He was running out of time. ''To answer your original question, yes, like all Native Americans and Asians and other members of the Mongoloid classification, my incisors are shovel-shaped,'' he said, surprising her. ''Now,'' he added, leaning down menacingly, ''are you going to ask how many scalps I carry on my war lance?''

Her eyes twinkled. ''Oh, that would be much too personal a question.'' she said with mock somberness.

He couldn't contain a chuckle. He turned and walked out of the café, shaking his head. If she'd been a little older, who knew what might have developed. As it was, he was a man on holiday doing a friend a favor. He had no time for cute college girls.

Armed with names and backgrounds, when he

reached his hotel room he removed his laptop computer from its padded briefcase, hooked it into the modem, and plugged it in. He accessed the mainframe in Washington, D.C., at FBI headquarters with his password and called up the information he needed.

The unit was attached to a small printer. He printed out hard copy of the data and disengaged the modem. How interesting, he thought. Burke had a record. Not only had he violated EPD regulations, he'd actually been charged twice already. The witnesses had never shown up to testify and he'd gotten off. But this time, Burke and his brother-in-law had left a trail. Who better to follow it than me, Cortez reasoned dryly.

He changed into jeans and boots and a blue checked shirt and let his hair down. He was going tracking. If people wanted to stare, let them.

The rental car he was driving was nice without being flashy. He enjoyed driving. Back at his home he had a banged-up pickup with a straight shift. He thought of it longingly.

As he started out of the city, he deliberately drove back by the café where he'd had lunch. He hated himself for the weakness of this impulse. Sure enough, it had paid off.

There was the young blonde, standing beside a muddied old Bronco. Her face was red and her hair was askew. She was kicking the flat rear tire repeatedly while asking God to do some pretty strange things to her vehicle.

Cortez pulled in behind her and cut off the engine. She hadn't even slowed down when he reached her.

''Flat tire, huh?'' he asked, nodding. ''I saw one of those once.''

She pushed back her tangled, windblown hair and looked up at him in disbelief. He looked so different with his hair down and wearing jeans that she didn't even recognize him at first.

He took off his sunglasses. ''You busy?'' he asked.

She was catching her breath from the exertion. ''Why? Are you going to offer to kick it—'' she indicated the flat tire ''—while I rest?''

''No. I thought you might come with me and help me track a truck.''

He caught her by the hand. Nice, he thought as he led her toward his car. She had good hands, strong and soft all at once. He opened the passenger door, but she hesitated.

With exaggerated patience, he pulled out his wallet and flipped it open, holding it under her eyes. He watched her expression change. That was another familiar sight. His credentials seemed to intimidate most people, who blurted out terrible secrets like unpaid parking tickets and promised immediate restitution.

"FBI," she stammered. Her face paled. "You can't be serious. You're going to arrest me for assaulting a Bronco?"

"Unprovoked assault on a horse," he agreed.

Her lower jaw fell.

He pursed his lips. "Okay. I'm deputizing you to assist me in an investigation. Better?"

"Me?"

"You."

She shrugged. "All right, but I'm not shooting anybody."

"Deal." He put up his wallet and inserted her into the passenger seat. Minutes later, they were on the way out of town.

"I have to find a place called Pirate's Marsh. Do you know it?"

As he'd guessed, she did. "Why, yes, it's just a few miles down the road. Turn right at the next intersection."

He grinned, glad that he'd followed his intuition. An archaeology student would know all the isolated spots. Or, most of them.

He followed her directions easily to a large area near the sea with huge live oaks dripping moss dotted around the shore. Two or three were uprooted.

"That's from Hurricane Hugo," she told him when they got out of the car and he stared at the felled giants. ''Amazing how powerful wind can be.''

''Wind, rain, all of nature,'' he murmured.

He started walking, his eyes on the ground. His little sojourn at Burke's had given him a good look at the sort of tires the man used on his dilapidated vehicles. They had an odd tread that he'd memorized. Plaster casts would be better, but he could do that later. He had some plaster in the car, and a jug of water. All he had to do now was find something in this bog and a tire track that he could link to Burke.

It was a link that he needed for the chain of evidence. He wasn't going to ignore blatant evidence of a federal infraction. It might not be his jurisdiction, but he knew a couple of the EPA boys. He'd had quite enough of white people polluting the earth with their industrial waste.

''What are you looking for?'' she asked. ''Maybe I could help.''

He glanced at her. ''Tire tracks. Something nasty in the water.''

''Okay.'' She started walking alongside him.

''Do you have a name?'' he asked suddenly.

She looked up. ''Of course I do,'' she said, and kept walking.

His lips tugged up. ''What is it?''

''Phoebe.''

He sighed audibly.

"Well, it is," she muttered, glaring at him. "What's wrong with being called Phoebe?"

"It's unusual, that's all."

"What are you called?"

"Wouldn't you like to know?" he challenged. He knelt and his eyes narrowed on a tire tread. Close, he thought, but not the right one. Not by a long shot.

"What are you called?" she persisted.

He got up, his eyes still on the ground. He pronounced a set of syllables with odd stops and a high tone. He glanced at her perplexed expression and smiled.

"It doesn't translate very well," he told her. "My mother saw a red-tailed hawk the morning I was born. If you translate it, it means something like 'He who came on the wings of the red-tailed hawk.'"

"That's beautiful."

"Sure." He knelt again to examine a print. This one was right on the money. "Bingo," he murmured to himself. He got up, ignoring the girl, and followed the tracks. When he came to a boggy place, he stopped and his keen eyes swept the expanse until he found what he was looking for: just the rusty edge of a barrel.

"Well, well," he said to himself. "Some days it all comes together."

"Did you find what you were looking for?" she asked, joining him.

"Yes. Thanks for your help."

She grinned. "Do I get a badge now?"

He laughed out loud. "No."

She sighed. "It was fun while it lasted."

He reached out and caught a strand of her hair, fingering it gently. "Is it naturally this colour?"

"Yes. Both my parents are very dark. They say that I'm a throwback to a Norwegian ancestor."

He let the hair go reluctantly. It was very soft, and he looked at her for a long moment, aware of some regrets. "How old are you?" he asked.

"Twenty-two. I was a late starter in college," she confessed.

"Not that late." His dark eyes slid over her body in the concealing thick coat and he wished that he had time to get to know her properly. "I'm almost thirty-six," he said. "The name I use with whites is Cortez."

She held out her hand. "It was nice to meet you."

"Same here. Thanks for the help."

Her fingers contracted briefly around his and he smiled down at her. "Two different worlds," he remarked quietly. "And too much age difference, not to mention the kind of life I lead."

"I was thinking the same thing," she confessed shyly.

His fingers gently caressed hers. ''Where do you go to school?''

''University of Tennessee at Knoxville,'' she said. ''But I'm off this summer, so I've been hanging around with some friends who study archaeology locally. I'm a senior at the university. I graduate next spring.''

''Then maybe I'll see you at graduation, college girl,'' he said unexpectedly.

Her expression was very still, and he dropped her hand.

''I'd stand out too much, wouldn't I?'' he asked curtly, turning on his heel.

''You bigot!'' she exclaimed, picking up a small dead limb and heaving it at his back. ''You take offense without any provocation whatsoever, you bristle before you even ask questions, you... you...!'' She found another limb.

He moved suddenly with the kind of speed that usually caught people off guard because his normal movements were so calculatedly slow. He gripped her wrist before she could throw the limb. ''Not nice,'' he chided. ''Don't throw things.''

''It isn't a thing, it's a tree limb,'' she pointed out, struggling against his strength. ''Let go my wrist!''

''Not on your life.'' He took the limb away effortlessly, but he didn't release her arm.

She stared up into his eyes with resignation and

faint excitement. He was very strong. "I would be honored if you came to my graduation, even if you came just as you are now," she said curtly. "I have friends of all colors and cultures, and it doesn't embarrass either me or my family to be seen with them!"

"I beg your pardon," he said genuinely.

"So you should!" she muttered.

"You kick vehicles with flat tires, you throw things at men...what other bad habits do you have, besides that nasty mouth?"

"It takes a few bad words to show a flat tire you mean business!"

He smiled. "Does it, really?"

"You don't curse. Not in your own tongue," she said smugly, surprising him. "I haven't come across a Native American language yet that contains nasty words."

"We don't need them to express ourselves," he said with a superior smile.

"Well, stand me in the rain and call me an umbrella!" she said, tongue in cheek.

"No time," he returned. He let go of her wrist and turned. "I'll drop you off at a garage. You'll need help changing that tire."

"You aren't going to offer to help?"

"I can't change a tire," he said matter-of-factly. "I was one of the last guys to serve in Vietnam, when they were evacuating refugees. I caught a burst of shrapnel in the shoulder. It did some damage. It doesn't slow me down, but I can't lift much.''

She winced. ''Oh, I'm sorry, I didn't mean to sound that way,'' she said miserably. ''I keep putting my foot in my mouth.''

''Pretty little feet,'' he mused, staring down at them. ''Boots suit them.''

She smiled. ''You aren't angry?''

He shook his head. ''Come on.''

He drove her to the garage nearest her Bronco and waited until she came around to his side of the car to tell him she was going back out with the mechanic.

''Thanks a lot,'' she told him.

He shrugged. ''My pleasure.''

She hesitated, but there wasn't really anything else to say. With a funny little smile, she waved and ran back to the waiting mechanic. Cortez forced his eyes away from her and drove on without a backward glance. He was already working on the proof he'd need to have Lombard and his company cited for violation of the environmental laws.

Nikki was sitting in the living room when Kane's friend Jake came to see him. Jake's eyebrows lifted, but he smiled when Kane introduced her only as ''Nikki.''

"Nice to meet you," he said politely. "Uh, Kane, I need to see you for a minute outside."

"Sure. Excuse me, Nikki." He left her on the sofa, wrapped up in her white chenille robe, and followed Jake out. It was hot today. Both men were in shorts, although Kane's legs were much better suited to them than his friend.

"Well, what is it?" Kane asked.

"I've got to replace the radio," he told the older man. "It's almost gone. I had an estimate on repairing it, but it's going to be less expensive in the long run just to replace it. Is it all right if I order that one we looked at and have it expressed down here?"

"Go ahead," Kane invited. "I have plans for her weekend after next." He glanced back toward the house, his face happier than Jake had seen it in months. "I thought I might take Nikki out on her."

Jake cleared his throat. "I guess you know your own mind, and I'm not one to interfere. But is it wise?"

Kane scowled. "What do you mean?"

"Well, she is your worst enemy's sister, isn't she? I would have thought that you wouldn't want to give Seymour any intimate glimpses into your life."

A big hand shot out and caught Jake's upper arm with bruising strength. "Seymour's sister?"

Jake nodded. "That's who she is, Nicole Seymour. My daughter is married to a senator from Virginia, remember. She and Nikki are casual friends and she's got photos of her. She's a dish, isn't she?"

Kane was feeling betrayed. He honestly hadn't had a clue who Nikki was. But if he knew her identity now...did she know his? He needed to find out. Afterward, whether she did or not, he had to get her out of his life and fast. He couldn't afford any connection whatsoever to his worst enemy.

"And to top it all off, she's a Republican," he said aloud.

"You win a few, you lose a few," Jake said philosophically. "Sorry to tell you about her, but you had to know sometime."

"Yes. I did." A hollow feeling claimed Kane as he dismissed Jake and walked back into the house. Nikki sat watching him with wide, curious eyes. Had she ever planned to tell him, he wondered. Or did she really not know who he was?

"We need a new radio on the boat," he told her, wary and curious now.

"Oh, I see." She smiled at him. "I really need to get back to my own cottage. I'm much better now, and I need to make a telephone call," she said. "I...my friend might come looking for me if he tries to phone me and I'm not there."

Kane's dark eyes narrowed. "What is your

friend, a mob hit man?'' he asked slowly, trying to draw her out.

''Oh, nothing like that,'' she said.

''You never did tell me. Is he impotent or gay?''

Her eyes fell. ''Neither,'' she said, and clammed up.

His eyes narrowed as he stirred his coffee. It was beginning to make sense, like puzzle pieces suddenly fitting. ''The man who owns that house, are you related to him by any chance?''

Her expression told him what he wanted to know. Her brother. Her brother Clayton Seymour owned it. He wanted to curse her for making him vulnerable, when she had to know there was no possible chance for them.

''You're very curious about him,'' she managed.

''Suppose you call him from here and have him come up?'' he asked. ''I'd like to meet him.''

''I couldn't possibly do that!'' she said, flushing. ''He's...I mean, he's very busy!''

Of course he was, Kane thought with venom. He was busy trying to take Kane down so that he wouldn't have to lose the election to their candidate. He was so angry that he only just controlled it. Nikki knew who he was. She'd probably known ever since he washed up on her beach.

''Is there anything you want to tell me?'' he asked coolly.

She lifted her gaze to meet his. "I do," she replied honestly. "But I can't."

He made an angry sound. She was getting under his skin. The longer he was around her, the more he wanted her. But his need was choked by the knowledge of her identity. It had to end here and now.

"You're very quiet," she pointed out.

He finished his coffee. "I have to get back to work," he said, averting his eyes. "I've been on holiday long enough."

Besides, he didn't dare tell her the real reason he had to get home. Not when her brother was going over his waste control methods with a magnifying glass. He faced a real challenge now. He had to get to the bottom of what could become a scandal if his idiot employee had engaged some guy with a pickup truck to haul off his industrial waste and dump it in a river somewhere. Once he hadn't believed that people could be so naive as to think they wouldn't be caught. Now he knew better. Wouldn't Seymour just love catching Lombard International with its hand in the toxic waste?

Nikki was thinking that she needed to go back to Charleston herself. She wasn't really feeling well enough to stay here by herself and he couldn't expect Kane to take care of her indefinitely.

"If you could drop me back by the beach house," she asked again.

His eyes lifted. ''Certainly,'' he said formally. ''Will he come and take care of you if I do?''

''He'll be there in a minute, as soon as he knows,'' she replied, wondering at his sudden, stark change of attitude toward her.

''In that case, I'll have my housekeeper get your things together,'' he said abruptly, and left her sitting there alone. She didn't move for several minutes, too shocked and hurt by his coolness to think rationally.

Half an hour later, she was back in the beach house, sitting on the sofa and gasping for breath. Pneumonia made the smallest walk feel like mountain-climbing, although she was no longer feverish and her chest was slowly clearing.

''If he doesn't come, telephone the house,'' Kane said, sounding as if the words were being dragged out of him.

''I won't need to, but thanks for the offer.''

He stood over her in white linen slacks and a yellow knit shirt, looking very handsome. ''It wouldn't work out,'' he told her.

She smiled sadly. ''I knew that from the beginning,'' she confided. ''But some things are very difficult to resist. You must know that you're devastating at close range.''

''So I've been told.'' His eyes narrowed. She was full of secrets and he couldn't find out even one. ''The man who couldn't—did you love him?'' he asked bluntly.

''Yes,'' she said, her voice faintly husky. She looked up unguardedly, and the pain in her eyes was briefly visible. ''I loved him more than my own life.''

''Didn't he even offer to have therapy?'' he persisted.

She laughed coldly. ''What good would that have done? You don't need therapy just because you can't feel desire for someone who loves you.''

Her pain disturbed him. He wanted to take her in his arms and comfort her, but that was out of the question now. She hadn't trusted him. He couldn't get past that.

''How long ago was it?'' he asked.

''Years and years. I've mostly avoided men until now.'' She glanced at him. ''Don't worry, I'm not fixated on you,'' she added when she saw his expression. ''I'm not going to dive off the roof or anything when you leave. I hope I didn't shock you. It's always best to be honest,'' she said, and felt a twinge of guilt because she hadn't been. But he was hardly likely to ever find that out.

''Yes, it is best to be honest,'' he said with involuntary anger as he studied her. ''But most people don't know how to tell the truth.'' He averted his angry eyes from her flushed face and looked around the room. "Can I get you anything before I go?"

"No, I'm fine. Thanks again for taking care of me, Kane. I won't forget you."

"I won't forget you, either. Get well, Nikki," he said pleasantly. "I'm glad I met you."

"The same goes for me. Goodbye, Kane."

He searched her face as if he wanted to memorize it. Then he smiled mockingly, and left. Nikki stared after him for a long time. She knew she'd done the right thing, especially for Clayton, but it didn't feel noble. It hurt. So did Kane's very cold attitude toward her. He didn't know who she was; it couldn't be that. Perhaps it was just that he didn't want to feel anything for her beyond physical attraction. Whatever his reasoning, he'd just killed any possibility of a future for them.

She lifted the receiver on the telephone by the sofa and dialed Clayton's number. It would be good to get back to Charleston, she told herself. And she could hardly stay here in her present condition.

Chapter Nine

Senator Mosby Torrance's aide John Haralson drove out to Pirate's Marsh the following day in his gray BMW. He was at the tail end of a convoy that combined local media with a team of EPA investigators, Cortez, and a shocked public health official.

"This marsh is practically in the Edisto River," the public health official gasped. "What is that?" he persisted as the investigators got the barrel out of the marsh and began to inspect it.

"Paint solvent," one said curtly, rubbing his gloved hand over the muck to read the stenciled legend on it. "Lombard, Incorporated," he added shortly. "Here's another one—antifreeze. And another, full of motor oil. Of all the cheap…there are provisions for disposal of substances like this.

Why, why, would he pay someone to dump it here instead?"

"To cut costs, of course. A man with a truck is plenty cheaper than an outfit qualified to handle toxic waste."

"Hold it right there and let me get a shot of it," one of the print media reporters called. He snapped the picture, including two dead water birds floating on the surface, waited for the film to advance automatically and took three more. The broadcast journalists were rolling their own videocameras furiously. "That should do it. Do you think this will make a case?" he asked the environmental people.

"Indeed it will," one of them commented.

Haralson dragged Cortez aside. He was wiping away sweat as he glared at the Comanche. "Busybody," he told his friend. "I didn't want to release this to EPD and the local newspapers and TV people until I had time to write a statement giving Seymour the credit!"

"Go to it. There's still time. And you'll never get a better opportunity than this," Cortez pointed out. "As to reporting what I found, I work for the federal government," Cortez reminded him. He produced his wallet. "See? I have a badge."

Haralson was thinking ahead. "This will be all over the state by morning."

"I do hope so," Cortez said easily. "A man who dumps this sort of garbage in a wildlife area should be drawn and quartered by the media, along with the people who hired him to do it!''

Haralson whipped out his pad and began to take down what he was gong to say. This was a heaven-sent opportunity, and it was going to stand Clayton Seymour in excellent stead with local voters. He began to smile.

''You must have proof of a connection,'' he mumbled jubilantly to Cortez. There was something in Haralson's eyes. Something Cortez almost questioned.

''I wouldn't have called all these people if I hadn't,'' Cortez said, gesturing as the EPD people pulled yet another drum out of the marsh. ''I can tie these tire treads to one of Burke's trucks, and one of Burke's own employees told me about the site.''

''This is one excellent piece of investigation.''

''Of course it is. I work for the…''

''…government!'' Haralson chuckled. ''Yes, I know. You eat, drink and sleep the job. How could I have forgotten?!''

''Think how well this is going to work out. Sam Hewett will lose the attention of his senior aide, Norman Lombard, with Kane Lombard fighting the environmental people. Seymour will win the election, Lombard will be prosecuted for environmental homicide, and Burke will be spending years as someone's girlfriend at Leavenworth.''

"You're right. It's going to work out very well indeed. I'll just get this release over to the press and wait for results. Now that we've got Lombard on the run, maybe we're safe."

"What was that?" Cortez asked curiously.

"Nothing," Haralson said. "Nothing at all. Thanks for your help."

"Thanks for selling me the gold piece. See you back in D.C."

"Yeah. Sure. Think nothing of it." Haralson was already walking away, grinning like a Cheshire cat as he bent his head to light a cigar. Cortez, watching him, wondered if the man had scruples. Maybe he thought keeping Seymour in office was worth sacrificing any he had left after years as a political insider. This had been so easy. Maybe too easy. His mind locked on it like a dog's jaw on a bone as he watched Haralson. He felt used suddenly, and he didn't like it.

Todd Lawson gleaned the situation when he heard the traffic on the CB radio receiver he always carried with him. Something big was going on out at Pirate's Marsh, one CB'er said, and proceeded to elaborate on what had been found. Industrial pollution, and linked to the newest industry in Charleston, Lombard's automobile manufacturing company.

Lawson felt his job passing before his eyes.

He'd tried to warn Kane, but apparently the other man hadn't thought there would be any rush. It was going to be hard to tell him what was going on. Seymour had all the aces this time.

Telling Kane wasn't as bad as Lawson had expected; it was worse. Kane ran out of foul language after the first five minutes of yelling down the telephone receiver at him. Then he got really nasty.

"My God, why didn't you know until now? How did you ever get to be an investigative reporter in the first place?" Kane snarled.

"I tried. I just couldn't get any doors to open for me," Lawson said quietly. "It was really bad out there," he added involuntarily. "They ran some footage here a few minutes ago. There are dozens of dead birds strewn around the marsh, and Congressman Seymour called a press conference to denounce you and promise retribution. Senator Mosby Torrance has started forming a committee to investigate..."

"Sweet Jesus," Kane exploded with something akin to reverence. "I'll kill Burke with my bare hands!"

"Get in line. Yours isn't the only company logo they found out there, although it was the most prominent. Listen, call a press conference of your own while there's still time. Give a statement. Tell people where you were those two days when you went missing and the solid waste manager changed waste disposal companies.''

Kane hesitated. He suddenly realized that if he did that he would have to tell the world that he'd let himself be knocked out and that a woman had nursed him alone for almost two days. Not only that, he'd have to admit that Nikki had stayed with him alone for three days. He pursed his lips and considered that it would give him some leverage later with Seymour if he needed it. He'd keep Nikki's dark secret, for now. Not that she deserved it, damn her. He could almost hate her for making a fool of him with her deception.

''I won't do that,'' Kane told Lawson.

''Why not?''

''Because there's a woman involved,'' Kane mused. ''And I might need that little tidbit later on. So I won't mention it now.''

''Seymour is going to hound you to death over that marsh,'' Lawson pointed out. ''You can't sit down and let him crucify you! You could go to jail, for God's sake!''

Kane stared blankly at the other man. ''Don't be absurd. I'll have to pay a fine, but it won't amount to more than that.''

''When Senator Torrance gets you in front of a microphone, it sure as hell will,'' Lawson said doggedly. He stared at the floor. ''Look, let me poke around and see if I can turn up anything fast.

I know there's a link between Torrance and Seymour that we can use. I just have to find it before Seymour gets you to Washington!"

"Go for it," Kane said heavily. "Lawson...I shouldn't have flown off the handle like that. It's been a hard week."

"Things will get better. I'll phone you in a couple of days. Sorry to be the bearer of such bad news."

He hung up and Kane stared down at the telephone, barely seeing it at all. Amazing how much had happened in these few days. He was surprised by the protective instincts that Nikki provoked in him. He could save himself so easily by just mentioning where he was, and the circumstances of his two-day absence. But if he did that, not only would he sacrifice his ace-in-the-hole, he had to consider what it would do to Nikki. She was ill. He couldn't land her in a scandal until she was in fighting shape. Then, though. Yes, by God, she was going to pay for ingratiating herself to him and pumping him for information. God knew what she'd managed to find out from his housekeeper and Jake during her residence. He'd have to grill both of them and make sure. Damn his own blindness! He'd been so attracted to her that he hadn't even considered that she might have ulterior motives.

He forced his mind back onto the problem at hand. Indiscriminate dumping was a long-standing problem. Many people had been charged with it. He hoped Lawson would turn up something else on Seymour. He didn't relish the thought of having to use Nikki's presence in his life as a weapon against her brother.

Derrie was cheerful in the office the next morning, having just heard the news.

"Nice going, boss," she chuckled.

"Don't thank me, thank Haralson and his friend, Cortez," Clayton returned, smiling at her as he put down his briefcase in the small office he kept for constituents in Charleston. It was part of a suite of law offices, but he rented a room. It was nicely furnished and very sedate. Everything a congressman's office should be, he thought approvingly. He had another in the state capital. A man couldn't gather too much support, and he had to be accessible everywhere.

"Was he personally responsible, do you think?" Derrie asked. "Mr. Lombard, I mean."

"What does that matter?" he asked, puzzled.

She frowned. "That doesn't sound like you."

Clayton sat down and stared at her. "I'm fighting for my political life," he said slowly, as if he were talking to an idiot. "If I don't get Lombard's back to the wall, his family may discover something about Nikki and Mosby and print it. Can you imagine in your wildest dreams what that would do to Nikki?"

"Yes, I can," Derrie said sadly. "But it hardly seems fair to destroy a man's whole life to spare your sister. Mr. Lombard's wife and little boy were killed in a car bombing in Lebanon just last year. He doesn't deserve to be crucified if he's not personally responsible."

"Of course he's personally responsible. I feel..." He stopped as the telephone rang, picking it up. "Seymour," he said. "What's that? You've had them blow up some photographs of those dead birds and put them on the placards they carry? Are you sure...okay. Well, listen, don't pay them any more than you have to, we're on a tight budget right now. Okay. You do that. Thanks, Haralson."

He hung up, a little hesitant about feeling triumphant. Haralson sounded very happy, but Clayton felt a sense of guilt. How absurd. He had to keep Lombard off his back and protect Nikki. This was the best way.

"Well, that should heat things up at Lombard's plant," he said thoughtfully. He glanced at Derrie. "You might call the local television stations," he told her. "Tell them we've heard that a group of environmentalists are about to start a picket line at Lombard's plant."

Derrie was just staring at him, her blue eyes incredulous. "You've paid people to picket him!"

"I haven't. Haralson's taking care of it," he said stiffly. "He says that by putting Lombard on the defensive, we can protect Nikki and Mosby from any tabloid threat."

"And you believe him? Clay, this isn't the way!" she cried. "For heaven's sake, this is dirty!"

"And you don't want to soil your lily-white hands?" he chided coldly. She pricked his conscience, brought out his own doubts and fears. He didn't like it.

"What you're doing is against everything I've ever believed in," she said quietly.

"Do you think you're irreplaceable?" he asked, furious with her scruples, her refusal to obey instructions. "Do you think I keep you on the payroll out of undying love? My God, the only reason you're still working here is because of your typing skills. You're so starchy that you rustle when you walk, Miss Prim! No wonder you can't get dates except with nearsighted acne lepers!"

She felt her chest expanding with incredulous temper. "How dare you!"

"You moralistic little prude, you belong in a convent somewhere," he continued hotly. "Always defending animals and plants, street people, and the like... Bett said that you're pathetic and she was right. I need someone in this office who can help me politically, not a far left conservative trying to undermine everything I do!"

"I won't support dishonesty and corruption, thank you very much," she fired back. "You've changed since you got thick with Mosby Torrance and that Haralson plague of his and Bett Watts. You've convinced yourself that your position is worth anyone else's sacrifice, haven't you, that a little lessening of principles is worth all the prestige and money?"

"I'm protecting my sister, and you know it," he said angrily.

"No, you aren't. You're protecting yourself against the Democratic challenger and trying to regain the points you lost by sacrificing the spotted owl on the altar of profit."

"Don't judge me!"

"Oh, I wouldn't dream of it," she agreed. "Your own conscience will hang you out to dry one day, if Ms. Watts doesn't pin it on the line right next to your manhood!"

He stood up abruptly, almost shaking with rage. "Get out!" he yelled.

"I'd be delighted!" she said fiercely, her small hands making fists beside her slender hips. "I was offered another job just a week or more ago, with a politician who has a conscience and a little moral fiber. I daresay he'd hire me in a minute!"

"Then feel free to join him!" Clayton growled.

She made him hate himself. He wanted her gone, now! ''If you want to go, go. And damn you and your pristine little conscience!''

She couldn't remember a time when he'd ever cursed her. She stood glaring at him with the blood draining out of her soft complexion. As her burst of temper dissipated, it dawned on her that he'd just fired her. After three years of hard work and hero worship, he'd admitted that he loathed her. She'd been fired, and he'd made it sound as if she were quitting. It didn't quite all register at once.

The ringing of the telephone startled them both. Automatically Derrie reached for it. She listened for a minute and in a taut voice announced, ''It's Nikki.'' She handed him the receiver and walked out, closing the door quietly behind her.

''Hello, Nikki, what do you want?'' he asked irritably.

There was a pause. ''I need you to come after me,'' she said, her voice hoarse and strained.

He was immediately concerned. ''What's wrong?''

''I had a relapse. It's pneumonia,'' she said heavily. ''I've seen a doctor and I have antibiotics,'' she added quickly, ''but I really can't stay here alone.''

''When was it diagnosed?''

''Three days ago...''

''And you haven't called me until now?'' he

raged. ''Nikki, in the name of God...I'll be there in two hours.''

He put down the receiver, worrying his thick hair as he stormed into the outer office. The path had been very clear in his mind—he'd tell Derrie to take over the office and he'd fly up and get Nikki. His plan altered immediately when he saw his aide.

Furious tears were streaming down Derrie's face. She'd already cleaned out her desk drawers and was picking up the small box that held the meager contents of her three years as his aide. All at once, he came to his senses.

''Derrie, no,'' Clayton said in shock. ''Listen, I didn't mean it,'' he added quickly, realizing that he'd said too much. ''I've had a bad morning...''

''I've had a worse one,'' she said icily, her blue eyes glaring at him. ''You can call the temporary agency. They'll replace me. I'll come back to retrain someone, but it's Friday and you have no pressing appointments today.'' She nodded toward the appointment book. ''The names and telephone numbers of your appointments are right there. I guess you can make a pot of coffee all by yourself if you have to,'' she added with bitter sarcasm.

''You can't leave,'' he groaned.

''No? Watch me. I'm sorry if it's inconvenient. You did invite me to leave,'' she reminded him with cold pleasure when he grimaced. ''But even if you hadn't, I can't work for a man who puts his political career above honor.'' Her soft eyes had gone hard, glaring at him. ''You've been around Ms. Watts and Senator Torrance too long, haven't you? Whatever they've got is contagious and you've caught it.''

''You can't leave!'' he ground out. Then he dashed all her illusions by adding, ''Damn it, Nikki's got pneumonia. I need you to stay here and hold down the office. I have to go up and get her at the beach house.''

He needed her to work. That was all it had ever been, all it would ever be. She'd loved him, and he had nothing to give her. Why had it taken so long for her to realize it? She sighed heavily. ''I'll go up and get her,'' she offered. ''I like Nikki.''

''What am I supposed to do in the meanwhile, type letters?'' he raged. ''That's what I pay you for!''

''Not any more,'' she said with quiet dignity. She shifted the box in her arms. ''If you'll have the pilot stand by, I'll go to the airport and then I'll bring Nikki home.''

He was furious. He couldn't hide it. Logic told him that he couldn't get a temporary girl in here and train her in the next thirty minutes. Derrie wasn't going to stay, but she would go and retrieve Nikki. She had him over a barrel.

''All right,'' he said gruffly. ''I'll phone the pilot.'' He indicated the box. ''Don't you want to leave that here?''

Her eyebrow lifted. ''Why? I'm not coming back.''

She turned and walked out the door, leaving it ajar because she had her hands full.

Clayton stood by the desk and stared after her with a mind that absolutely refused to register what had happened. He'd never had to worry about leaving the office before, because Derrie was so competent and capable. She could handle anything. Now she was gone. He'd fired her. He would have to replace her. He wondered if he could. His delight over Seymour's downfall was overshadowed by his emptiness at losing the best assistant he'd ever had. Bett would be delighted, he realized, because she'd never liked Derrie. But Clayton felt a growing sense of great loss. And not only that, now he was faced with the unpleasant task of learning how to make his own coffee.

Nikki was surprised to see Derrie at the door when she answered it.

''Clayton didn't come with you?'' Nikki asked weakly.

''He has to answer the telephone and make coffee,'' Derrie said with forced carelessness. ''You see, this is my last official act as his secretary. I quit.''

Nikki stared at her, seeing the faint swelling around her eyes and the visible pain of her decision.

"Why?"

"Because your brother is letting Torrance and Bett Watts mold him in their image," the younger woman said quietly. "He's helping to dispossess the spotted owl out west, and now he's using some underhanded methods to crucify Kane Lombard for something he may not even be guilty of."

Nikki's heart jumped wildly in her chest. "Lombard...what did he do?"

"You don't have television here, do you?" Derrie asked. "Well, it's all over the news. Mr. Lombard has been charged with several counts of industrial pollution of a major tributary. They say he cut costs by throwing out a reputable waste disposal company and replacing it with some local who was notorious for dumping vats of pollutants in deserted fields and marshes. There's been terrible damage to wildlife. Dead birds everywhere. The Resource Conservation and Recovery Act and the Toxic Substance Control Act of 1976 make it a felony to dump toxic wastes illegally."

"Oh, my God," Nikki said shakily.

Without registering Derrie's curiosity, she wobbled to the phone, picked it up and blindly dialed Kane's number without considering the consequences.

His housekeeper answered, and all she would tell Nikki was that Mr. Lombard had been called urgently back to Charleston.

Nikki put down the receiver. She'd never felt quite so bad. "He wouldn't do such a thing," she said.

"I know that," Derrie said. "The poor man's had so much... Wait a minute, how do you know he wouldn't?"

Nikki started. "I've read about him," she began.

"Of course," Derrie said with an apologetic laugh. "So have I. He seems like a decent sort of man." Her smiled vanished. "Your brother is losing all his values, you know. I said I'd come and get you, but I'm through entertaining Ms. Watts and making coffee and I'm not sacrificing my conscience for the sake of any job. I have a good brain and it's going to waste."

Nikki managed a wan smile. "Indeed you have, but I fear for my brother's future if you aren't in it. You were a moderating force. Now, Bett will be telling him how to tie his ties."

"I know." Derrie's eyes were sad as she recalled the things Clayton had said to her, but she forced the misery away. "We have to get you back to Charleston. What can I do?"

"Help me pack," Nikki said. "Then I'll dress and we'll get underway. Are we flying?"

"Afraid not. You know you can't fly in a pressurized cabin with pneumonia, you'd have to be taken off by an ambulance when we got to Charleston. I hired a limo."

"Extravagant..."

"Very." Derrie smiled. "I hope your brother has a migraine when he sees the bill."

Nikki was too sick to argue, but she couldn't help but wonder what Clayton had done to make loyal Derrie quit.

Kane Lombard met the vicious publicity head-on. He knew what was going to happen from the minute Lawson had called to tell him the news. He wasn't guilty, but by the time the media got through with him, he'd look it.

It wouldn't be a nine-day wonder, either, he realized when he saw the headlines. Seymour had jumped in feetfirst with charges that Lombard was a prime example of the capitalist who put profit before conservation. He was going to make an example of Kane. He had strong support, too, from every local environmental group and a few national ones. When Kane got to his plant, he had to get through placard-carrying mobs of people who had probably been hired by some of Torrance's crowd for the benefit of the TV cameras that were strategically placed.

Many of the same public officials who had paved his way when he opened the automobile plant were now lined up visibly with the opposition.

"It's going to be a circus," Kane remarked, looking down on the mob at the gates of the plant from his sixth-story window.

Gert Yardley, his elderly executive secretary nodded. "I'm afraid so. And the news people are clamoring for interviews. You'll have to give a statement, sir."

"I know that. What kind of statement do you recommend? How about, 'I'm innocent'?" he asked, turning to face her.

"I have no doubt whatsoever about your innocence," Mrs. Yardley said, and smiled sympathetically. "Neither does Jenny," she added, naming the junior secretary who shared an office with her. "Convincing yon ravenous wolves outside is going to be the problem."

He stuck his hands in his slacks pockets and turned away from the furor below. "Get my father on the line, will you?"

"I can't, sir," she said. "He telephoned two hours ago and said to tell you that he's on the way down here."

"Great." He lifted his eyes skyward. "My father is just what I need to make a bad day worse. I can handle my own problems."

"I'm sure he knows that. He said you might need a little moral support," she added with a smile. "A man who's being publicly hanged shouldn't turn away a friend. Even a related one."

"I guess you're right." His dark eyes narrowed. "I want to see that new waste disposal man, what's his name, Jurkins. Get him up here."

"He's out sick," she returned grimly. "And Ed Nelson is still recuperating from his kidney stone operation. He and Mr. Jurkins both called in, both also protesting their ignorance of Burke's true operation."

"They would, wouldn't they? God forbid they should try to cross the picket line. All right, call Bob Wilson and get him over here," he said, naming the head of the legal firm that represented Lombard, Inc.

"I anticipated that," she said. "He should be here momentarily."

"Thanks, Gert," he replied.

She smiled. "What's a good secretary for, if not to help the boss? I'll buzz you when Mr. Wilson arrives."

She left him, and he turned back to the window. It was threatening rain. Maybe it would dissuade some of the lesser-paid protesters, he mused. He thought about Nikki and allowed himself to wish that she was here. He'd cut her out of his life, and he couldn't sacrifice her even to save his reputation. He wondered how badly he was going to regret that decision, even as he firmed it in his mind.

* * *

"As far as the company goes, you haven't got a legal leg to stand on," Bob Wilson told him regretfully a few minutes later. "I'm sorry, but they've got ironclad evidence linking Lombard, Inc., with Burke's and the illegal dumping site. The fact that you didn't personally make the decision to hire him doesn't negate the fact that you approved your subordinate's hiring of him. The buck stops at you. The company is in violation of several environmental laws, federal, local and state, and it will be prosecuted for at least one felony count, probably more as the investigation continues and they find more of Burke's handiwork. A fine is the least of your worries right now."

"In other words, even if I was willing to prove that I was incapacitated at the time of the hiring, it wouldn't lessen my responsibility in the eyes of the law."

"That's exactly right." Wilson frowned. "Of course, Burke will be prosecuted along with you. He's an accessory."

"Good. I hope they hang him out to dry. His brother-in-law Jurkins is my new solid waste manager, but I didn't know about any relationship between the two of them until this came up. How am I supposed to know things like that?" He glanced at Wilson. "Can I prosecute Jurkins for making that decision without my preliminary approval?"

"You did approve it," Wilson said with forced patience. "Jurkins denies any wrongdoing. He said that he told you what he'd done and you said it was all right."

"But, my God, I had no idea who Burke was or that CWC's record had been misrepresented to me!"

"Jurkins swears that he can show you on paper what CWC did to discredit them. He also swears that he didn't know Burke had been in any trouble, whether or not that's true. You're still culpable, regardless of that," Wilson informed him. "I'm sorry. I can't see any legal way out of this. You'll have to plead guilty and hope that we can negotiate a reasonable settlement."

"While that SOB gets away scot-free?"

"Which one?"

"Burke."

"We're investigating," Wilson assured him.

"Could kickbacks be involved here?" he asked suddenly, staring at his legal counsel. "If they were, there'll be proof, won't there?" Kane persisted.

"Well..." He grimaced, sticking his hands deep in his pockets. "We can't find any evidence that anyone who works for you has had any drastic change in lifestyles. We're checking into employee backgrounds right now, though. If there is anything, we'll turn it up."

Kane leaned back against his desk. "You mean that this whole situation was innocently arrived at?" he asked.

"I can't prove that it wasn't at this point."

"Suppose I fire Jurkins?"

"What for?" Wilson replied. "He's done nothing except make a mistake in judgment, allegedly trying to save you money on operating expense. He's full of apologies and explanations and excuses."

"We could take the case to the newspapers. My father's, in fact."

"You aren't thinking," the other man said patiently. "Burke may be a scalawag, but he's a working man with a family to support. If you start persecuting him, despite what he's done, it's only going to reinforce the negative image of your company as a money-hungry exploiter of working people. People will overlook his illegal dumping because you're picking on him. In fact, the press will turn it around and make a hero of him—the little guy trying to make a buck, being persecuted by big business."

"I don't believe this!"

"I've seen it done. Being rich is its own punishment sometimes."

"I've provided hundreds of new jobs here," Kane thundered. "I've employed minorities without government pressure and put them in top executive positions. I've donated to civic projects, I've helped renovate depressed areas...doesn't any of that work in my favor?''

''When the hanging fever dies down, it probably will. You only have to live through the interim.''

''You're just full of optimism, aren't you?''

Wilson got to his feet and went to shake hands with Kane. ''I know it must look as if we're all against you. Don't give up. It's early days yet.''

Kane glowered at him. ''And when it rains, it pours. Get out there and save my neck.''

''I'll do my best,'' he promised.

Nikki was exhausted when she and Derrie reached the old Victorian family home in the Battery.

''You'd better sack out in the downstairs bedroom until you're more fit to climb those stairs,'' Derrie pointed out.

''I guess so,'' Nikki returned, with a wistful look at the gracefully curving staircase with its sedate gray carpet.

Derrie helped Nikki into the bedroom and then unpacked for her while Nikki got into her pajamas and climbed in bed. ''Good thing Mrs. B. has been here.''

''If it wasn't for Mrs. B. three times a week, I couldn't keep this place,'' Nikki pointed out. ''She was a young girl when she kept house for Dad, but even middle age hasn't slowed her down. Doesn't she do a good job?"

"Wonderful." Derrie put the last of the dirty clothes in the laundry hamper. "You said that you'd had pneumonia for four days. However did you manage alone?"

Nikki averted her eyes. "I didn't eat much," she said, "and I had a jug of bottled water by the bed. The antibiotics worked very fast."

"Oh, that's right, you have a doctor for a neighbor up there, how silly of me to have forgotten," Derrie said.

"That's right, Chad Holman lives just down the road," Nikki assured her, relieved. It was highly unlikely that Derrie would run into Dr. Chad Holman to ask about Nikki's return bout of pneumonia. Kane's intervention would never have to be mentioned.

"I told you that you were doing too much at Spoleto," Derrie chided, glancing at the other woman as she lounged in the bed. "Summer pneumonia can be the very devil."

"I'm on the mend. I got chilled, that's all. I'll be more careful."

"You need to take better care of yourself," Derrie chided.

"Yes, ma'am," Nikki said. "Stop brooding. You've stopped working for my stupid brother, so you're hardly required to worry about me."

"I'll miss your stupid brother," Derrie said sadly, as she looked at Nikki and smiled. "But it wasn't because of him that I've been your friend."

"I know that. I'm sorry Clayton ever let himself get mixed up with Mosby," Nikki said quietly. "My ex-husband is a desperate man, and Bett Watts makes a vicious coconspirator. They're going to take my brother down if he isn't very careful. This fight with Kane Lombard could be just the thing to do it, too. Mr. Lombard doesn't strike me as the kind of man who takes anything lying down, and his family owns one vicious tabloid in New York."

"Mr. Lombard is very much on the defensive right now," Derrie observed. "They say his plant is surrounded by rabid environmentalists with blown-up photos of the dead birds in that marsh."

Nikki winced. She could imagine how Kane would feel. She'd learned enough about him during their acquaintance to tell that he was a man who loved wildlife. He'd been against the lumbering bill when her own brother wasn't. If he wanted to preserve the owl, certainly he wouldn't do anything deliberately to kill birds.

"I think you should know," Derrie began slowly, "that some of those protestors who are picketing Mr. Lombard's plant were hired to do it."

Nikki's lips parted as she let out a sudden breath. ''Does Clayton know?''

Derrie turned, uncomfortable and uneasy. ''Well, you see, that's why I quit. It was your brother who hired them.''

Chapter Ten

Nikki couldn't believe what she was hearing. But she knew that Derrie wouldn't lie.

"But Clayton has always been so concerned for the environment, especially here at home," she said. "It's Haralson, isn't it?" she asked quietly. "He's fighting in the way he knows best. But meanwhile, Clay is allowing himself to be used for what he thinks is political power."

"He thinks he's doing it to protect you from a scandal," Derrie replied, frowning. "Nikki, do you have a skeleton that Kane could rattle?"

"Doesn't everyone?" Nikki asked uncertainly. She chewed on a fingernail. "What are we going to do?"

"Talk to Clay," Derrie invited. "Perhaps he'll listen to you. He's gone deaf with me."

"I'm sorry you won't stay," Nikki murmured.

"I can't. He wanted me to call the television stations and get them over to Mr. Lombard's plant." She grimaced. "That was Haralson's suggestion, too, I'm pretty sure, but Clayton was willing to do it."

"I see." Nikki didn't recognize these tactics. Not only were they not like Clayton, they weren't like Mosby, either. Mosby wasn't a malicious man. Even in his antienvironment stance, his goal was to save jobs, to put people to work. He wasn't working for personal gain. He never had. But he'd sent Haralson to help Clayton's campaign. Why?

"I would have refused to call the TV stations, too," she said when Derrie appeared to be waiting for reassurance.

Derrie forced herself to smile. "It feels funny to be without a job," she said slowly.

"What will you do?"

"Something I may regret. I'm going to work for the competition. Sam Hewett asked me to work for him when the race started. He's very pro-women's rights and I know his family," she said, grimacing at Nikki's pained look. "He's a good man and he won't fight dirty. He has integrity—the sort of integrity that your brother always had until that Haralson man came along and started helping him." She lowered her eyes. "I'm very sorry. I wish it hadn't come to this."

''So do I. Let me talk to Clayton before you rush into anything,'' Nikki pleaded.

Derrie moved closer, a hand going to her tangle of blond hair. ''You don't understand, Nikki,'' she began. ''He told me what he really thought of me. I guess because we joked so much I never took him seriously when he teased me about being a prude. But he was really mad this morning. He said the only reason he kept me around was because I was efficient.'' She shook her head. ''I didn't realize how much I cared until then. It's hopeless, you see,'' she said with a sad smile. ''I can't make him love me.''

Nikki knew how that felt. Her own heart was still raw from Kane's unexpected rejection. ''Oh, Derrie,'' Nikki said miserably. ''Whoever he gets as a replacement won't come close to you. You're the only long-term staff member he's kept from the old days in the state house of representatives.''

''I know. Well, I hope you and I will still be friends.''

''Don't be absurd, of course we will. Thank you for helping me get home, Derrie.''

''Any time.'' She picked up her purse and moved to the door. It was all beginning to hit her now. ''I'll call Mr. Hewett and then have a nice lazy weekend before I start back to work, if he still wants me, that is.''

''I have no doubt that he will.''

Nikki looked concerned and Derrie instantly knew why. ‘‘I’m not going to sell out Clayton, even if he is a rat.’’

Nikki flushed. ‘‘Derrie, I wasn’t thinking…’’

‘‘Yes, you were, it’s quite natural to. But I’m not that mad. Mostly, I’m hurt.’’ She breathed heavily. ‘‘I’ll get over it. Life happens.’’

‘‘Doesn’t it just?’’ Nikki said sadly, remembering Kane and what she’d had to sacrifice. ‘‘I want to know how things work out for you.’’

Derrie smiled at her. ‘‘You will, I promise.’’

Clayton came that night to see about Nikki. He looked drawn and preoccupied.

‘‘Worn out from learning to make coffee?’’ Nikki asked mockingly when he walked into the living room, curled up on the couch waiting for him.

‘‘So she told you,’’ he said. He dropped heavily into his armchair and stared at her. ‘‘You look awful.’’

‘‘I feel better than I did,’’ she replied. ‘‘I caught a chill. Stupid of me, under the circumstances, but I’m better now.’’

‘‘I’m glad. I would have come, but Derrie made it impossible,’’ he said angrily.

She laughed in spite of herself. He looked as he had when they were children and someone took something he treasured away from him. The two of them looked very much alike except for the darkness of Nikki's skin. He shared her dark hair but he had blue eyes, and she had green ones, a legacy from both sides of the family.

"She quit," he muttered. "Can you imagine? I asked her to do one little thing beyond her regular duties, and she walked out!"

"I know why she walked out," Nikki returned. "I'd have walked out, too. Haralson is destroying you, Clay. You've changed more than you realize."

He glared at her. "If the Lombards get hold of your marriage, do you have any idea what they'll do to you and Mosby in that supermarket sleaze sheet they've made millions on?"

"Yes, I know," she agreed quietly. "And I'd rather face that than watch you use the same tactics to get reelected."

"You have to play hardball sometimes. Haralson knows what he's doing. Maybe his methods are a little ruthless, but Lombard is ruthless, too."

"Not like this," she said. "If he hit you, you'd see him coming."

His face cleared. He stared at her for a long moment. "How do you know?" he asked quietly.

She hesitated. "I've read some very interesting things about him," she said. She couldn't tell her brother that she'd spent several days alone with Kane Lombard, or that she'd been falling in love with him. In Clayton's current frame of mind, that would have been foolish.

"No more Derrie," Clayton was mumbling dully. "I can't even believe it! She's been with me for years, from when I was first elected to the state legislature until I was elected to Congress, she was always there. And now she walks out over a triviality."

"It isn't a triviality," she said.

He glanced at her curiously. "Wake up, Nikki. You know what politics is like. Neither of us has ever been blind to what went on behind the curtains."

"Yes, but Clay, you've never been part of that before. You were an idealist."

"I can't change anything until I garner some political clout, and I can't do that until I'm reelected. Two years terms for Congressmen are outrageous, we aren't even settled in office before we have to run for reelection. I want back in. I have plans, an itinerary," he said, talking to himself. "How I win isn't that important. Once I'm reelected, I've learned that nothing changes, no matter how hard you work," he said dully.

"Unemployment is growing by the day." His face hardened. "Derrie's worried about an owl and I'm trying to save jobs. Well, I can recoup my support right here in my own state. All I have to do is throw Lombard to the wolves. He's been dumping chemicals in a marsh. The media is having a field day at his expense,'' he added, brightening. ''This is the first break I've had since the campaign began. I got full credit for helping catch him.''

''Do you know what Mr. Lombard's been through in the past year?''

''Who doesn't?'' he said shortly, rising. He held up his hand when she threatened to continue. ''Enough, Nikki. It doesn't change facts. He's guilty and I'm going to nail him to the wall.''

''Mosby is behind you, I gather,'' she said coldly.

''He loaned me Haralson. He always liked me.''

Nikki averted her eyes. Yes, he had. Mosby even liked Nikki, but that was all. She couldn't forget the revulsion in Mosby's eyes the one time she'd tried desperately to arouse him by stripping in front of him. The damage he'd done, without any malice at all, to her image as a woman was never going to be fully erased. Kane might have helped, but he had his own emotional barriers.

''You've forgiven Mosby,'' Clayton said slowly.

''Yes,'' Nikki replied softly. ''He couldn't help it.''

Clayton winced. ''If it got out, he'd kill himself,'' he told her. ''He's a decent man, a very private man. He supports job programs and minorities, even if sometimes he only does it for political gain. The environmentalists may hate him, but they're the only ones. He's kind, in his way.''

''Yes, I remember,'' she said. Her heart was still bruised, and it didn't help to recall Mosby with an injured bird on his lap driving wildly to the nearest veterinarian's office to have it treated.

''You never even suspected, did you?'' Clayton said sadly. ''Dad did, I think, but he wouldn't admit it even to himself. He was too bent on saving his own skin. Mosby needed a wife, and Dad needed Mosby.''

''And the only one who suffered was me,'' Nikki said miserably.

''That's not quite true,'' Clayton told her. ''Mosby was devastated when he realized exactly how you felt. It took him a long time to get over it. He's more sensitive than most, and he doesn't like hurting anyone.''

''I know that,'' she said. She looked at Clay. ''But Bett doesn't mind hurting people. She's trained you so that you're the same way lately.''

He glared at her. ''Bett is my business. And she doesn't like you, either.''

''Heavens, should that surprise me?'' Nikki laughed. ''I don't think she owns anything except pin-striped suits and ties. I'll bet you've never seen her in a dress.''

Clayton scowled. "What does that have to do with anything?"

"I like dresses," she replied, her green eyes sparkling. "I don't have to prove that I'm better than a man. I already know that I am," she added wickedly.

He sighed, shaking his head. "Nikki, you're hopeless."

"Probably. Don't lose yourself in the political maze," she pleaded. "Don't lose sight of why you ran for the office in the first place. You're on the Energy and National Resources Subcommittee and the energy committee. You've made suggestions that won you more support on the hill. I'm very proud of you. Don't blow all that to keep Mosby and Bett on the good side of the timber lobby."

"I'll reconsider my position," he told her. "Now. When you get back on your feet, I thought we'd throw a few gala parties."

"I know, beginning with one in Washington, D.C., in September," she added, feeling brighter and happier as she considered the motif for the first party.

"The primary election will be over by then," he said uncomfortably.

"And we'll win," she assured him, smiling. "And the party will be a celebration."

He hoped so, but didn't put it into words.

"I do love politics, Clay."

"So do I," he seconded. "And I'll try not to disillusion you too much with my campaign. Just remember, Nikki, we both have a lot to fear from Lombard. If he's occupied with defending himself against the EPA rules, his family will be too busy trying to help him to pay much attention to you and Mosby before the primary. It's only a delaying tactic, and he's filthy rich. They won't hang him too high."

Nikki didn't like agreeing with him, but he was probably right. All the same, she wondered at what it was already costing him to adhere to his new policy. The first casualty was Derrie. She wondered how many would follow.

Mosby Torrance sipped wine as he stood in front of his lofty window overlooking the traffic of nighttime Washington. He was barefooted, wearing a silver and gold robe that emphasized his blond good looks.

He felt triumphant over Haralson's victory against Lombard in Charleston. Now Lombard had his hands full trying to defend himself. The very action of keeping Lombard's family occupied would keep Mosby off the line of fire as the campaign escalated.

He couldn't afford to let Clayton lose the election. The Democratic contender was mild-mannered, but still a liberal who had no sympathy with Mosby's position on the real major issues like tax incentives for industry and a bigger military budget and supporting the lumbering industry. He needed all the support he could get from the House, and Clayton was shaping up very well as an environmental candidate and a strong national defense ally.

Mosby needed that wedge on his team, because he didn't support environmental programs; he supported industry and expansion and growth to provide much-needed jobs for the unemployed. Privately, he thought that Clayton did, too, but it was politically correct at the moment to be an environmental candidate. And until Mosby had coaxed Clayton into helping him with the timber bill, the congressman had a spotless record of environmental championship. It had been a shame to blot that record, but Mosby had needed Clayton's support. Besides, the Lombard scandal was going to make everyone forget that Clayton hadn't helped the spotted owl.

Mosby leaned his head wearily against the cool glass. It was good not to have the Lombards after him. He was older than Clayton, raised in a generation with stifling attitudes toward anyone different from the norm. His parents had hidden his flaw from other relatives. They had made Mosby ashamed of it. Because of his upbringing, he'd always had to hide what he was. No one would have understood. At least, that's what his parents had said. Often he'd wondered what Nikki would have said, if she'd known. He'd had to steel himself not to show desire for her, not to let her know, ever, how attractive he found her. All he could have given her was a travesty of the real thing and, inevitably, she'd have wondered why he couldn't function as a man. It was better this way, he told himself. Much better.

He was dignified and very conservative on the outside, and that won him votes. But inside, he was a frightened, insecure man who dreaded the new climate that threatened to expose any politician who kept a secret. Mosby had exacted many sacrifices. He would do anything to keep his private life secret, and he had; he'd married Nikki. He winced, remembering. It had been hopeless from the very beginning.

His fist clenched on the glass. Poor Nikki. Poor, poor Nikki, to be so much in love and have all her dreams shattered. He'd engineered that sight she had of his private life, that fiction of himself as a gay man. He'd known that it would drive her away, and it had. But he also knew that she'd never become serious about anyone since their divorce, and he knew why. He regretted hurting Nikki most of all.

It was all over long ago, he told himself. He just had to live with it, and with the fear of exposure.

The thing now was to get Clayton ahead in the polls while keeping the pressure on Lombard. That last part was Haralson's idea, just as it had been Haralson's idea to go to South Carolina and help with Clayton's campaign. In fact, Haralson said that he knew the truth about Mosby and wouldn't hesitate to give it to the media if Mosby didn't send him to Charleston to help Clayton.

He scowled. Haralson was a wild man just lately, into all sorts of shady things that Mosby had tried not to notice. But the man was like a loose cannon. Mosby had a bad feeling about his obsession with getting something on Lombard. He didn't know why he should. After all, Lombard was no friend of Mosby's, with his family sticking its nose into his past. But just the same, Mosby didn't like the idea of doing anything illegal. Perhaps he should take a closer look at Haralson's methods. If worse came to worse, there might be a way to nudge Haralson into a corner and keep him quiet about what he knew of Mosby's worst secret.

He picked up the telephone and dialed a number.

While he waited for the connection, he remembered his first year in the Senate, a young idealist with so many hopes and dreams that an unfortunate bit of publicity—a hint about his sexual preferences—had almost ended. His marriage had saved him, at Nikki's expense. But even marriage would no longer protect him, not if Lombard got wind of his past. The dreams and ideals had gotten lost in the shuffle to protect his secret, until now it was almost second nature to him. Perhaps his three terms in the Senate had jaded him, he thought miserably. He lived in a closed society, despite his frequent trips to his home state to keep in touch with his constituents. But the longer he lived in the Capitol, the more distasteful the outside world became to him. He was safe here. For the time being, at least. As long as he had Haralson out of his hair for a few weeks while the campaign picked up steam. He'd have to find some leverage to use against Haralson if it became necessary. If he dared, he'd warn Clayton about him as well, but that wouldn't be wise at this point.

"Hello," came a quiet voice on the other line.

"I need a favor," Mosby said. "I want you to do a little digging for me, strictly on the QT."

There was a pause. "Okay. Shoot."

He gave the man Haralson's name and background.

"Isn't this the one who's working for Seymour down in Charleston, the one who just exposed some nasty mess concerning Kane Lombard?" the man asked.

"The same."

"Well, well. Now isn't this interesting?"

"What is?"

There was a low chuckle. "I'll tell you all about

it in a few weeks. Haralson got careless. That's all you need to know right now.''

''This...carelessness. Is it to my advantage?''

''Yes, indeed. And as you say, that message is on the QT. I'll be in touch.'' The receiver went dead with a gentle click.

That sounded as if Haralson could find himself in water over his head very soon. As he'd said about the Lombards, if pressure was put on a man he was less likely to find time to smear anyone else. The best defense, in other words, was a good offense. Try that on for size, Haralson, he mused. Mosby put down his wineglass, relief draining away the fear. He slid the robe away from his body and walked, smiling, back to bed.

The wheels of justice were slow, but relentless. Kane Lombard spent a lot of time with his attorneys and his production people and managers, trying to sort out the nightmarish complications of his own negligence. Both Will Jurkins and Ed Nelson came back to work. Nelson was feeble, but involved himself in the defense of his company. Jurkins provided the paperwork that showed CWC's lack of efficiency and showed a reason for firing them. However, Kane couldn't help notice that Jurkins had dark circles under his eyes and asked if the man wasn't sleeping well. Jurkins had mentioned something about a sick child and had gone back to his office, looking haggard. Like the rest of the staff, Kane decided, Jurkins was feeling the pressure of public animosity. All of them had to pass through the picket lines daily, and only the security force kept them safe at all.

The day of the primary came, and Nikki went with Clay to their local precinct to vote. Crowds were already standing in line at eight in the morning, and Nikki's heart lifted. It did look as if he had the Republican seat firmly in hand.

She had collaborated with one of Washington's leading hostesses to concoct some sort of party that people would be talking about years from now. Assuming that Clay won the primary, there were other parties planned for Charleston, fund-raisers and banquets and social evenings to garner more support. Nikki expected to be worn to a frazzle, but it would be worth it. If only he would win the primary!

"This looks encouraging," she said.

Clayton didn't agree. The turnout frightened him. He'd made a major blunder by supporting the timber bill, and he prayed that people were going to remember that he'd helped nab a local industrial polluter. Usually when so many people went to vote, it was because they were angry and wanted to get someone out of office. He'd actually known some old-timers who only ever voted against—not for—candidates.

''Don't look so nervous,'' she chided.

An African American lady next to them grinned. ''That's right, it's not against the law to vote for the candidate of your choice.''

Clay grinned. ''Picked the best man, have you?'' he teased.

''Oh, yes, sir,'' she said. ''Going to have a new president this fall, so I figure we may as well get those other rascals out of there and put in some people who can get something done. I have no insurance. I can't make my house payment this month. I can't even afford to buy a new pair of shoes.''

The woman looked down at them, worn on both sides and scuffed. ''The plant I worked for moved down into the Caribbean so it could get cheap labor and make more money. It don't bother the government that I wouldn't have a job,'' she added. ''What a pity that we pay those people so much to represent us and they just forget how hard life is outside the capitol.''

She nodded politely and moved on as her line shortened. Clayton had gone pale. Nikki touched his arm and tried to encourage him, but he felt bad. Why hadn't he realized what was happening? These people wanted change because their economic situation was a nightmare. They weren't going in that polling place to vote for him, they were going to vote him out of office!

All those plants that had closed down their domestic operations and moved to other countries, all those jobs lost, all those unemployed people hadn't seemed to register with him before. He saw the homeless people and he slipped them a dollar from time to time, but he never noticed that they had no house to go to. Where had his mind been? On the spotted owl, he thought, and on keeping Kane Lombard's family off Mosby Torrance's neck. He'd spent almost two years feathering his own nest and thinking of his own political future and satisfying his own ambitions. He'd forgotten that most important thing of all; that these people had elected him to represent their interests in Washington. How could he have been so blind?

"Derrie tried to tell me," he began.

Nikki looked at him and her eyes asked a question.

"I hope it's not too late," he said quietly.

"What do you mean?"

But the line moved, and so did they, and the question was drowned out by the low buzz of conversation.

The polls closed at seven, but there were still lines of people waiting to get into the polling booths. Early returns gave Sam Hewett a tremendous lead in the Democratic primary, but on the Republican side, Clayton was running neck and neck with a well-known Charleston attorney. It was much too tight a race for comfort. It meant that voters were unsatisfied.

"Will you stop pacing and worrying?" Nikki chided, sweeping into the hotel room in his headquarters in a blue-and-green-silk pantsuit that suited her dark complexion.

Clayton, with his hands in his slacks pockets, standing flanked by Haralson and Bett, glowered at her. "Do you see these figures?" he asked.

She handed him a cup of coffee in a foam cup. "You're not going to lose."

Bett glanced at her. "You sound very sure."

Nikki smiled. "He's the best man, isn't he?"

"Of course," Bett agreed.

"Then he'll win." Nikki moved her eyes back to the television screen. "It's early yet, and these are small typically Democratic precincts they're reporting. Wait until we get the urban vote. That's where Clay's strength is."

Bett was surprised. "How do you know so much about politics?"

"I have three and a half years of college," Nikki said. "I'm only a semester short of having my degree."

"I didn't realize that."

"No, you were much too busy resenting my—how did you put it?—empty-headed hostessing."

It was a challenge from a face dominated by

sparkling green eyes. Bett had character enough to admit when she was wrong. She smiled ruefully.

"Sorry about that."

"Oh, we're all guilty of making snap judgments," Nikki said mischievously. "I won't mention what I asked Clay about you when I first met you."

"Thank you," Bett murmured sheepishly.

"Clay!" Haralson called suddenly. "Look!"

They all turned their attention to the television screen where new figures were being posted. The urban precincts were just beginning to be reported and Clay's two-percent lead had just turned into a twenty-percent lead.

"Hallelujah!" Clayton shouted.

"See?" Nikki asked, smiling, "I told you so."

Chapter Eleven

The celebrating went on all night. The Republican opposition conceded early on, and Clayton and Bett and Nikki bathed in the adulation from his supporters.

At midnight, Clayton went on television to make his acceptance speech for the Republican nomination.

"I want you to know that I'm going to fight hard to win this time," he told the camera. "And I'm not going to sit on my record. I've had my eyes opened today about issues I haven't confronted. People are out of work because of jobs going to other countries. We have such people, right here in our city. It's time we did something about the economy and learned to balance the budget. I've seen the light. I'm going to blind you with it until

I get back into Washington, and then I'm going to tackle a new agenda. The environment is still an important issue to me, but the thing is to get our people back to work. That's going to be my number one priority. Thank you all for your support. Let's go on and win in November!"

The supporters cheered wildly. Clayton smiled, but there was a new fire in his eyes that everyone around him noticed. Bett saw it with trepidation, because she also represented a lobby that supported foreign expansion of American businesses. Her smile was a little strained as she contemplated the future.

Nikki was oblivious to the other woman's thoughts. Her eyes were on her brother, and she was bursting with pride. Her only sadness was what was happening to Kane Lombard. She knew that he wasn't responsible for that dumping. But how to convince everyone else was the problem. It had to have happened while he was lying injured in her beach house. She wondered if he'd kept that quiet because he was trying to protect her reputation. After all, he didn't know who she was. He'd think she was just a beachcomber.

She often thought of him and remembered the joy of being with him. It had ended all too soon. He haunted her dreams, and made her sad. Not since Mosby had she felt quite so valueless. Apparently her only worth to men was as a decoration, and that attraction soon paled. Mosby had wanted a storefront. Kane had wanted a careless lover. She was suited to be neither.

She'd seen Kane on television several times, and she'd felt sickened by the trials he was facing because of her brother's supporters. She knew that Clay hadn't engineered the incident, but he was certainly using it to his advantage. She wondered if it had made Kane hate him even more, and what form of retribution he might select in reprisal. It worried her so much that she almost telephoned Kane once to discuss it with him. But he didn't know who she was, and she didn't want him to. He'd surely hate her if he knew the truth, especially after what had happened. So many secrets lay behind all this sparkling hoopla of politics. Everyone had a skeleton in the closet. Some skeletons were even able to speak.

The elder Lombard puffed angrily on his big cigar as he paced around his son Kane's office.

"Damned stupidity," he muttered, glancing at his eldest son to make sure he was being listened to. "You know better than to run off on vacation and leave the business unattended. Think I've ever done that?"

Kane didn't answer. This speech was familiar. His father always asked the same question. The elder Lombard didn't make mistakes, always knew what to do, and was there on the spot with an I-told-you-so whenever he deemed it necessary.

"In my day, we'd have had that employee drawn and quartered," he continued hotly. "No questions asked, either, mind you. And the press would have been muzzled!"

"You're the press," his son pointed out.

The old man made a dismissive gesture with a big, wrinkled hand. His hands were almost out of proportion to his tall, spare frame. "I'm not that kind of press, I'm not easily led and fed lies. I print the truth!"

"No, you don't."

Fred Lombard glared down his thin nose at Kane. "I print it sometimes," he clarified, "when I think it needs printing. The rest of the time people expect to be entertained, and they pay through the nose for it. Don't you appreciate how to sell news?"

"Sure. Put two heads on the victim and draw in a flying saucer on a photograph, blow it up, and cover the front page with it," Kane returned.

Fred chuckled. "Sure, that's how you do it."

"You won't win a Pulitzer."

"I'm crying all the way to the Swiss bank where I keep my money," Fred returned. "No interest, but total confidentiality, and I like that. Don't expect to inherit everything," he added. "You have two brothers."

"I don't need to inherit anything," came the cynical reply. "I'm set for life already. I'll have free room and board and three meals a day at Leavenworth."

"Bosh." Fred waved the cigar at him. "They can't put you in prison for something an employee did in all innocence."

"Illegal dumping is a felony, didn't you hear the attorney?"

"Sure I did, but I'm telling you that the current administration is so slow about investigations that you'll be my age before any charges are brought."

"That could be true. But what if this administration loses in November?"

"Then we're all in a lot of trouble. Especially you, because that young fellow not only has some bright ideas about the economy and the jobless, he's keen on keeping the earth unpolluted."

"More power to him," Kane replied. "I feel the same way. But even if I didn't do the dumping, I allowed it. It's my responsibility to make sure my employees hire disposal people who obey the law. I didn't."

"You weren't here," Fred returned. "I keep reminding you, you weren't here! If you want to take long vacations, sell the business!"

Kane sat down on the edge of his desk with a heavy breath. "I've got the company attorneys working night and day on a defense, but my heart isn't in it. Did you see the photographs?'' he asked, anger and sadness in his dark eyes. ''My God, all that destruction. I hope they lock that idiot up in one of his own trucks and push him into a swamp.''

''He'd pollute the environment,'' came the dry reply.

''I suppose so,'' Kane agreed reluctantly.

''Cheer up. I'm working on a way to save you.''

Kane's head cocked. ''If you dare put a picture of a flying saucer over a photograph of that marsh and print it...''

''Son, would I do that?''

''Hell, yes.''

''Not this time,'' Fred promised. ''I've got that fellow Lawson investigating some ties of Seymour's to Senator Torrance.''

Kane scowled. ''What sort of ties?''

''It's very interesting. Did you know that seven years ago, Seymour's only sister married Mosby Torrance?''

Kane felt his heart turn over. *''What?''*

''The marriage lasted six months. After a quiet divorce, there was talk that Torrance had only married to stop some gossip about his continuing bachelor status.''

Kane's mind was spinning as he connected what he was being told. Nikki had been married. She hadn't told him that, but she'd said that she was involved with a man who couldn't touch her. Torrance? Could it have been Torrance?

Fred stopped pacing and stared at him. ''What are you brooding about?''

''What do we know about Torrance?''

''Not much. He's a secretive devil. I've got Lawson doing some discreet backtracking. We know that Torrance grew up in a little community near Aiken. Lawson has gone up there to talk to some people. If Torrance is hiding anything, that's where we'll find it.''

''And if you do find something, what are you going to do?'' Kane asked suspiciously.

''Use it as leverage,'' came the terse reply. ''You and I both know that it's Torrance more than Seymour who's after you. I suspect it's to keep your back to the wall so that you won't have time to do any digging and point any fingers in his direction. He needs Seymour, but he'd jettison him in a minute to get us off his back. That's what I'm counting on. I want leverage.''

''You're an underhanded man,'' Kane said after a minute.

''Luckily for you,'' his father replied. ''Your lofty principles would land you in the hoosegow for sure if I wasn't!''

Kane wasn't so certain that his father's lack of them wouldn't land him there, but he kept quiet. His mind was on Nikki and the time they'd been together, when he'd felt safe for the first time in his adult life. It seemed very far away right now, with his business in turmoil. He should have been honest with her from the beginning, and let her be honest with him. If he hadn't been so wary of commitment, anything could have happened. Now, there were too many barriers. His eyes narrowed and his temper flared. What had Torrance done to her?

When Clayton went back to Washington, Nikki went along and moved into the small cottage at the Royce Blair estate which Madge Blair had made available to her. Madge was contributing the setting for a gala evening to celebrate Clayton's party nomination and also to garner support for his campaign. Nikki's genius for organization was being put to good use as she hired caterers, made arrangements for entertainment, and played overseer for the immaculate theme decorations that were being installed in the mansion's great ballroom.

"You never cease to amaze me, Nikki," Madge confessed while she helped hang delicate silver filigree musical notes against a background of golden staffs on white satin. "A theme party built around opera, with all the guests to come dressed as their favorite singer or operatic character. I expect we'll have twenty Pavarottis," she confessed, laughing.

"Where's Claude?" Nikki asked, looking around the room.

"In hiding with the cats," Madge said, laughing. "He does so detest parties, my poor darling. He's shut himself in the library with the Siamese twins and he's furiously reading Greek tragedies. It inspires him, he says."

"Madge, he writes sexy murder mysteries," she commented. "He's world-famous. Everything he writes is made into a major motion picture. There's one debuting next month."

"I know, dear, I'm married to him," Madge returned, tongue in cheek.

Nikki laughed. "Is he going to come to the party, at least? He does live here."

"He might. But rest assured that he'll roll himself in flour and come as something disgusting like the ghost in that Mozart opera I hate." She tacked a note into place. "Who are you coming as? I know—Madama Butterfly! With that jet-black hair, you'd be a natural."

"Actually, I'm going to wear a gauzy gown and come as Camille. I feel tragic."

"Oh, Nikki, not you. You always sparkle so."

"I've had my share of sadness."

Madge glanced at her. "Indeed you have. But your face doesn't show it. You look almost untouched."

Nikki could have howled. She was, but Madge

didn't know why; she only knew that Nikki had a failed marriage behind her.

"Hand me that stapler, could you?" Nikki asked.

"Here, dear. The invitations have all gone out, and we're very nearly through here. Only a few more hours. Clayton and Bett will be on time, won't they?" she added worriedly.

"They promised."

"Nikki, Claude insisted that we add a couple of names to the list, so I sent out a few extra invitations. I hope you don't mind?"

"How silly. It's your house and you're our friends. You're even loaning us your home for this oh-so-discreet fund-raiser. How could I possibly mind?"

"It's just that Clayton is at odds with Kane right now. But, Kane and Claude belonged to the same yacht club at one time, and they're still very good friends. I hope you won't hate him..." Madge said worriedly. "Why, Nikki, are you all right?"

Nikki had dropped the stapler and almost fell off the ladder where she was perched. "Kane Lombard? Claude invited Kane Lombard?" she asked, shaken.

"They're friends, you see. Oh, dear, I did try to stop him. He invited Kane's woman friend, too. They're almost inseparable these past few weeks since he's had such terrible problems—not that

Clayton should be blamed for them, of course.'' She sighed. ''Oh, Nikki, Claude doesn't think. He means well. It's those four cats,'' she added darkly. ''Two Siamese and two Persians, and they drive me mad! How he can write with those furry assassins all over his desk is beyond me!''

Nikki's heart was beating madly. Kane was coming here. He'd see her. He'd find out who she really was. She'd have to watch him with the lover he'd told her about, the faceless woman who had part of him that Nikki would never know.

''Perhaps you should go and lie down,'' Madge suggested.

Nikki's wide eyes met the green ones of her blond friend. ''No. Really. I'm fine. I just got a little dizzy. I haven't eaten anything.''

''Then you must have a sandwich. Come with me. I'll have Lucie make you one of her famous Philly steak sandwiches and cottage fries.''

''Thanks just the same, but I really don't want to die of cholesterol poisoning,'' Nikki chuckled. ''Make that a small salad and some bread sticks instead, if you could.''

''You sparrow, you.'' Madge smoothed her hands over her ample hips with a grimace. ''If I liked lettuce leaves, I could look like you in places, at least.''

''You're very nice as you are, as I'm sure

Claude tells you constantly.'' She linked her arm with Madge's. ''Now, let's go over these catered items just once more.''

The day's activity, frantic though it was, didn't take her mind off the coming confrontation with Kane. She nibbled at her fingernails until she almost gnawed one into the quick. She looked around the room at the arrangements, satisfied, and went toward the staircase. It was nearing time for people to start arriving. If only it would go smoothly. She always worried about the food and musicians arriving on time.

''I can see the wheels turning in your head,'' Claude observed, coming into the hall with a cat under one arm. One of the felines was a big, chocolate-point Siamese with blue eyes that appraised Nikki and found her uninteresting. He closed his big eyes and curled closer into Claude's jacket.

''Mudd is hopeless,'' he remarked, nodding toward the sleeping cat. ''He only wakes up to eat. He's so lazy that he even lets the others bathe him. His psychologist says it's because he's depressed. He isn't let outside you know, and it's frustrating him.''

Nikki didn't dare grin. Claude took Mudd's therapy sessions very seriously indeed.

''How is he progressing?'' she asked cautiously.

''Well, I don't notice much change, but at least he's stopped chewing on my computer keyboard.

Damnedest thing, all those toothmarks. Jealousy, you know. Yes, that's right, he's jealous of the computer when I'm writing.''

It was impossible to be mad at Claude for long. Nikki, like everyone who knew him, adored him. She'd manage to stay out of Kane's way. He didn't know who she was, really, and in costume, perhaps she could go unrecognized. ''Are you coming to the party?'' Nikki asked her host.

''I might. I think I'll come as Ravel, with a cat under each arm,'' he added. ''Ravel kept cats, you know. Dozens of cats. He even spoke to them.''

''I used to speak to my cat,'' Nikki pointed out.

''Not in its own language,'' he returned with a wicked grin.

''Puff understood me well enough. He could hear the sound of a can being opened from the balcony upstairs,'' Nikki recalled wistfully. Puff had died of old age a few weeks back, and she was still sad about it.

''You need a new cat,'' he said gently.

She shrugged. ''I'm too busy for cats,'' she lied. It was unthinkable to replace Puff so soon.

''Why do you look so sad?'' he remarked. ''Clayton won the nomination.''

''That isn't what I feel sad about.''

''He'll discover that Bett isn't right for him and marry that Derrie of his one day,'' Claude chuckled.

"Derrie quit, and Bett's already announced their engagement. She isn't so bad."

"She's a lobbyist. If she marries Clayton there will be a major conflict of interest and she'll lose her job. She's an ambitious lady. When she had to make the final choice, she'll leave him."

"How do you know so much about people?" Nikki asked, aghast.

"My dear girl, I'm a writer. Who knows more about people than we do?"

"Good point."

"Didn't Camille have a cat?" he asked, frowning. "Madge told me that's who you're going dressed as. You could carry a cat, too."

"I think having a woman with tuberculosis carry a cat would be a bit...how shall I put it... unexpected?"

"Oh, yes. I see." He chuckled. "Bad suggestion. I know! I'll see if I can get Madge to dress as something Egyptian or even Babylonian—from the Rossini opera *Semiramide,* you know—and *she* can carry a cat under each arm."

"Why does someone besides you have to carry a cat?"

"Two cats," he corrected. "I have four. They get in my box of fanfold paper and eat it if I leave them alone. Or they chew up manuscripts. Mudd can open the cabinet under the desk, remember."

"You need a filing cabinet."

He frowned. ''That's cruel.''

''What is?''

''Suggesting that I lock my cats up in a filing cabinet!''

Nikki gave him an exasperated look and dashed upstairs to the sound of mischievous laughter. Poor Madge, she had to live with him!

The gauzy white costume suited Nikki. She felt as if she were a floating island of sand among all the brightly colored costumes of the guests. Clayton and Bett had arrived, dressed as Carmen and her soldier. Clayton looked uncomfortable in the high-collared uniform while Bett was unconvincing as a peasant girl in the revealing blouse that showed little more than her extreme emaciation.

There was no sign of Kane as yet, and Nikki entertained a faint hope that he might not come. He didn't like Clayton, after all, and he must know that the party was being given in Clayton's honor. Nikki hadn't told Clayton that his archenemy was expected. She might not have to, she thought, as time passed and still Kane didn't make an appearance. She began to relax a little.

Claude and Madge were exceptionally colorful as Maurice Ravel and Madama Butterfly. Claude had Mudd under one arm. A quick scrutiny of the other guests revealed three more carrying cats. She smiled to herself. Claude was exceptionally persuasive, and the cats were like children—they loved being held.

"It's the odd couple," Nikki quipped when they joined her.

"Look who's insulting whom, the coughing courtesan," Claude returned, clutching Mudd under an arm. Mudd was wide-awake and very obviously irritated at the company he was having to keep. He gave his human friend a pie-eyed glare and suddenly sank his teeth into Claude's arm.

"Ouch!" Claude cried.

"Repressed hostility can stunt mental growth," Nikki said, nodding. "Better allow him freedom of expression. We wouldn't want to inhibit him."

"I'll inhibit him into a *boeuf bourbonnais* if he does that again," Claude said, glaring at the cat.

"Don't be absurd, dear, you can't cook a cat with red wine, it's so bourgeoisie," Madge told him.

Nikki laughed. These two were the closest friends she'd ever had, and the most loyal. They didn't know of her background, but it wouldn't have mattered if they had. They were the least judgmental people she'd ever known.

"What a crowd," Clayton murmured, joining them. He scowled at his sister with her stark white complexion and painted cheeks. "What are you supposed to be, Vampira?"

''I'm dying of tuberculosis, can't you tell?'' she muttered at him. ''I'm Camille.''

''I hate opera,'' Clayton remarked to no one in particular.

''You'll learn to like it when we're married,'' Bett said carelessly. ''I love opera, so we'll be going quite often.''

Nikki didn't say a word, but she raised an eloquent eyebrow for her brother's benefit. He gave her a hard glare.

''Why isn't Derrie with the two of you tonight?'' Claude asked suddenly. ''Did she have other plans?''

Bett looked murderous. Clayton cleared his throat.

''Derrie quit and went to work for the competition,'' Nikki replied. ''She found that her job description didn't quite cover what the boss expected her to do.''

''She wouldn't follow orders so I fired her,'' Clayton said, daring Nikki to argue. ''She was a turncoat.''

''Indeed she was,'' Bett agreed eagerly. ''I never trusted her.''

''I did,'' Nikki replied, staring at them both levelly. ''She was the most loyal employee Clay ever had. She stayed with him through thick and thin, even when his office was attacked because of some unfavorable legislation he introduced in the state house of representatives, before he even dreamed of going to Washington. Derrie was threatened, but she still wouldn't quit.'' Her tone became fierce as she stood up for her friend. ''She worked twelve-hour days without complaint, gave up her home to move to Washington with Clay to oversee his personal and constituent staff. She even sacrificed her personal life to do it. Untrustworthy? Well, if that's how you define it, I think we need more people like her.''

Clayton fidgeted uncomfortably under his sister's hot glare. ''You're very loyal to your friends, Nikki, but you don't understand the situation at all.''

''Do explain it to me,'' she challenged.

''Please,'' he laughed. ''Don't rock the boat, sis. A lot is riding on this. I need more support if I'm going to get back in the saddle come January.''

''Mosby and I are drumming up all sorts of support for you,'' Bett told him.

''Where is Mosby?'' Madge asked.

''He had other plans and sent his regrets,'' Clayton said quickly. ''He's not much of a mixer. Parties make him nervous.''

''It's because all the women throw themselves at his feet,'' Madge said with a wicked smile. ''He's so handsome, isn't he? Oh, my, even my knees go weak when I look at him.''

Nikki's had once, too. But now she thought of

Mosby with sadness and pain. She didn't reply. Bett knew about the marriage, but only that it had existed. Apparently Clayton didn't trust her very much, either.

"Look, more guests are arriving," Claude said enthusiastically. "I must mingle, my dears. Here. Have a cat."

He handed Mudd to a protesting Clayton, who promptly dumped him into Nikki's arms with a grin.

"You know you love cats," he reminded her. "You have Puff."

"I *had* Puff," she amended. "I do miss him." She petted Mudd, who narrowed his eyes and began to growl.

"He's expressing his buried hostility," Clayton pointed out.

"He's asking to be put down. I wonder if I dare?" she mused, looking around for Claude.

"If you do, and he gets into Claude's manuscript, you'd better have an escape plan," her brother said.

"Why can't you hold him?" she muttered.

"He doesn't like me."

He was growling louder now, and Nikki held him out from her dress. His gleaming claws began to flex.

"Take him, Clay," she pleaded.

"He matches your costume better than he

matches mine,'' he protested. ''Spanish officers hated cats, didn't you know?''

''They did?''

''How many paintings of Spanish officers holding cats have you ever seen?'' he queried.

Nikki had to admit that she hadn't seen any. She was about to protest his sly escape when she heard a voice she'd never expected to hear again.

Catching Mudd from behind so that he couldn't bite or claw, she turned and looked straight into a pair of black eyes that held no shock or surprise whatsoever.

Chapter Twelve

Nikki felt her knees go rubbery underneath her. It was Kane. He wasn't paying much attention to the elegant woman standing close at hand that he was with. His whole attention was focused on Nikki, and there was accusation and anger and pain in his dark eyes.

She didn't understand the anger. He couldn't know she was Clayton's sister. Her own heart was turning over. She'd hoped to avoid him, although that was absurd. There weren't so many guests that she could have gone unrecognized.

"Hello, Kane," Claude greeted, clapping the other man on the shoulder. "No costume, I see."

"He wouldn't put one on," Chris said carelessly. "I see that I don't have dibs on *Semiramide*," she added with a raised eyebrow at Madge's costume. They were both wearing the same colors, but Chris's smug smile was justified. Madge looked too chunky in her gear, while Chris's showed off her slender figure to advantage.

"Ah, but you don't have a cat, my dear," Claude purred.

She gave the cat in his arms an unpleasant look. "I hate cats," she said. "Nasty, sneaky things."

Claude was affronted. He clutched Mudd closer and started to speak.

"Why, there's Ronald!" Chris said suddenly, brightening as she waved to a dark young man across the room. "Kane, do come and meet him. His father is chairman of an oil company."

"I'll be along," Kane said, refusing to be led.

Chris shrugged and went off by herself, her whole expression seductive as she wrapped herself around the younger man and then spoiled the effect by looking back to see if Kane noticed.

He didn't. His eyes were on Nikki.

"Expensive company for a beachcomber," he remarked.

She flushed. "Well, you see..."

"Don't bother thinking up lies," he continued curtly. "I know who you are. I knew before you left the beach house."

"You never said a word," she accused.

He stuck his hands in his slacks pockets. "I was

waiting to see why you were playing games,'' he said.

''It wasn't a game. I didn't know how to tell you,'' she replied quietly. Her green eyes searched his face, learning it all over again as the silence stretched between them. ''You look so tired. It's been terrible, hasn't it?''

He lifted one thick eyebrow and smiled cynically. ''Gathering tidbits to feed your brother?''

She drew herself up to her full height. ''No. I was asking about the health of a friend,'' she returned. ''You were that, for a brief time.''

''And you weren't playing me for a sucker,'' he agreed mockingly.

''Would that be possible, even if I'd wanted to?'' she asked. She smiled wistfully. ''You'd have seen right through me.''

He felt the ground going out from under him as he looked at her. He'd missed her. Being with Chris, even in the beginning, was nothing compared to the high he felt with Nikki. ''Are you completely well this time?'' he asked.

The concern thrilled her. ''I think so. I've been taking it easy.''

He looked around. ''So I see. Everyone knows that Madge can't organize. If she could, Claude's desk wouldn't be in such a deplorable mess. You did all this, I presume?''

“Madge helped,” she said in defense of her friend.

“And Claude reads Greek tragedies and listens to opera and pets cats when he isn’t murdering people to entertain the public.”

“Shame on you. Claude’s your friend.”

“Indeed.” His eyes scanned the room until he saw Clayton, and then they narrowed angrily. “Your brother plays dirty pool. He’s going to discover that the mud sticks when it’s thrown. Remind him what my people do for a living,” he added, glancing back down at her so quickly that she started. “And tell him that I said not to get overconfident. I’m on the firing line because one of my employees made an error in judgment. Your brother could be there for another reason entirely, along with his major cohort.”

Nikki felt the blood draining out of her face. Major cohort. Mosby!

“Whatever Clayton’s done—and I’m not defending him blindly—you have no right to hurt Mosby.”

Her defense of her ex-husband irritated him. “Why not? He’s behind this effort to discredit me, and don’t think I don’t know why. He’s got a secret, hasn’t he, Miss Seymour? And he thinks keeping my neck under his foot will keep us from digging for it while he uses every gutter tactic in the book to put Clayton Seymour back in office!”

''Mosby isn't underhanded,'' she began.

''One member of his staff is. And the honorable senator is putting pressure on me from a new angle,'' he said suddenly. ''He has powerful contacts, you see, and he's using them all. Now it seems that I'm about to be investigated for income tax evasion. And guess who's heading the IRS in my direction?''

She just stared at him. It was inconceivable that Mosby would go so far unless he was really afraid. What did Kane know?

She moved closer to him, looking up with a plea in her eyes. ''Don't hurt him,'' she said softly. ''He isn't what you think. He's not like that.''

''What is he like?'' he demanded. ''You ought to know, you married him, didn't you?'' He caught her arm tightly and his dark eyes glittered down into hers. ''Was he the one who didn't want you, Nikki? Did he only marry you to keep the gossip columnists finding out that he was involved with some married member's wife, was that it?''

She gasped.

''I thought so,'' he said coldly. He dropped her arm as if it offended him to touch her. ''And you want along like a lamb. Did you love him?''

She bit her lower lip until she tasted blood. Her eyes were huge, tragic.

''Well, did you?'' he demanded.

''Yes!''

"But he didn't love you, did he? Or want you." His eyes ran over her with involuntary appreciation, almost hunger. "But you still want him. You can't let go, can you? There hasn't been another man in your life since the divorce. Oh, yes," he said smugly, "we checked."

"We?"

"My father owns a tabloid," he reminded her. He smiled slowly. "There's nothing he can't find out. In fact," he added, "he's on the trail of something very big. If he finds it, your brother may be very sorry indeed that he took advantage of my unfortunate circumstances to feather his own political nest."

"Clayton wasn't thinking beyond winning the race," she said, defending Clayton, as she always had. "Sometimes he gets tunnel vision. But he's a good man, and he does care about his constituents."

"I'm one of his constituents," he reminded her. "He didn't show me any of that concern."

"You're supporting his major opponent, a Democrat," she pointed out.

"And I'll support him even more, now," he returned. His face went even harder. "I'm going to see your brother thrown out of office in November. I promise you I am, no matter what it takes."

She felt chills run down her arms. "Revenge, Kane?" she asked.

''Call it what you like.'' He studied her beauty in the costume and felt regret like a wound. ''Why didn't you tell me the truth?'' he asked raggedly.

''It wouldn't have mattered,'' she replied. Her eyes were haunted. ''All you had to offer was an affair, and I'm not heart-whole anymore. It was never meant to be.''

One big, lean hand came out of his pocket. He reached out and touched her cheek, as lightly as a breath. She flinched, but she didn't pull back from it. Her soft, misty eyes sought his and gloried in their admiration of her beauty.

''Did you know what he planned to do?'' he asked.

Her mouth pulled into a sad smile. ''What do you think?''

''You're too honest for your own good in some ways, and a little liar in others. It hurt me to let you go, Nikki.''

The pain she felt was naked on her face. ''It hurt me more,'' she whispered unsteadily. ''I don't have a lover hidden away to console me.''

His jaw tightened and he dropped his hand. ''She's convenient and she doesn't make demands,'' he said.

''I thought she made you impotent,'' she shot back, green eyes sparking with jealous rage.

He smiled in spite of himself. ''You hope,'' he taunted.

"I loathe you," she spat under her breath.

"Go ahead," he challenged. His eyes were black, bright with wicked delight. "Hit me, Nikki. Come on." He stepped closer. "Throw a punch. You want to."

"If I hit you, it will be with a lamp!"

"You won't get that far. Know why?" He bent down, so that only she could hear him. "Because the minute you lift your hand to me, I'll back you up against a wall and kiss you blind."

"Is that how you manage women, Mr. Lombard?" she choked.

"It's how I'd manage you," he replied, so arrogant that her leg positively ached to kick him where it hurt most. "I haven't forgotten the way you looked at me that first morning," he added, his eyes narrow with masculine glee. "You lusted after me, Nikki. And the one time I kissed you, do you remember who pulled my mouth down to your..."

"Isn't it warm in here?!" she croaked, fanning herself with the feather boa around her neck.

"Come out onto the balcony," he invited. "We'll...reminisce."

She could imagine how he'd do it. She had visions of being crushed between his powerful body and the stone wall, and her knees went rubbery. It wasn't fair. She was an independent, grown woman. He was making the sort of sexist remarks that required her to pick up the nearest blunt object and lay his head open. If only her body would cooperate with her dizzy hormones.

"The ambitious senator obviously can't or won't do you any good," he said huskily. His dark eyes slid down to the low neckline of her dress. "But I could. I know how to make love, Nikki."

"I'll bet you do!" she said fiercely. "How many women did it take?"

"Not as many as you're thinking," he mused. "And I'm not promiscuous, either. There'll be no accidents and no risk."

"There'll be nothing, period," she said shortly. "I'm not about to replace Miss Ribs in your bed."

"Does your brother know about us?" he asked with pure honey in his deep voice.

Her face gave her away. That was an unexpected riposte.

"I didn't think so. Why didn't you tell him, Nikki?"

"Because I knew he'd have a screaming fit, that's why," she said. Her eyes searched his and she felt the hunger for him all over again. It was an odd hunger; something gnawing and deep that was more than glands and hormones. "Why didn't you tell the reporters?" she asked. "It would have hurt Clayton in the polls."

"It would have hurt you more. I don't have to stoop that low to win fights." He traced her cheek down to the small, pointed chin, and he smiled as he touched the faint hollow in her long, graceful neck. "I won't sacrifice you. Not even to save myself."

The shock of what he was saying went all the way down to her toes. She stared at him with aching need, with a terrible sense of loss. She could have loved this man more than she ever dreamed. But her brother stood between them.

"Clayton won't stop. Neither will Mosby," she said miserably. "They'll carry the pollution charges all the way to the court of last resort if they have to."

"It was a nasty piece of work, wasn't it, Nikki?" he asked quietly. "I hated the photographs, the damage it did. It wasn't my fault, but I can't prove that."

"If you told about the accident, on the beach..."

He shook his head, smiling. "Even that wouldn't exonerate me. I told you. I won't sacrifice you."

"Why not? Everyone else has, at one time or another," she said bitterly. First her father, then Mosby.

"I'm saving you for a special occasion," he replied. "I miss you, Nikki."

"I miss you, too," she said sadly.

His dark eyes slid over her with a kind of possession. "You look lovely. Your brother is glaring at us."

"My brother is glaring at you," she corrected. "He likes me."

He smiled. "So do I. I'm sorry it didn't work out."

"We never had a chance," she replied.

The band was playing, and out of the corner of his eye, he could see Chris draping herself against the oil millionaire's son on the dance floor.

He caught Nikki's hand. "We're going to be burned at the stake before the evening's over," he said. "We might as well enjoy it. Come here."

He drew her into his arms, into his body, and wrapped her up tight as he began to move to the lazy two-step. Nikki shivered and tried to stop.

"Why?" he whispered at her ear.

"I can't," she ground out, clutching his lapel.

His big arm contracted, bringing her breasts right into his shirtfront. "Relax," he said huskily, his voice deep and sultry in the space between them. "It's all right to let me see that you want me. I want you, too."

Her legs trembled as they brushed his. She couldn't remember feeling anything so explosive since Mosby had first come into her life. But Mosby hadn't wanted her close like this. Mosby hadn't made her feel like this. She shivered as she let it happen, and her body melted into the warm strength and power of Kane's.

"Chemistry," he said deeply, feeling her tremble. "We mix like oxygen and hydrogen, bubbling where we touch. Blood rushing into empty spaces, churning, making heat and magic. Feel it, Nikki?" he asked, and his arm dropped just a fraction, rubbing her against the suddenly changed contours of him.

She gasped and instinctively started to step back, but he laughed deep in his throat and held her firmly in place.

"Now you know, don't you?" he whispered. "There's only one secret left. And if we go outside in the shadows, I can ease up that voluminous skirt and we can have each other against the wall I mentioned earlier."

Her fingers curled into his chest under the dark evening jacket, against his spotless white silk shirt. She could feel the thick hair under it, the warmth. "No."

"No," he repeated. "It's unrealistic, isn't it? But I know how it would feel. So do you." He moved, deliberately letting her feel the power of his body as his cheek lay against hers and his breath feathered the hair at her ear. The music, the people, the world vanished in the heat of what they were sharing. Her eyes closed. She felt him in every cell of her aching body.

"Come closer," he said, his voice harsh.

She pressed into him, shivering.

"Move, Nikki," he challenged. His hand slid to her lower back, pulling, pressing.

"Kane," she protested once, the fragile sound lost in a gasp as she felt herself going helplessly on tiptoe to search for a more intimate contact.

His other hand clenched in the thick hair at her nape and he made a muted, hoarse sound at her ear.

"Oh, God," he groaned, shivering.

She couldn't stop. She hoped they weren't being watched, because she couldn't stop what was happening. The sheer heat they were generating was becoming a throbbing pleasure that outweighed every single thought of modesty.

The sudden change of tempo in the music was a shock like ice on fire, and Kane's head lifted to see that people around them were beginning to shift gears into a complicated disco pattern.

"I can't dance anymore." Nikki's voice sounded choked, as she looked up at Kane.

His face was faintly flushed, high on his cheekbones. His dark eyes were fierce as they searched her face. "We'll have to," he said huskily. "Would you like to look down and see why?"

She felt her cheeks color. "No need, thanks," she said huskily, and forced a smile. "I won't ever dance with you again, you know."

"I would very much like to take you into a closet or a bathroom or even a recess in the wall and make love to you until you fainted," he said roughly.

"You have someone to do that with," she pointed out, fighting for control.

"I don't want her," he said passionately. "My God, I don't want anybody else. You. Only you."

"My brother, your father, Mosby, the other candidate," she moaned. "It's too complicated."

He felt his body begin to unclench as he concentrated on the music to the exclusion of everything else. "What do you want to do, then?" he demanded. "Forget it?"

"We have to." She looked up into his eyes. "We have to, Kane. I can't hurt my brother."

"But you can hurt me?"

"It isn't that way." She dropped her eyes to the swift, hard rise and fall of his chest. "You just want me. It will pass. I'm sure you felt that for Miss Ribs at the beginning."

"Not like this," he confessed curtly. "I'm on fire for you."

"I'm an unknown quantity, that's all. That's all it is!"

"Oh, I see," he said mockingly. "You're a virgin, so I can't wait to get you into bed, hurt you, force your body to accept me, and enjoy the suffering I'm going to see in your face. Is that what you think I need?''

Her eyes widened. ''No!''

''I'm glad. I don't see virginity as a sacred quest,'' he said shortly. ''It intimidates me. I'd prefer you with enough experience at least to welcome me.'' His eyes slid over her narrowly. ''You were married. Didn't he even...?''

She stopped dancing. The memories were painful. ''Let's sit down.''

He restrained her. ''Tell me.''

''He didn't want any part of me, Kane,'' she said wearily. ''He found me totally undesirable. So undesirable that I never had the nerve or the confidence to let another man that close. Until you came along,'' she added bitterly, her green eyes accusing. ''And look what happened.''

''Yes,'' he mused. ''Look what happened,'' he agreed, glancing back toward the dance floor. ''You're very sexy.''

''You're just looking for a good time.''

''It wouldn't be, for you,'' he remarked.

''I believe some women actually have a very easy time of it,'' she countered.

He thought about that and began to nod. ''Yes, if you wanted me enough, you might.'' He smiled slowly. ''And you did. My God, you did, Nikki.''

She dragged her eyes away. ''I need to sit down.''

"Thank your lucky stars that what you feel isn't noticeable," he said with dry humor.

She cleared her throat, refusing to look at him as he escorted her off the floor and toward the refreshment table.

Clayton and Bett were glaring at them. Kane didn't even acknowledge Clayton. He lifted Nikki's hand to his mouth and kissed the back of it with flair and seductive grace. He left her, striding back toward a livid Chris.

"Did you have to embarrass me on the dance floor?" Clayton demanded petulantly. "You were practically devouring each other."

"We most certainly were not!" Nikki said. "We were talking."

"That's a new name for it," Bett mused. "He's very attractive, but he does have a mistress, Nikki. I hardly think you'll displace her. An acquaintance of mine says that she's been with him since even before his wife was killed."

Nikki searched the other woman's face. "He isn't that sort of man."

Clayton was very still. "How do you know?"

"I just do. I'm going to circulate, Clay. You'd better, too."

"Could you manage not to make love to my worst enemy on the dance floor for the rest of the evening?" he asked sarcastically.

"It doesn't help the campaign, you know, Nikki," Bett added her piece.

"Neither does slinging mud," Nikki said flatly.

She avoided Clayton and Bett for the rest of the evening, which was just as well. She'd made an enemy there, she thought, watching Bett cling to Clayton. And now Bett would have the inside track. She'd be able to influence Clayton all over again, just when Nikki had almost made him see the error of his ways. She regretted that Derrie had left. The younger woman had always been able to reason with him before Bett came along. But it was too late for that now. Mosby and Bett had spun a nice web around Clayton.

Derrie was enjoying her new job, but she missed Clayton terribly. It had been like cutting out her heart to leave him. Every time he appeared on television, he had Bett with him. Her place in his life was obvious now. Not that Derrie could have competed, even so. She was a repressed prude, after all.

She was leaving the office, on her way to catch the bus, just behind a junior aide to the candidate for whom she now worked. She watched him cross the next street over, and suddenly she spotted Senator Torrance's man, Haralson, standing on the curb talking to a dark man in an even darker suit, wearing sunglasses. Haralson didn't see Derrie, who'd come out the side door. He was watching Curt Morgan, Sam Hewett's junior legislative counsel, and when the aide got past him, Haralson said something to his companion and gestured toward Curt's retreating back. The man nodded and began walking. There was a stealth in what they were doing that disturbed Derrie.

Haralson knew her on sight, but the other man wouldn't. She waited for Haralson to get into a cab and for it to drive away. Then she dashed down the street after the mysterious man.

He was trailing someone. She knew it instinctively. Clutching her purse close, she tried to remember all the things she'd heard and read about following people. Don't be seen was number one. Get lost if you're discovered was number two. Somewhere after that, there were other rules of thumb that she'd already forgotten.

She pushed back her blond hair and moved a little closer, pretending to be looking for an address. She held an old grocery list from her coat pocket in her hand and pretended to compare it with street numbers. Meanwhile, she was moving right along with the crowd, behind the strange man who went from one street to another, waiting for traffic lights to change.

He had an odd walk. He seemed to glide as he went along, as if he were used to long distances and knew how to navigate them with the least effort. He looked foreign. She wondered if he was.

At the next corner, just when she thought she was getting close, she lost him.

She stopped looking at the paper in her hand and began looking all around, her blue eyes curious and wary. The wind blew her soft blond hair from its bun in wisps around her oval face, and she felt exposed, standing there in her close-fitting pale gray suit and white blouse.

She was attracting attention, too, worse luck. Well, she'd lost him. But it was very curious. Why would Haralson have someone following a man who worked for her new boss?

Chapter Thirteen

Derrie made a mental note that she'd have to tell Sam Hewett about the strange occurrence. She wondered if Clayton was behind the snooping. She'd seen him stoop pretty low lately. But why would he be interested in the comings and goings of Sam's staff?

She walked back the way she'd come, toward the bus stop. As she got on the bus, she felt a strange tingling at the back of her neck. She laughed at her own suspicious nature. She'd been watching too many detective shows.

But when she got off at her apartment house, she had the same odd feeling. She couldn't shake it. As she started to use her key in the apartment building door, she suddenly turned and came face-to-face with the dark man in the suit. At close range, he was very tall and fit, and there was something quite intimidating in the untamed look of him. Her first thought, uncoordinated, was that he might be a mugger. She dropped the key and fell back against the door, ready to defend herself if she had to.

"Don't scream," he cautioned.

He sounded whimsical. She stilled. "Why not?" she asked.

"Because I don't want to have to show my credentials to a police officer. I'm supposed to be on vacation." He bent and picked up the key, handing it to her. "Here. I need to talk to you."

"You were with Haralson," she said, accusingly. "I won't tell you anything. I don't work for Clayton Seymour anymore."

"Neither do I, in the sense you mean." He lifted his hand and took off the dark glasses. His eyes were large and very black, like coal. The shape of his face up close was clearly American Indian. She stared at him, fascinated and realized he must be the mysterious stranger her niece Phoebe had encountered recently.

"Yes, I'm a Native American," he said with exaggerated patience, as if he'd grown weary of repeating it. "I don't have a tomahawk. I don't speak Sioux. I never hunted buffalo in my life. I don't take scalps except on Saturday. This is Friday."

She smiled. She liked him. ''Okay. Do you drink coffee?''

''Only if I can't get firewater or peyote...''

''Will you stop?'' she muttered. ''Honest to goodness, you'd think I didn't even know what an Indian was.''

''Native American. Indigenous aborigine, if you prefer,'' he said smoothly. ''Do you have many in South Carolina?''

''I don't think we have any. North Carolina has some Cherokee people.'' She glanced back at him. ''I really don't want to do the laundry and wash dishes. Do you take prisoners?'' she asked hopefully.

''Sorry.''

She sighed with resignation. ''You win some, you lose some,'' she said.

She led him into the small apartment. There was a framed photo of Clayton, in color, smiling at her from the mantel. She turned it facedown. ''Traitor,'' she muttered at it, and went to make coffee. She felt proud of herself for doing that until she realized that she'd only put it back up later. She was such a wimp.

''Still mad at your ex-boss?'' he asked, leaning against the door to watch her.

''Yes,'' she said, glancing back at him. He seemed to know all about the reason Clayton was her ex-boss. But then Phoebe had told her that he was a government agent. She had to hide a smile, remembering the odd light in her usually calm niece's eyes.

"Make yourself at home while I fix the coffee," she invited.

He smiled, taking her at her word. He slid off his jacket, tossed it on the sofa, loosened his tie, rolled up his sleeves, and took the rawhide tie out of his ponytail. His thick, jet-black hair fell into clean, graceful strands all around his shoulders.

"You said to make myself at home," he pointed out. "This is how I relax at home."

Derrie paused with the coffeepot in one hand, laughing. "Fair enough. I've never seen hair like yours," she said. "It's very thick, isn't it? Why do you wear it in a ponytail?"

"Because people stare less," he said simply.

"Sorry," she said with a rueful smile. "But it suits you." She averted her eyes away from his handsome face and the powerful lines of his tall, muscular body. She could see why Phoebe was attracted to him. If Derrie hadn't been crazy about her ex-boss, who knew how she might have felt?

"Flattery will get you nowhere," he said. "I'm used to women throwing themselves at me because of my hair."

She laughed. "Do they?" She spooned coffee into the crinkly paper lining of the filter cup and inserted it in the coffeemaker. She missed it the first time, muttered, and finally maneuvered it into the slots. She glanced back at him. "It must be terrible for you sometimes, though, all kidding aside," she said.

"What, trying to act white?" he asked bluntly.

"Yes." She started the coffeemaker and busied herself getting down cups and saucers and put them neatly beside the coffeemaker. "What do you do, when you aren't tracking down people?" she asked, just to see how much he'd tell her.

"I belong to the Justice Department."

She whistled, glancing back at him. "Weren't you just in a movie with Val Kilmer?" she teased.

"Nope, I'm not FBI."

That was interesting, she thought, because he'd told Phoebe he was. "You look like a younger version of him. He's very handsome."

"I look like a younger version of Val Kilmer?" he asked, aghast.

"You look like a younger version of Graham Greene, who is one of my favorite actors," she replied.

He liked the face and the sense of humor. She reminded him of the archaeology student he'd met, but she was older and more mature. He'd always been drawn to blondes, although he fought the attraction these days; fiercely when he'd caught himself staring at the archaeology student. Besides, he was here on business.

He pursed his lips. "I don't know if I like smart-mouthed blondes or not," he said, thinking aloud.

She poured coffee into cups. "We're even. I'm not at all sure that I like indigenous aborigines." She sat down and motioned him into a chair. He turned it around and straddled it, his hand idly smoothing over the coffee cup. It was hot.

"Why were you watching Sam's aide?" she asked.

He traced around the rim of the coffee cup. He had long fingers, flat-nailed, very dark and quite immaculate. Her eyes followed the movement. "Haralson asked me to. He's a casual friend of mine."

"That isn't a reason, really."

He lifted his dark eyes to hers. The humor was gone. He was serious. "Can you keep a secret, or are you too much in love with Clayton Seymour to keep things from him?"

She felt her breath catch "What do you know about me?"

"I did a check on Seymour. You're one of his executive administrative people, so naturally you came under scrutiny. Your name is Deirdre Alexandra Marie Keller, but you're called Derrie. You have a degree in political science with a minor in sociology. You worked for Seymour from the time you graduated high school all the way through college, attending classes at odd times and different colleges when you could until you got your degree, a little later than your old classmates. You lived in Washington until just recently, and now you've been named executive administrative assistant to Sam Hewett. Not only that,'' he added with a curious smile, ''but for the first time your intellectual capability is actually being fully utilized.''

She flushed and averted her eyes to her coffee cup. She didn't like being reminded that Clayton had never thought her capable of much besides designating tasks to secretarial staff.

''My, what one can learn about people.''

''My, yes,'' he mocked. ''Come on. Can I trust you or not?''

She met his eyes. ''I don't carry tales. Not even for men I've been in...been fond of,'' she amended.

''Which says a lot. Okay, here's the lowdown. Haralson thinks he has me in his pocket. He's letting a lot of things slip that he's going to regret. One of them is that Curt Morgan is directly connected to Senator Mosby Torrance, and is feeding him secret information about Hewett's campaign to be passed on to Haralson.''

''Oh, my God!'' She was aghast.

''What do you know about the boy?''

''Nothing,'' she stammered. She pushed back her blond hair. ''Well, not much,'' she amended. ''He's very handsome, and rather nice. He left a paid position as a senate intern to work for Sam's campaign. He came highly recommended..."

"By whom?"

She stared at him. "I don't know by whom. Mr. Hewett said he was. I didn't double-check because I didn't have a reason to." She frowned. "Listen, if Haralson's a friend of yours, then you're no friend of ours. That man is dirty. Really dirty."

"No kidding?"

She glowered at his exaggerated surprise. "Come on, what are you really trying to do, get us to throw out an essential staff member on the word of somebody from the enemy camp?"

"That's the problem. That's what it sounds like, doesn't it?" He leaned back in his chair and his dark eyes studied her with a rather unnerving, unblinking scrutiny. "I can't help noticing that you very much resemble a young woman I met in Charleston recently...an archaeology student named..."

"...Phoebe?" She laughed at his look of surprise. "Yes, she told me. It's very natural that she'd have made a beeline for you. She's fascinated by Native Americans."

"So I noticed."

"I hope she didn't embarrass you. She doesn't mean to insult people. She's only eager and enthusiastic about her studies."

"How do you know her?"

"She's my niece," she said, smiling.

He snapped his fingers. "You're the aunt!" He shook his head. "I must not have been listening. She said her aunt worked for a politician, but I never made the connection."

"She told me all about you," she returned. "She's my brother's only child. He was killed in Lebanon a few years ago. Remember the Marine barracks that was bombed during the Reagan administration?"

"Yes. I'm sorry."

"So were we. My parents are still alive. They live in Georgetown. My sister-in-law remarried, so Phoebe comes to see me fairly often. We do resemble each other, don't we? But she's very pretty..."

"She's very young," he said, smiling back.

"She'll mature."

He didn't want to think about the college girl. He crossed one long leg over the other. "If you know anything about Haralson, you'd better tell me."

"Said the fox to the chicken."

"I'm not directly involved in this," he said. "And I don't want to be. But if Haralson's mixed up in something illegal, I'm not going to be caught holding any bags. I did him what I thought was a simple favor. I found a toxic waste dump. But I didn't know he was going to use it to destroy a local businessman. That wasn't a civic duty, it was an assassination attempt. Lombard isn't a polluter, for God's sake, he's a card-carrying environmentalist."

"I didn't know that, but I never approved of what Clayton did. In fact, that's why I'm working for Mr. Hewett."

"I know," he returned. "I work for the government."

"The Justice Department, you said. What part of the Justice Department?"

"I'm a spy."

"Right."

"No, I am."

"Go on," she said, turning her head slightly away from him. "Spies aren't real. They're figments of Ian Fleming's imagination."

A corner of his mouth tugged up. "Sorry to disillusion you. They're not." He took out his wallet, opened it, and tossed it across the table to her.

She read the credentials, her eyes softening as they lifted back to his. "Jeremiah Cortez."

He shrugged. "My mother was studying biblical history when I was born. I have a brother named Isaac."

She handed the wallet back. "If Haralson is your friend, why are you checking up on him?"

"Force of habit. Even friends aren't exempt. I

think Haralson set the thing up. I can't prove it, but that's what I think."

"Wouldn't it make more sense to tell Kane Lombard?"

He made a disgusted sound, deep in his throat. "Right. I tell him and he tells his father and the next day I read in the tabloid, Comanche Spy Accuses Senate Aide Of Desecrating Ancestral Burial Ground."

Derrie almost fell out of the chair laughing.

He glared at her. "That's right, chuckle, but that's what they'd say. I'm not going to be a human interest story. Don't you know anything about spies? We're supposed to keep a low profile."

"That's why you wear your hair long and dress in a suit in Charleston in midsummer."

He pursed his lips and one eye narrowed. "If I cut my hair and wore jeans, do you really think I'd fit in any better here?"

"No, you'd just look as if you were trying to be something you're not," she replied honestly. "I like the way you look," she added, smiling.

"You and your niece are unusual," he said thoughtfully. "You're very honest."

"So are you, and I think that's going to be a real problem when you start pointing fingers at Haralson, because he's not. That picket mob at Lombard's was his idea."

He was suddenly intent, every trace of amusement wiped from his face. "Can you prove that?" he asked.

She shook her head. "He talked to Clayton. All I heard was what Clayton said to him, and my ex-boss wouldn't admit that in public in a million years. Haralson has him well-trained," she added bitterly.

"Apparently he has Senator Torrance well-trained, too," he said. "Because what I'm finding out about Haralson is that he's been given a more or less free hand to do what he likes. Until the past year or so, he was on the borderline of legality in his methods, but in this campaign he's crossed the line."

"What do you think he's up to?" she asked.

"I don't know. I'm going to find out."

"Do you think Senator Torrance has put him up to it," she persisted.

He scowled. "Torrance has a nasty tongue and he's probusiness all the way, but he's as honest a man as I've ever heard of. No, he wouldn't use that sort of underhanded method to win his own election, much less to help Seymour win his."

She hesitated. "Seymour's sister Nikki didn't seem to think so. She didn't seem surprised at the tactics."

"She doesn't know everything that's going on," he returned.

Plots. Plots within plots. There was something

in this man's face that was secretive, careful. "Are you really just on vacation?" she asked slowly.

He answered her with a question of his own. "What do you know about Torrance's marriage to Seymour's sister?"

She hesitated.

"Derrie," he said, using her name for the first time, "I understand loyalty. If we're going to do anybody any good, you're going to have to trust me."

"That's hard."

"I know."

His eyes were without guile, without secrets. He didn't look away or fidget, and she read his body language very well.

"It's something to do with his marriage to Nikki," she said finally. "I never knew what, because nobody ever talked about it. All I know is that Nikki doesn't date or get serious about men since then." She paused, searching his face. "Don't hurt Nikki. She's an independent woman, but she's so fragile."

"That won't be necessary. Haralson is who I'm after." Dark lights flashed in his eyes and she got a glimpse of what it would be to have him for an enemy. The look made her nervous, even though it was meant for someone else. "He's up to his neck in this, but what I don't know is how and why. It has to be more than just making sure Seymour wins the election."

"Does Senator Torrance know more than you do?"

His dark eyes narrowed. "I'm not sure that he does. The senator doesn't follow Haralson's movements too closely. That's an error in judgment, surely, but I don't think he's malicious enough to deliberately discredit someone. Haralson, now, he is."

"You're his friend, aren't you?" she asked.

"I was a casual friend," he corrected. "I collect old coins. Haralson found out and we traded a time or two. He offered to sell me a piece I've been coveting for my collection in return for finding an illegal dumping site for him." He leaned back again. "I didn't know what he was up to at the time. When I realized it, it was too late. Now I'm plenty sore and out to settle the score."

"What can you do?"

"What can *we* do," he corrected.

She gaped at him. "Oh, no! I'm not getting mixed up in this," she said abruptly, standing up.

He got up, too. He was tall, muscular, powerful-looking. "You're already involved. Your boss stands to lose the election if that double-dealer gets his way. Seymour should stand or fall by his platform and its relevance to the voters, not by dirty tricks."

She grimaced. "The Seymours are still my friends."

"That won't change."

"Yes, it will. Haralson is helping Clayton. If I go against him, I'll hurt Clay," she said, wincing involuntarily.

"Are you in love with him?" he said quietly. "Or is he just a habit you can't quite break? Of course, love erases all faults, doesn't it?"

She lifted her eyes and found a sudden stark bitterness in his face. "You aren't quite as carefree as you pretend, are you?" she asked bluntly.

His thick eyebrows shot up. "My life is none of your business."

The curt, short remark made her smile. Poor Phoebe, if she got mixed up with this man. "Fair enough."

He picked up his jacket and shouldered into it. Then he straightened his tie, pausing to loop the rawhide around his hair again.

"Are you going to help me?" he asked.

"What do you want me to do?" she asked with resignation.

"Watch Curt. That's all. Nothing heavy."

"For how long?"

"A few days. I've only got another week of vacation."

She didn't want to do it. It seemed so disloyal to Nikki and Clay. But if Haralson was up to no good, it was just as well to find out the extent of it.

"All right." She looked up at him curiously. "You aren't going to get in trouble for doing this, are you?" she asked.

He seemed to withdraw, although he hadn't moved. He turned away. "I told you, I'm on vacation. If I want to watch people, so what? I'll be in touch."

She watched him walk to the door, intrigued by that somber remoteness when he seemed at first acquaintance like a clown.

"You're a very complex man, Mr. Cortez," she said quietly.

He opened the door and turned, his dark eyes meeting hers. "I think you ought to know that the rumors are flying about Seymour and Bett Watts. Gossip has it that she's setting a wedding date."

Her pain was almost tangible. Her eyes glittered with it, but she smiled nevertheless. "Thank you. I needed that."

He scowled. "Yes," he agreed, "you did. Bett is a lady with her eye to the main chance. She's no goldfish, she's a barracuda. If you care about Seymour, why don't you do something about breaking up that relationship?"

"You're very personal for a man I've only just met," she pointed out.

"You're the kind of person I feel comfortable

with—you and Phoebe,'' he said. ''A man can't have too many friends.''

She relaxed her outraged stance and smiled sheepishly. ''Well, no one can,'' she agreed. ''Maybe you're right. But Bett's got a lot going for her.''

''So have you,'' he said, and smiled.

She smiled back. ''Thanks, pal.''

He shrugged. *''De nada,''* he murmured in Spanish. ''Don't let Morgan know you're watching him, will you?''

''I'll be very careful.'' She cocked her head. ''You're very intelligent for a spy.''

He smiled amusedly. ''Am I? Good night, Derrie.''

''Good night.''

He was a curious man, she thought as she went to pour herself a cup of coffee. He'd shown her some credentials, but Phoebe had said he was FBI, and the identification Derrie had seen simply said Justice Department. What if he was neither? What if he was mixed up with Haralson and trying to get something on Sam Hewett? Or what if he was really after Clayton?

She picked up the telephone and dialed Phoebe.

''Hi, Aunt Derrie! What's up?'' Phoebe asked.

''Cortez was just here,'' she said bluntly. ''Listen, didn't you say that he showed you FBI credentials?''

Phoebe brushed back her long hair and felt a faint twinge of jealousy that surprised her. Why had Cortez gone to see Derrie? "Yes, I did," she said.

"Tell me what the two of you did."

"He pushed me down in the long grass and ripped off my blouse..." Phoebe began wickedly.

"Phoebe! This is serious," she added. "And strictly business, if that's what's unsettled you. You know how I feel about Clayton."

"Yes, I do. I'm sorry. Isn't it silly to feel possessive about a man you've only seen two times in your life? And he's too old and too different, I know all that," she added before Derrie could.

Derrie, oddly, didn't agree with her. "I know he was looking for the waste dumping site. Think hard, dear, when you saw those drums, do you remember seeing a logo on them?"

Phoebe hesitated, trying to force her mind back. "Well, yes, I do," she said. "It was faint, though. Very faint..."

"That's all I wanted to know. Thank you." There was a pause. "Why are you sitting at home?"

"I'm not, really. I'm going out with some of the gang. We have to pick up Dale. He lives next door to the Seymours."

"I don't suppose you'd stop by there and tell Nikki to call me?"

"Why can't you telephone her?"

"Mainly because they've changed the unlisted number," Derrie said, hating to admit it. "I guess Clayton was afraid I might pester him on the phone or something! I can't get the new number from the operator, you know, and I certainly can't call Clay and ask for it."

"I see your point," Phoebe mused. "Okay. I'll do it. Uh...Cortez didn't mention me, did he?" she added offhandedly.

"In fact, he did," she returned. "He thinks you're very attractive."

"Oh." Phoebe's heart lifted. She smiled to herself. "Good night, Aunt Derrie."

There was a smile in the voice that replied, "Good night, my dear."

Chapter Fourteen

Nikki was deeply worried about the way Clayton was acting. He hadn't been the same since the party at the Blairs, and he was increasingly preoccupied.

They were back in Charleston the next weekend, and the campaign was escalating. There were new headlines in the paper about the legal battles Kane Lombard was facing with the South Carolina environmental people. He was probably not going to face criminal charges, but his company was in violation of several statues of the Hazardous Waste Management Act, not to mention the Pollution Control Act overseen by the people at the Department of Health and Environmental Control. She couldn't help feeling sorry for him, and faintly irritated with her brother for making a campaign issue of it.

"Quite a dish Lombard had in tow that night," Clayton remarked over a small supper that night.

"Yes, wasn't she?"

He was watching her, waiting for a show of jealousy. "Her name is Christine Walker. She's a clinical psychologist. Incredible, isn't it, with a figure and face like that? She could have made a fortune modeling."

"I didn't notice."

"Of course you noticed, Nikki!" he said angrily, slamming down his fork. "You were practically making love on the dance floor, you and Lombard. You've got to tell me what's going on!"

She stared at him coolly. "If you must know, he was injured and washed up on the beach. Chad and I looked after him."

"Chad Holman?"

"That's right."

He studied her. "Chad stayed at the beach house with both of you?"

Her eyes met his levelly. "No."

"Oh. My God, you didn't stay there alone with him?"

"He had concussion," she said stiffly. "I had no choice."

"Of course you had a choice, damn it! You

could have put him in the hospital and left him there!''

She slammed down her own fork. ''No, I couldn't! I wouldn't leave a man I hated in that condition.''

''My sister. My sister slept with my worst enemy...!''

''You hold it right there!'' She stood up. Her green eyes flashed angrily at him. ''I did not, ever, sleep with him. You know it, and you know why!''

He moved away uneasily, eyeing her. ''All right,'' he said. ''I know it. But nobody else would believe it, not with Lombard's reputation.''

''I don't care what people think.''

''I have to. Nikki, I'm running for reelection. This isn't some great cosmopolitan city, it's Charleston, where reputations and family honor still mean something! If news of that got out, it could ruin me!''

''It's not going to get out,'' she said stiffly.

''No? What if Lombard is faced with a jail sentence for that dumping?''

She gasped. ''No. They'll fine him, but they wouldn't...!''

''Illegal dumping of toxic waste is a felony. CEOs and presidents of companies have gone to jail for it. Lombard could, too. Faced with years in prison, he'd throw you to the wolves without a second thought. He and his family would use any wedge they had to prevent that!''

''It wouldn't help him,'' she pointed out. ''Even if I'd slept in the same bed with him on Seabrook Island, it wouldn't do him any good to tell it!''

''It would if he could claim that his accident prevented him from finding out the truth about what was going on back in Charleston.''

''Nothing was going on,'' she said. ''That employee of Lombard International's who hired Burke's swore he didn't know about Burke's bad environment record. They interviewed him on television, don't you remember?''

''Nevertheless, he can be charged for that,'' Clayton said with an attorney's knowledge of penalties. He'd studied environmental law. ''The fact that he didn't check out Burke's is enough to make him liable under the environmental statutes. He's guilty of negligence, if nothing more criminal. The environmental people are very militant these days, and they should be. Pollution is easy to cause, hard to correct. Prevention is the only way we can insure future supplies of clean water and air.''

''But it's okay if we wipe out a species of owl to temporarily save loggers' jobs,'' she said deliberately.

''You and Derrie! Damn Derrie!''

''You miss her, do you?'' Nikki asked mischievously.

He didn't want to think about Derrie. He hated his office since she'd left it, he was more alone now than ever. He stuck his hands in his slacks pockets and wandered around the room, his eyes lingering on familiar things, family heirlooms like the Early American furniture and the antique coffee mill and the grandfather clock that had been left behind when their parents died. He touched the clock, noticed that it wasn't running at proper tempo. He opened the case, picked up the key, and wound it.

"I remember the sound of that clock chiming when I was very small," Nikki recalled, smiling. "I always thought a little man lived inside."

"So did I." He put the key down and closed the case. His fingers lingered on it. "I feel alone sometimes. Do you?"

"Yes." She joined him, her arms wrapped around her chest. "It's different when you don't have parents. It's hard to talk to people who do."

"Have you...heard from Derrie?" he asked without looking at her.

She averted her amused eyes. "Not since just after the primary election. I guess she's getting settled." She glanced at him. "Mr. Hewett is well-liked," she said. "Don't get overconfident, or do anything illegal, will you?"

"I haven't." He sounded insulted.

She sighed. "Clay, you're walking right on the edge. Don't you know it?"

"I have to win."

"Why?" she asked bluntly. "Why do you *have* to win?"

He hesitated. Now that she was putting it in those terms, into words, he wasn't really sure. The campaign had been important to him, of course, but only in the past two or three months had it become the most important thing in his life. He stared at her.

"Well, because I want to go back to Washington, I suppose," he began. "I have programs I haven't been able to implement, unfinished projects to work on..."

"You weren't like this until John Haralson came down and started working for you."

"Mosby suggested it. Haralson has always worked well for him."

"Mosby walks around in a fog," she said. "He doesn't want to know how things are done, just that they get done. He's very naive in some ways, and altogether too trusting."

"You aren't still...?"

She laughed gently. "Still grieving for him? Oh, no. I have scars, but I gave up hope long ago. Mosby can't help it, can he?"

"No." He looked at his shoes. "He's never been found out. That's the most amazing thing of all. He pretends to like women, then he pretends to like men. He's managed to keep anyone from finding out."

"How, do you suppose?" she asked quietly. "I mean, how would he keep someone from noticing, in bed..."

"He kept you from noticing, didn't he? You're a babe in the woods, sis," he said without malice. "It's just as well that you are. How about a movie?"

She shook her head. "I'm tired. Washington wrung me out."

He dug in his pocket for his keys. "Bett's still there, on business again." He hesitated. "I might go and see Derrie."

"That would be interesting."

He laughed unamusedly. "Yes. I guess it will." He started out, then paused and looked back at Nikki. She looked fragile these days. "When you had pneumonia, was it really Chad who looked after you?"

She hesitated.

"You'd better tell me. I see him occasionally."

"No," she confessed quietly. "It was Kane. It was so far gone that I could barely remember Morse Code. He knew immediately that it must be me. He came and got me. I don't remember much except that I came to in an oxygen tent."

He stared at her, realizing how dangerously ill

she must have been. Kane had saved her life. She hadn't said anything, but she must have bitterly resented the way Clayton had treated Lombard in the press. She owed her life to him.

Clayton felt guilty, and that made him angry. He didn't want to be beholden to his worst enemy. That reporter from the Lombard tabloid was still in Charleston and snooping around, and Haralson was getting pretty nervous. Too many undercurrents were at work here, he thought.

"I need to win the election. I can't have the Lombards digging into our pasts."

"Clay, if they published everything they know, they still wouldn't have a story," she said quietly. "It's Haralson's head that would roll. Mosby is a victim. It would hurt him if things came out, but perhaps not as much as you think. He's hardly a drinking, lecherous playboy."

"Not at all."

"Haralson is keeping you on a very short fuse," she said bluntly. "He's the one who's obsessed with winning the election. Why don't you find out why?"

He frowned. "I know why. He's trying to help me."

"Clay..."

"I'll be in later," he said, smiling easily. "Don't worry. It will be all right. So long as you keep away from Lombard," he said firmly. "Don't let me down, Nikki, please? No fraternizing with the enemy, regardless of what you owe him."

"All right."

She sounded subdued, but he trusted her. He winked lazily and left the house. Paying Derrie a visit had been on his mind for a long time. It wouldn't hurt to see how she was faring. Besides, he thought, Haralson had mentioned something about Curt Morgan and having him followed. If Morgan was doing anything suspicious, perhaps he could get Derrie to let it slip.

Nikki was more worried than ever as she sat watching the evening news. The environmental people had found another toxic waste dump on a deserted piece of farmland. Burke wasn't implicated in this one, and there were no logos on the old oil drums full of toxic waste they found there.

The cleanup crew was putting the drums in overpacks—metal envelopes the purpose of which was to prevent further leaking. Hundreds of gallons of the unidentified toxic substances had already leaked out, however, and leached into the soil. The extent of the damage would be found over time, but first the waste had to be analyzed and identified, and then cleanup operations would begin. The on-site EPA coordinator was hopping mad, promising retribution for this latest "midnight dump" and prosecution to the fullest extent of the law.

Along with the new report was a rehash of the site that Burke's disposal operation and Lombard International were accused of creating. Charges were pending, and there had already been a red flag beside the company on the EPA list because of an earlier sewage leak. The news report made that one sound deliberate now, which was, Nikki thought, sure to make Kane's defense even harder. Her eyes narrowed. How strange that the company should change waste handlers on the heels of the leak, and that Burke's should be so easily traced to the site; how fortunate for the environmental people that the dumping site had been so quickly and easily located. And that the logos from Lombard International had been very readable, indeed. And painted on in orange...

She got up from her chair and moved to the telephone without a single thought in her mind except that it had to be a frame. Why hadn't anybody else thought of it? Why hadn't Kane?

She knew the number of his beach house on Seabrook Island. He probably wouldn't be there, but perhaps she could coax his housekeeper into giving her the number.

What if his lover answered? She panicked and almost put down the receiver. It was too dangerous. What if she hurt Clayton by doing this, what if Kane decided to use their time together against her, what if...

"Lombard."

It was Kane himself. The shock of his deep voice, unexpected, almost caused her to drop the receiver. She fumbled it back to her ear.

"Who is it?" came a curt demand.

"It's...Nikki."

There was a pause. "Are you all right?" he asked, and his voice was soft as velvet.

Tears stung her eyes. She blinked them away. The concern was awesome.

"I'm fine," she said. "How are you?"

"Notorious," he returned dryly. "I trust your brother is enjoying the public renumeration of my alleged sins in connection with this latest dumping scandal?"

"He isn't here."

There was another pause. "Dangerous, isn't it? Calling the enemy just to talk?"

"Could I see you?" she asked.

"Sure. They're showing a file photo of my back on TV right now. Turn on channel..."

"Kane, don't joke. I've...found out something. Thought out something," she corrected. "I have to talk to you."

"I don't trust you, Nikki," he said flatly. "And you shouldn't trust me."

"You saved my life," she said simply. "Think of it as the repayment of a debt. I don't have anything to say that could compromise you any more than you've already been compromised. But I think you should listen to me."

"Go ahead," he invited.

She started to speak and then thought about possibilities. The telephone could be bugged. It would be a simple thing for someone with Haralson's contacts to do. In fact, he had connections in the Justice Department, Clayton had said…

"Suppose I meet you somewhere?" she asked.

"Risky."

"It's more risky to talk on the telephone. Someone might be listening."

"That's true," Kane said. "Okay. Where?"

"Where I found you."

"When?"

She was getting the hang of this. It was almost fun. "At the same time you got to the party in Washington."

"I'll be there."

Nikki put on a pair of dark jeans and a white sweatshirt with a jeweled rose on the front. This was going to take a little stealth. She'd looked out and the service truck she'd noticed earlier was still sitting there. It could be legitimate, of course, but she didn't think it was. There was some cloak-and-dagger stuff going on here. If someone was trying to follow her, for any reason, she was going to make it very difficult.

She went out through the basement. The back

lot had two big live oaks in it, with the sidewalk just beyond, on the narrow street by the bay. There were some young people in a crowd going along it. In fact they were headed toward her house. She intercepted them, finding Phoebe Keller and a handsome young man and another couple in her path.

"Nikki!" Phoebe said, grinning. "I was just coming to see you. I couldn't get Derrie on the phone and I thought she might be over here. It was just a whim, we were out walking..."

"Come along with me for a minute, will you?" Nikki asked, glancing beyond them. A man was leaning out of the truck window watching another man steal toward her house.

"What's going on?" Phoebe asked.

"I'm not sure. But I need to get away from the house without being seen."

"Hey, no problem," Phoebe's companion said. "Where do you want to go?"

"To Seabrook Island. I have to get a cab..."

"We'll take you down," Phoebe said gaily. "I love the island!"

"Will they let us on it?" the boy asked.

"I have my pass," Nikki assured them. "And the refrigerator's full..."

"Say no more," Phoebe said, clutching the boy's hand tightly. "Nikki, you angel, we haven't even had supper!"

"Don't expect haute cuisine," she teased. This was an unexpected bonus. For all intents and purposes, she'd be out with her friend's niece and the young crowd on the island. There was nothing to connect her with Kane, so far.

"Hamburgers are cuisine to us," Phoebe's male companion said, chuckling.

The beach house was all alight an hour later. Nikki took Phoebe to one side and turned up the radio. She couldn't take a chance that the beach house might be bugged, too. They weren't followed, she knew that. She'd watched all the way down here.

"Listen," she told Phoebe. "I've got to go down to the beach for a few minutes. Make a lot of noise, and if anyone comes asking for me, I'm lying down with a headache."

"Are you in trouble? Can I help?" Phoebe asked gently. "I know someone in law enforcement—well, sort of," she amended, remembering the new friend she'd made. She didn't know where to find him, but her aunt had mentioned talking to him. That had surprised—and disturbed—Phoebe. She knew her aunt Derrie was still in love with Clayton Seymour. But it bothered her that Cortez had gone to see Derrie, despite the fact that Derrie said it was just business talk. She felt rather proprietorial about Cortez, despite the age difference.

She shouldn't, but knowing it didn't help. She'd gone out with this young crowd tonight for no other reason than to force Cortez out of her mind.

Nikki cleared her throat impatiently.

"I'm sorry," Phoebe said. "I tend to drift off. Nikki, you're not in any trouble, are you?"

"Not yet. I may be soon, though," came the rueful reply. "Never mind. I'll be back in a little while."

"It's not too safe alone on that beach."

"I won't be alone." Nikki smiled and darted out the door.

Kane was leaning against a moss-dripping live oak, smoking a cigarette. It was his second.

"I didn't know that you smoked," Nikki said.

He turned and moved to meet her. They were in the shelter of the tree at the water's edge and couldn't be seen from the beach house or the neighbor's houses.

"I stopped smoking," he said. "Until a few weeks ago."

She wrapped her arms around herself. She couldn't see him very well in the moonlit darkness, but she felt the warmth and size of him and felt secure despite the hostility between them.

"There was a truck parked outside my house when I started to leave. I think the phone is bugged and I think I'm being watched."

"Were you followed?"

She shook her head. "I made sure." She looked up at him. "Something is going on. I seem to be in the middle of it, and so are you."

"Explain."

She leaned against the tree beside him, her eyes soft on what she could see of his face. She wanted so badly to go up close to him and slide her arms around him and let him hold her. It had been a long time since he'd held her so intimately at the party.

"Someone is framing you."

"What?"

"Haven't you figured it out?" she asked. "The leak may have been accidental. But the dumping came right on its heels, as if somebody knew you'd be on the EPA's hit list for a prior offense. The dumping site was found with ridiculous ease. The logo of your company was stenciled on those containers in bright orange fresh paint. Add it up."

His cigarette was hanging in midair. He'd been so upset by the charges and the publicity and the unrelenting persecution that his ability to reason had been impaired. She was right. He hadn't appraised his situation at all. He'd been too busy defending it.

He shifted closer to her, and bent to talk more softly. "If your brother was behind it, would you tell me?"

"I love my brother," she said quietly. "I'd do almost anything for him. He doesn't realize that he's become entangled in this mess, too, but I do. Someone is using the campaign as an excuse to destroy your company and your credibility. I get cold chills just thinking about what could happen. It's cold-blooded and shrewd, and there has to be a very intelligent purpose behind it. I just can't think what. But it has to be more than an underhanded way to help Clayton win the election, don't you see?"

His eyes narrowed as he finished the cigarette and ground it out under his heel. "What good would it do to put me in front of the media as a target?"

"I don't know. But there must be some reason. Kane, I know you weren't responsible for what happened," she said fiercely.

He searched what he could see of her features. His head turned then and he stared out over the bay, toward the ocean, his eyes unseeing on the moonlight that sparkled in the waves.

"Why don't you think I did it?" he asked.

She sighed as she leaned her head against the tree to study him. "You love the ocean, don't you?" she asked. "You're a naturalist through and through. People like that don't try to destroy the environment."

His head turned toward her. ''You're perceptive.''

''I suppose so, at times. What will you do?''

''Nothing, except to keep my eyes and ears open.''

''Kane, you won't go to jail, will you?'' she asked worriedly.

''There's very little chance of that. Why?'' he added. ''Are you afraid I might drag your name into it for an alibi?''

''I know you wouldn't,'' she said quietly. ''But I'd let you, if it meant a jail sentence otherwise.''

His heard jumped, ''And throw your brother's political career into the garbage?''

She didn't blink. ''Yes.''

He felt himself moving, without conscious volition. He reached for her, lifted her, riveted her to his powerful body. Then he kissed her, with the wind blowing in from the bay rippling her hair.

He backed her into the tree and edged himself between her jean-clad legs, shifting her abruptly so that the core of her was suddenly pressed to his raging arousal.

She gasped, but he didn't slow down. If anything, he became more ardent. She felt his hands on her thighs, under her taut bottom, lifting and pulling her into his hips so that only the fabric kept his body from penetrating hers right there.

''The bark would hurt your bare back,'' he said

tightly, his breath moving against her lips as he spoke. "That's the only reason I haven't unzipped your jeans."

Her senses were dimmed, but returning. She shivered. The contact was so intimate that she was glad he couldn't see her face.

He moved sensually against her hips and she heard his breathing deepen. "Feel it?" he whispered. "I'm going to explode any minute."

She did blush, and buried her face in his throat.

Curiosity suddenly overcame his desire. His body stilled. "Nikki...what's wrong?"

She made a gesture with her head, and her burning face pressed closer.

He was remembering things. Confessions she'd made, little hints about a man she'd loved. She'd been married, but she'd said that her husband never wanted her. She'd said at one time that the man she loved...couldn't.

He felt his chest collapse under a rush of breath. He eased the crushing weight of himself away from her softness and rested gently on her, instead.

"You'd better tell me, Nikki," he said slowly.

She drew her closed eyelids against the furious pulse in his throat. "You know already," she whispered. "You're very experienced, aren't you?"

"Experienced enough to know that I've shocked you. Nikki, I don't think you know what sex is. Am I right?"

"Oh, I'd say I have a pretty good idea of what it is, right now," she managed with black humor.

He lifted his head and moved her so that he could see her flushed face in the moonlight. He eased her up, pressed to the tree, and softly thrust against her. Her expression was unmistakable.

"So many emotions," he remarked while he fought for control. "I see fear and shock and, beyond it, desire. But I don't think I could make you desperate enough to forget the consequences, could I?"

"No," she whispered.

He let her slide down the tree. The bark was rough at the back of her sweatshirt. He held her by the waist, not quite touching him, and studied her.

"You've avoided men since the divorce, they say," he said. "Why? Because he couldn't and you didn't want to end up in the same trap again, wanting a man who couldn't take you? There's no possibility of that happening with me. I'm capable, in every way there is."

"So I noticed," she replied sheepishly.

"Nor do I practice irresponsible sex," he persisted. He was almost shaking with passion. His hands contracted. "My house is empty. Deserted. And it's not bugged. You could scream if you wanted to," he whispered seductively. "I might even make you want to."

She remembered the feel of him against her and the sound she'd made. It was a little embarrassing.

He smoothed back her disheveled hair with hands that had a faint tremor. Then he began to unbutton his shirt, slowly, letting her see his chest come into view. There were beads of sweat clinging to the thick hairs that covered him to the collarbone, and his bronzed muscles were damp.

"You're sweating," she remarked nervously.

"I want you," he replied simply. "A man's body reacts in various ways to a woman's allure. It becomes damp, it trembles. When he's very much aroused, he swells." He caught her hand and pulled it gently to him, pressing it the length of his arousal.

She tried to jerk her hand away, but he held it securely.

"Relax," he said softly. "Just relax. Don't be embarrassed. It's as natural as the waves rolling onto the beach, as the wind blowing. Touch me, Nikki."

He pulled her cheek to his bare chest and smoothed her hair, kissing her forehead while his free hand curved around hers and helped her learn his body.

"Not so frightening now, is it?" he whispered. He loosened his grasp and lightly stroked the fingers that touched him. He caught his breath and laughed at her expression. "You didn't hurt me."

She drew her hand away just the same and he let her. His big hands slid around her, under the sweatshirt, against her bare back. They unclipped her bra. When she started to protest, he bent and brushed his open lips lightly against her mouth. The action stayed her movement.

"You know what I feel like," he whispered as his hands moved around her. "Now I want to know what you feel like."

She stood very still, barely breathing. His hands moved around her rib cage and tenderly lifted the slight weight of her firm breasts. His thumbs slipped over the hardening tips and stroked them lightly while he kissed her.

"Lean back, Nikki," he whispered. He eased her spine to the trunk of the tree. His hands bunched the fabric of the sweatshirt and slid it up, with her bra, baring her pearly breasts in the moonlight.

She shivered. It was the most erotic sensation she'd ever had, the breeze on her bare breasts and a man's sultry gaze appreciating them.

"Arch your back, little one," he whispered. "Offer them to me."

She must be crazy. She was certain that she was. Her back began to arch slowly, her breath coming rapidly through parted lips. She shivered in the breeze, and then his warm, moist mouth was covering her, his tongue moving softly over the hard nipple, making her body undulate while she moaned with helpless pleasure.

"The poor fool," he whispered hoarsely. His hands fought snaps and a zipper while his mouth made a banquet of her. "God, the poor...man!"

He was touching her! She tried to resist, but his mouth on her breasts made her too weak with pleasure. Her legs parted for him and she sobbed as he worked witchcraft on her aching, helpless body. She clutched his mouth to her breast and shivered again and again as he brought jolts of white-hot pleasure that robbed her of breath and strength.

She couldn't bear it. The tension was making her frantic. She lifted to him, her hands clawing at his shoulders as she tried to make it happen, tried to make the tension snap...

She cried out, stiffening. His mouth quickly covered hers to silence the sharp little cries. She shuddered again and again and he laughed against her lips with arrogant, wicked delight.

When she softened in his arms, he kissed her hungrily and she heard the sound of another zipper moving. The pressure of his mouth grew suddenly insistent. She was his. There was no thought of resisting now, when she knew what he was going to give her.

The hard thrust shocked her, but the pain was fleeting and as he lifted her, she felt him all the way inside her body.

She made a sound, a gasp, and he felt her tighten.

"Gently," he whispered into her lips. His body was faintly tremulous, like his voice. He was stimulated beyond stopping, beyond reason. He wanted the mindless pleasure he'd given her. He wanted to feel it like silver knives through his powerful body.

His hands cupped her bottom, protecting it from the tree bark. He kissed her and lifted, thrust, with smooth motions of his hips that very quickly made her his conspirator. She shivered with each slow movement, barely able to breathe, her lips touching his as he guided her body back to his again and again.

"I've never done it like this," he whispered huskily. "I've never felt it like this. I can't be tender enough, I can't touch you…inside…deeply enough," he choked. His hands contracted and he groaned in hoarse anguish, his legs shivering as hers wrapped around his hips. "Nikki, make… it…happen…to…me!"

His hands gripped her painfully and he began to shudder, to sob, as his mouth claimed hers. She felt the jolt of fulfillment all the way through her as he went over the edge. The sound he made into her mouth was shocking in its inhibition, and she wondered if she would be riveted to him forever. It felt like that. He was still moving, and what she'd felt at first began to build in her. But there wasn't enough time. He'd let her back to her feet and he was leaning against the tree beside her, shuddering in the aftermath, gasping for breath.

She wanted to cry. He hadn't used any protection and she hadn't tried to stop him. She'd promised herself that this would never happen to her, that she would never allow herself into a situation where she might lose her head and give in to a man's ardor. Now she had. The first wave of terror hit her like acid.

Her hands fumbled with fabric and fasteners. He was quicker than she was. Seconds later, dressed again, he helped right her clothing.

"Don't cry," he whispered gently, brushing at her eyes. "It's all right."

"No, it's not! I let you...!"

He picked her up in his arms and began to kiss her, with breathless tenderness. "I lost my little boy," he said at her mouth, his voice unsteady. "Give me a baby, Nikki."

Chapter Fifteen

Nikki couldn't believe she'd heard him right. Her body felt stiff and sore and bruised. He wasn't letting go, though. He moved to the other side of the tree, where its roots stretched toward the beach, and eased her down. Sitting down beside her, he pulled her across his lap and leaned his back on the tree trunk while he held her cradled against him.

"You don't believe in promiscuous sex," he said. "Neither do I. You love the environment. You like politics. There are hundreds of other things we have in common. The baby will be the foremost thing."

"It's happening too fast," she began dizzily.

"I know it is. I wanted you too much. Next time,

I'll give you what I had.'' He looked down at her. ''Did it hurt very much, Nikki?''

She flushed. ''I wasn't talking about...that. I meant talking about marriage and babies...''

His big hand pressed down on her belly. ''It was your first time,'' he murmured with unforgivable smugness. ''I read somewhere that virgins always get pregnant the first time.''

She hit his chest. ''I am not going to have a child out of wedlock in Charleston!''

''We'll get married,'' he said. ''The sooner the better, in fact.''

She gasped. ''My brother would kill you before he'd let me marry you!''

''Not when we tell him you're pregnant,'' he said smugly.

''I am not!''

His eyebrows lifted. ''How do you know?''

''Because I didn't...I mean, there wasn't... time,'' she finished, drowning in confusion.

''Because you didn't climax when I took you?'' he asked bluntly, chuckling at her expression. ''You will next time. I'm sorry to tell you that pleasure isn't a necessary requirement for conception.''

''It was only one time,'' she said stubbornly.

He smiled slowly. He eased her down on the grass-covered soil under the tree. ''So far,'' he murmured.

"You can't!" she said frantically.

He pulled her hand to him and grinned at her surprise. "Yes, I can." His mouth covered hers and he eased between her legs, feeling her tremble. He whispered into her lips, "If it hurts, you'd better tell me now, while I can still stop." He pushed down and she bit her lip.

He sighed, a little sad. "I was afraid that might happen. I was overeager, wasn't I?" He rolled over onto his back and tugged her so that she was resting on his chest. "All this raging masculinity, wasted," he sighed, pressing her hips down to his. "Ah, well, there's always our wedding night. I hope you like short engagements, because we can be married in three days. And we will be," he added when she looked inclined to argue. "I don't know what's going on around here and I don't give a damn, but you're going to live with me until we're finding out."

"I have to go home!"

"Why?"

The feel of his body under hers made her warm and cozy. She lay down and sighed as he absorbed her weight. "Because I can't be underhanded. I'm not ashamed of the way I feel about you."

He was still. His hand smoothed at the nape of her neck. "And how is that?"

"Deeply affectionate. Passionately desirous. I'd think up more adjectives, but I'm sleepy."

"Making love is tiring," he whispered, and his voice smiled. "You won't come home with me?"

"I want to. Oh, I want to! But let's do it properly," she pleaded. "If you're sure you want to marry me, that is."

He lifted an eyebrow. "I'm sure, all right," he said solemnly. "The baby would be a nice consequence, but it's my backbone I'm thinking of mostly."

"Your what?"

"My backbone," he murmured with deep satisfaction. "I like having it melt and blaze up like fireworks. Couldn't you tell how much pleasure you gave me, or is rictus still too new to you?" She looked puzzled and he laughed, whispering in her ear.

"Oh," she gasped.

"You won't be so easily shocked a few weeks from now," he whispered. "In fact, there's every possibility that you'll be shocking me."

"I wouldn't bet on it." Her fingers curled into his chest. She stared out at the movements of the ocean. It was all so sudden. She felt as if she had emotional whiplash.

"Don't brood," he said lazily. "What's wrong?"

"You're still sleeping with your mistress."

"No, I'm not," he said firmly. He rolled her over onto her back so that he could see her face.

"I haven't touched her since the day I washed up on your beach. Not even to kiss her, Nikki."

She frowned. "But..."

"I took her around with me, yes," he said. "I didn't want it to get back to you that I was mourning because you left."

She smiled. "Oh."

His fingers traced over her face, down to her mouth. "And I was," he added somberly. "Mourning, I mean. I've grieved for you, Nikki, night and day. It knocked me for a loop when I found out who you were, but that didn't stop the longing. Seeing you at the Blair's party was the most painful thing that's happened to me in recent months."

"You didn't call me," she pointed out.

"How could I? Your brother would like to see me in prison. I have no love for him, either. I didn't want to put you in the middle, put you in the position of having to choose between us."

"I only wanted to warn you," she said. "I really didn't mean to, well, to let this happen."

"'This' was delicious," he murmured deeply. "Have you any idea what it felt like to have you, to feel you having me, wanting me?"

"A little," she said, her eyes bright.

"I cheated you of fulfillment," he said, "but..."

She put her fingers over his mouth and had them

soundly kissed. "You didn't," she said. "Before you made love to me, you gave me that."

"It started out to be unselfish," he said ruefully. "I was going to let you see what we could have. But when I watched you at the last, I couldn't control myself. I had to have you."

"There's no need to feel guilty," she said. "I let you."

"Sweetheart, you couldn't have stopped me," he replied quietly. "I honestly didn't mean to let it go that far. I meant for you to have a white wedding, and a proper wedding night."

"I'll have both. Even the puritans allowed intimacy between engaged people," she whispered. She lifted her mouth to his and kissed him softly. Her body sought the length of his and pressed there gently, feeling him wanting her. "You're very big," she whispered daringly, and heard him groan as he answered the kiss. It was a long time before he lifted his head.

"You have to go home," he said harshly.

"You don't want me to go home," she said. She nuzzled close. "I don't want to leave you. But I must."

His hands trembled as they held her head to his chest. He ached from head to toe. "I could have protected you if I hadn't lost my head. I had something in my wallet."

She closed her eyes, thinking about a baby. Her fingers traced the collar button of his shirt and drifted down to tangle in the exciting thickness of hair that covered his chest. ''You miss your family, don't you, Kane?'' she asked softly.

''I miss my son,'' he confessed. His hand tightened on her head. ''I miss him like hell. God, Nikki, I want another child!''

He rolled over and she opened her arms, cradling him against her. Perhaps grief was making him vulnerable, but she loved him. Given time, he might come to love her, particularly if there was a child.

She reached up and kissed him with slow tenderness. ''I'll give you one,'' she whispered.

He searched her eyes. His hand pressed back the strands of dark hair that clung to her cheeks. She looked beautiful and untamed, and faintly pagan lying there on the grass. He could picture her, nude and wanton, her body undulating slowly.

She heard him gasp. ''What is it?'' she asked.

''I was thinking about how it would be, to have you here, naked on the grass.''

''I don't look as good without my clothes as you do without yours,'' she said, smiling. ''I love to look at you.''

He made a rough sound in his throat, and for an instant the chemistry between them almost exploded.

"We were lucky," she whispered. "But someone might come down here looking for me."

He shivered. "And you're not decent."

"And I'm not decent," she agreed. She moved and winced a little, smiling sheepishly. "It felt good."

Color flared along his high cheekbones, but he laughed. "Yes. It felt good."

He got to his feet reluctantly and helped her up. As he held her in front of him, his eyes were watchful. "You look different. Radiant."

She searched his eyes. "You meant it? About wanting to get married, to have a baby with me?"

"I meant every word," he said softly. His expression was breathlessly tender, and he seemed suddenly shocked as he looked at her. "I adore you!" he whispered huskily.

She smiled, her eyes misty with feeling, with delight. "Will you call me tomorrow?"

He nodded. "Like a shot. Come home with me. I'll strip you and myself and we'll lie naked in each other's arms until morning, even if that's all we can do."

"I have to go home." She nuzzled her face against his chest. She wanted to say the words, but he hadn't. It was too soon. But she owned him now. He was hers. She looked up and possession was written on her face. "Leave that slinky brunette alone,'' she said quietly. ''You belong to me now.''

''Honey, I couldn't touch another woman now if my life depended on it,'' he said evenly. ''You can't imagine what you did to me.''

''I'll get better with practice,'' she said.

He laughed delightedly. ''Could I survive if it did?''

She smiled back. ''Good night.''

He caught her hand and lifted it, palm up, to his lips. ''Dream of what we did.''

He walked back toward the beach, where he'd left the small motor launch that he'd piloted over to see Nikki. She watched him go, her body tingling, her heart full. Life was very good, she thought. She couldn't regret what had happened. She was a woman now, and soon she'd be a wife. Kane Lombard's wife. Her feet hardly touched the ground all the way back up to the beach house.

Nobody noticed that she was back. Phoebe and her male companion were dancing to loud music and munching potato chips. Nikki curled up on the sofa and dreamed of the future until it was time to go back into Charleston.

The telephone call early the next morning was so unexpected that at first she simply held on to the receiver and stared blindly at the wall.

''What did you say?'' she stammered.

"I said, I got some very racy photos of you and Lombard last night. Hot stuff, lady. Suppose I turn them over to the tabloids?"

"Kane Lombard's father owns a tabloid," she said quickly.

"Not the only one. He doesn't mind slandering other people. But how is he going to like having his own son on the front page of somebody else's tabloid? Sister of congressional candidate makes out with her brother's worst enemy on the beach," he rattled off. "What headlines!"

She slid down the wall to the floor. "What do you want?" she stammered. If the telephone was bugged, she was dead. Her whole life flashed before her eyes.

"I want you to stay away from Lombard," he said. "And I want you to keep your mouth shut about why."

"But…!"

"You don't really think he wants to marry you?" he chided. "I've got some juicy photos of him with his mistress, the one he hasn't touched, remember? Taken two days ago. They were on the yacht, naked. Do you want me to send over some prints?"

She felt sick. She wrapped her arms around her legs. "You're perverted."

"Who isn't?" came the mocking reply. "If you go near Lombard, those pix go straight to the papers, with four-column cutlines. And we'll be watching. So be a good girl."

The line went dead. If only she'd had the presence of mind to tape it! She hadn't been followed. She knew she hadn't been followed. So how had they found her?

She buried her face in her hands. This couldn't be happening! Kane wanted to marry her. What would he think when she wouldn't talk to him, or see him? What if he caused a scene and these people were hiding outside with cameras to capture it all on film? Her heart stopped. It would be on all the news shows. Irate lover attacks congressional candidate's sister. Publicity. Bad publicity. Clayton would be knocked out at the polls with such sordid goings-on.

But Kane's character would be even more blackened, wouldn't it? She didn't know what to do now.

Derrie answered the knock on her door wearing a beige and gold and white caftan with her hair trailing down her back. She was ready for an early night, and not expecting company. It did occur to her that it might be Cortez, and because she thought of him as a friend, she opened the door a little eagerly.

When she found Clayton Seymour standing there, her heart skipped wildly. She'd actually thought it was over, that she felt nothing! How silly. Loving him was a bad habit, she thought miserably. If only she could break it!

The sight of her made Clayton stop in his tracks and just stare. He'd rarely ever seen Derrie like this. For some reason, he found it much more affecting than he should have. He smiled lazily. "Well, hello. Have you missed me?"

"Not particularly," she said. Her legs were trembling, but she managed to keep him from seeing.

He sighed. "Ah, well. I suppose Hewett's given you the big head, appointing you executive advisor. Maybe I should have done that myself."

"But you didn't think women were capable of handling that much responsibility."

"Bett is," he said maddeningly. "I didn't think you were. More fool, me." He stopped just inside the door and frowned as he looked at her. "I only asked you to call the television stations. Someone else would have done it anyway, you know."

"I do know. But it wasn't going to be me. What do you want, Clay?"

He shrugged, jamming his hands deep into his pockets. He hadn't realized until now how much he'd missed her. She was different now. More confident. Much less intimidated. He found himself attracted, more than ever. "I thought I might persuade you to come back."

She shook her head. ''Not a chance. Especially not as long as you've got Haralson on your staff.''

''What's wrong with Haralson?'' he asked defensively. ''Everybody attacks him lately. First Nikki, now you!''

''We're intuitive. You aren't. He'll drag you right down if you aren't careful,'' she said slowly. ''You have no idea how much trouble you could be in because of him.''

''Because he knows how to take advantage of a weakness in my worst enemy?'' he laughed. ''For heaven's sake, he's a political advisor. He's good at his job. Better at it than you were,'' he added. ''I've never had so much media attention.''

''You may get more than you want one day.''

''If it's what I said about you, I've already apologized,'' he said, eyeing her. ''You've changed, haven't you?'' he asked suddenly. ''You're different, somehow.''

No doubt, she thought. Having responsibility and praise were new to her. Sam Hewett appreciated her abilities as Clay never had. As Cortez had said, she was only now fully utilizing her brain and her expensive college education.

''We all grow,'' she said noncommittally.

''You've done some wonderful things for Hewett,'' he tried again. ''I like your promotional ideas. They're solid without being sensational.'' He hesitated. "You could come back and we could try a few of them."

She smiled at him. He sounded almost boyish. "How's Bett?"

He grimaced, snapping his hands into his pockets. "She wants to get married," he said roughly. "She was the one woman in the world whom I never expected to think of it."

So Cortez had been right. Her heart sank. She would never have gotten Clay, not in a million years. Bett would always have the inside track.

Her face gave her thoughts away. Clayton winced as he looked at her. Derrie had loved him. Why hadn't he realized it in time? Now he was tangled up with Bett and Derrie was lost to him. She wasn't immune, but she was fighting the old attraction. As she grew in power and strength, she would meet other men. She would marry and have a family...

"I've been unfair to you in every way there is, haven't I?" he asked quietly. His pale eyes searched hers. "I used you, took you for granted, finally threw you out of the office and my life. And do you know what, Derrie?" He laughed bitterly. "The girl I hired to replace you is afraid to open her mouth. She can type, but she can't spell. She's pretty and sweet. But she isn't you."

"Why don't you let Bett run the office for you?" she asked dully. "She'd be a natural."

"Bett doesn't want to work for me. She wants to remain a lobbyist. She likes the money, you see. Even my salary can't compare to what she makes." He turned away to the window and stared out it. "She's deciding where we're going to live even now. What a girl."

"I'm sorry if you aren't happy," Derrie said. "But it's really none of my business."

He turned, his face solemn. "It was once."

"Those days are gone. I miss working for you, but I'm very challenged with Sam. He's a good boss." She forced a smile. "And we're going to beat your socks off at the polls in November."

His eyebrows levered up. "I'm no lost cause."

"Keep Haralson on and I can guarantee that you will be."

"He's spending the weekend in Washington."

He drew in a long, slow breath, and his eyes were hungry as they searched over her. "She tells me where she wants to go, what she wants to do. She even tells me what to do in bed." He smiled sadly. "Did you ever wonder how it would feel to sleep with me?"

She wouldn't blush. She wouldn't! "Once or twice," she confessed tautly.

His eyes narrowed and he smiled. "You're blushing. You haven't ever done it, have you?"

She hated that superior attitude, the way he was looking at her. "I dated a college boy in my senior year in high school,'' she said curtly. ''He was handsome and very persuasive, and I was stupid. I slept with him, one time, and that's why I haven't slept with anybody since,'' she said, shocking him.

He moved closer, scowling. ''Why?''

She shifted uneasily. She didn't like remembering. ''Because I didn't want to. He parked the car and I thought we were just going to make out a little. But he pushed me down and before I even realized what was happening, he was...'' She wrapped her arms tightly around her breasts. ''I hated it! He was in a hurry and it hurt awfully. Then he said that if I didn't like it, it was my own fault, because I'd led him on. All the girls did it, he said, so why should he have thought I was any different from them?''

He felt outraged. He'd never even suspected. He'd always thought that Derrie was a prude, that she never dated because she was afraid of being seduced. He hadn't thought it would be a reason like this.

''You should have taken him to court,'' he said curtly.

''What defense would I have used?'' she asked bitterly. ''I was in love with him, or so I thought. Everyone knew we were a couple. It would have been my word against his and he was captain of the football team and the eldest son of one of the most influential families in Charleston.''

"I begin to see the light."

"I thought you might," she replied. "They talk about equality and justice. Let me tell you, the wealthy people make the laws and decide who pays the penalties. If you don't believe that, look at the inmates in any prison and see how many rich kids you find there."

"Were there consequences?" he asked.

"Luckily, no," she said heavily. "I didn't get pregnant and I had myself tested for HIV twice, months apart. But it scared me to death. I never wanted to take the same chance twice."

"You worked for me for six years," he said. "Why didn't you ever talk to me about it? It must have only just happened when I hired you, the first year I ran for the state legislature."

"It had," she said. "But I couldn't even tell my parents. How could I have told you?"

"He should have been arrested," he said angrily.

"Ironically, he died in an automobile accident the very next year," she said, lifting her eyes to his. "I didn't even cry when I heard. I guess I didn't have any tears left."

"Why should you?" His eyes slid down the caftan, lingering where her breasts thrust against it. Her silky hair flowed like waves of gold around her shoulders. She wasn't a beautiful girl, but she was disturbingly attractive. She was sexy, he decided finally. He'd forced himself not to notice that before. He was involved with Bett, and he'd thought Derrie a virgin. But inside, he was churning, changing. He felt himself growing uncomfortable as the sensuality of her appearance worked on him.

"Derrie, do you know anything about Haralson?" he asked suddenly.

She moved away from him toward the kitchen. "Nothing that you won't find out eventually," she said, remembering her promise to Cortez to say nothing, even to Clay. Why she should trust a man she'd just met was strange, but she did. She knew somehow that he wasn't going to do anything to hurt the Seymours. He had it in for Haralson, though, and Derrie wasn't going to lift a finger to save that dirty dog.

He paused in the doorway, leaning against it while she put coffee on to brew. His face was troubled. "What you aren't telling me could cost me the election."

She turned. "Would that bother me, when I work for your closest competitor?" she asked mischievously.

He pursed his lips, smiling faintly. She was sexy when she smiled like that.

He shouldered away from the door and moved toward her, intent in his eyes.

"You stop right there," she told him, wielding

the scoop she was using to put coffee into the filter basket. "I'm seeing someone else. He's from Washington and he's very handsome..."

He didn't even slow down. She kept talking until he took the scoop and tossed it aside and suddenly pushed her back into the counter with the weight of his hips.

"Shut up..." he murmured against her mouth.

She stiffened at the unfamiliar contact with his aroused body. She hadn't even known that he got aroused in the six years she'd worked for him, although it was certain that he did with Bett.

Bett. She had to remember Bett. She did try, but his hands were framing her face, his thumbs coaxing her lips apart so that his mouth could press between them. He smelled of spice and soap and he tasted of coffee. She could taste the woody tang of it on her tongue when his mouth began to open and she breathed him.

A sound passed her lips, but he ignored it. His mouth grew slowly more insistent until she stopped fighting the pleasure and gave in to it. He was warm and strong and he smelled good. She relaxed into his aroused body with a little sigh and felt his arms enfolding her.

Not until his long leg began to insinuate itself between hers through the caftan did her drowning mind come swimming back to reality.

"No," she gasped under his mouth.

He lifted his head. His eyes were as turbulent as hers. He frowned slightly. His gaze fell to her mouth and further down. He eased her back so that he could see the stiff peaks of her breasts and their jerky, quick rise and fall. If he was aroused, so was she. He hadn't lost her. He hadn't!

His eyes lifted to hers. "Derrie," he said huskily, savoring the sound of her name on his tongue.

"I won't...sleep with you," she choked.

He moved back, just a little, his eyes curious, puzzled. He smiled. "I know. But you want to," he said, amazed.

"I've wanted to with a lot of men! It isn't just you!"

He knew better. He smiled, a little sadly. "I'm getting married, you know," he said wistfully. "And I've just realized that I don't want to. The thought of a lifetime with Bett makes me want to throw the election and sail to Bermuda."

"Sam Hewett and the rest of us would appreciate it," she managed breathlessly.

He chuckled. He felt better and brighter than he had for a long time. And all because of Derrie!

He let her go with flattering reluctance. "You still taste like a virgin, despite that cowardly so-and-so back in high school," he said quietly. "Suppose I give Bett the heave-ho and come back? What would you do?"

"Nothing until after the election," she said

abruptly, although she was bluffing and they both knew it. ''I won't fraternize with the enemy.''

He lifted an eyebrow. He was still tingling all over and finding it hard to breathe. ''How about after the election?''

She folded her arms over her telltale breasts and laughed jerkily. ''Well, we'll see.''

He smiled wickedly. ''That's worth waiting for.'' He turned toward the door, paused and turned back, surveying her. ''I guess I've turned a blind eye to Haralson, just as Mosby has. It's time we did something before it's too late.''

''I can't possibly agree with you, because I work for the opposition,'' she stated.

''So I noticed.'' He drawled it, his smile sensuous and teasing.

She flushed and glowered all at once.

He laughed at her bridled fury. ''Pretty thing,'' he murmured. ''Now I know why the world went dark when you left.''

''Why?''

''I'll tell you,'' he promised, going out the door. He stuck his head back in. ''*After* the election!''

Chapter Sixteen

Nikki avoided calling Kane all morning. She also avoided answering the telephone every time it rang. But that night it started and refused to stop. She put on the answering machine. That was worse.

"Answer me, Nikki," Kane growled. "I know you're there. What the hell is wrong with you? Have you had second thoughts? Changed your mind?"

She swallowed. In order to save Clay—and Kane—she was going to have to lie. There was no other way. The thought of those sleazy photographs in the tabloids made her sick. She couldn't bear it.

She picked up the receiver and fought down nausea. "Kane, I have had second thoughts," she said in a dull, defeated tone. "I'm sorry. I really can't do this to Clayton."

"Your brother has his own life to live," he pointed out. "Nikki, we made love!"

"Yes. Th-thank you for the tutoring," she stammered, clutching the receiver. "I'll put it to good use."

There was a shocked pause. The receiver slammed down in her face. So much, she thought, for victories.

Clayton noticed Nikki's pallor, but he didn't understand what had caused it. She was so secretive lately, so tense. And he had problems of his own. Derrie and Haralson came immediately to mind, although in different ways.

"Are you all right?" he asked.

"Sure. How was Derrie?" she returned.

He smiled with soft pleasure. "Delicious, thank you," he murmured. "Odd that I never noticed her in six long years, isn't it?"

Nikki brightened at the look on his face. "Yes, I always thought so," she confessed.

"She's full of surprises, our Derrie." His smile faded and he began to look worried. "I wish I had time to explore them all. But there's a campaign waiting to be won and a few problems to solve. I'm not going to marry Bett," he said abruptly, facing his sister.

"Will wonders never cease?" Nikki sighed, smiling.

"I know, you never liked her."

"I never trusted her," came the dry reply. "Women can usually see through other women, Clay. She was never quite what she seemed, and it was pretty obvious to me that she liked *what* you were more than she liked *who* you were. As a congressman, you were of great value to her. If you'd lost the election, I'm afraid it would have been another story. She doesn't look at you like a woman in love should look at a man."

He searched her green eyes and realized abruptly what she meant. The way she'd been with Kane Lombard when they danced had been a revelation to him. Not since Mosby had Nikki looked like that. He felt rather sad that he'd been so adamant about keeping her apart from the industrialist. On the other hand, Lombard was a polluter and deserved everything he got. But there was still the problem of Haralson. He owed the man for his help; especially his help unmasking Lombard's polluting of the natural environment. But Haralson was becoming a liability that he couldn't afford. It was just a question of time before the man was going to cross the line and do something illegal.

His eyes narrowed. "I've had time to do some serious thinking about Haralson, especially since Derrie seems to agree with you. I've decided that you're right. I'm going to send him back to Washington and get someone else to run my campaign."

She brightened a little. "Oh, Clay. I'm so glad. You're doing the right thing!"

"I suppose so. But he was a hell of a campaign coordinator. Who's going to replace him?"

"Me."

His eyebrows lifted and then he chuckled. "Yes! Why not? You'd be a natural!"

He wouldn't have thought so even a week ago, but apparently the way he'd misjudged Derrie had turned his attitude around. Nikki knew that she could do a better job than Haralson, and in a less underhanded way.

Nikki watched him move toward the door. "Where are you going?"

"To give Haralson his walking papers, of course," he returned. He grinned at her. "I'll expect you at the office at eight sharp tomorrow morning, Miss Seymour. You are now a working stiff."

"You can count on me," she assured him.

She could only hope that with Haralson out of the picture, the threat of those photographs hanging over her might conveniently disappear.

Kane was half out of his mind over Nikki's change of heart. He could hardly believe that she cared so little for him. He'd been certain last night that she loved him.

But what if guilt was making her turn away from him? She was a virgin, and he hadn't known. He'd backed her into a corner, all but forced her. Did she hate him? He had to know! But how was he going to find out?

Mrs. Yardley knocked on the door and peeked around it. "It's Mr. Jurkins, sir," she said. "He'd like a word with you, if it's convenient."

"It's convenient," he said dully. "Send him in."

Will Jurkins was wearing a two-year-old suit with scuffed shoes. He looked the least prosperous of any employee Kane had. He stared at the other man for a long moment. If he'd suspected Jurkins of taking kickbacks to change solid waste companies, it was hardly evident.

"Yes, Jurkins? What can I do for you?" he asked with faint impatience.

"I keep hearing gossip," the other man said slowly. He was twisting a paper clip in his nervous fingers. "I just would like to know if they plan to try to put you in jail over this, sir."

"Bob Wilson says that it's unlikely," Kane replied. He perched himself on the edge of his desk. "Probably we'll be fined. But that sewage leak didn't do us any favors with the state and federal environmental people."

"Yes, I know, and that's my fault. That leak was a legitimate accident, Mr. Lombard," Jurkins said earnestly. "I wouldn't do anything illegal. I mean I wouldn't have. I have a little girl, six years old," he stammered. "She has leukemia. I can take her to St. Jude's for treatment, you see, and it's free. But there's the medicine and she has to see doctors locally and the insurance I had at my old job ran out. She isn't covered under the insurance here. It's that preexisting conditions clause," he added apologetically.

"I know about that," Kane replied. "Almost thirty million Americans have no health insurance, you know, and people with preexisting conditions can't get any, period. If we get a new administration in November, perhaps we'll have a chance of changing all that."

"I hope so, sir. But that wasn't why I came."

Kane lifted a questioning eyebrow. Jurkins was almost shaking. "Sit down, Jurkins," he said, gesturing to a chair.

Jurkins looked oddly thin and frail in the big leather armchair. He was still twisting the paper clip. "I hope you won't get in too much trouble."

"At least they aren't going to shut us down," Kane returned.

Jurkins hesitated. He looked up and opened his mouth. He wanted to speak. But he couldn't make the words come out. He got to his feet again, jerkily, red-faced.

"I'll, uh, get back to work now, sir," he said. His voice was unsteady. So was the smile. "I hope it works out."

"So do I." Kane sat on the edge of the desk when the man left and kept going over the odd conversation. Something was definitely wrong there. Jurkins knew something and he was afraid to tell it. He pushed the intercom button. "Get me Bob Wilson," he said.

"Yes, sir," came the quick reply.

Haralson stared at Clayton Seymour as if he couldn't believe his own ears.

"You're firing me?" he asked the other man. "Are you serious?"

"I'm afraid so. I'm going to give Nikki your job."

Haralson, always so cordial and kind, suddenly turned nasty. He sat up in the chair, holding his cigar between his cold fingers, and reached into his desk drawer. "No, you aren't. Want to know why?"

"Do tell me," Clayton invited with smiling, cool confidence.

Haralson drew a photograph, an 8 x 10 glossy, out of the drawer and tossed it across the desk to Clayton.

"If you want to see that on the front page of every tabloid in the country, fire me."

Clayton gasped. It wasn't blatant, for a photograph of that sort, but it made innuendoes that were unmistakable. That was Kane Lombard—and his sister!

"I'm sure you'll see things my way," Haralson said pleasantly. "I'm going to get you back in office, of course, that's a byproduct. But my main purpose is to bury Lombard. He cost my father his cabinet position. He found out that my father was having an affair with an intern and he told his family and they spilled it to the whole damned world!

"I was in my last year of school when it happened, but I never forgot. We lived in a small town in Texas, and that sleazy tabloid ran the story week after week after week! My mother killed herself over it, and I swore I'd make Lombard and his family pay! It's all been a means to an end—my job with Torrance, everything! Torrance had no choice but to hire me, and to send me here to help you when I told him to," he added, laughing. "You see, I have friends who know the ins and outs of the detecting game. And I know all about Mosby Torrance."

"What do you know, exactly?" Clayton asked.

"That he's gay."

Clayton couldn't reply. He didn't dare say a word. The man was unbalanced, and if he wanted to believe that about Mosby for the time being, it might be safer than the truth. He looked down at the photo.

"Take it with you," Haralson invited. "I still have the negatives. And tell your sister she'll have no opportunity to make that monster, Lombard, happy. I told her on the phone that she'd see those pictures published if she took one step toward Lombard. I won't let him have any happiness. He's going to pay and pay and keep on paying until he's as dead as my mother is!"

Clayton wandered back to his office with his mind in limbo. Haralson was dangerous. How could he have missed the signs? Mosby was afraid of the man because he thought Haralson knew the truth. In fact, he didn't, but that hardly mattered if he had Mosby on the run. Now he had Nikki on the run. Clayton didn't know what to do. If he showed the photo to Nikki in her present state of mind, she might lose it.

The election was less than a month away. Haralson had something else up his sleeve. No doubt he was going to publish those photos anyway. He'd probably wait until the last possible minute and then let fly. The scandal would destroy Nikki socially. It would ruin Lombard in the process. It might even do enough damage to Sam Hewett's campaign—because Kane's brother was his campaign manager—to cost Hewett the election. Clayton wanted to win. But not that way!

He only knew of one possible thing to do, to stop Haralson in time. It was probably the mistake of his life. He got in his car and drove out to Seabrook, to the new Lombard beach house.

If Kane Lombard was shocked to find Clayton Seymour standing on his doorstep, he hid it quickly. He had a glass of scotch and ice in one big hand. His eyebrow jerked as he stood aside to let the shorter man enter.

The beach house was luxurious, Clayton thought, and right on the marina. It must have cost a fortune. Well, Kane had one.

''Is this a social call?'' Kane drawled.

''Thank your lucky stars that I'm not homicidal,'' Clayton returned. He glanced around. ''Are you alone?''

Kane nodded. ''What is it?''

''I think you'd better have a look at this.'' He took the photograph from the inside of his suit jacket and tossed it on the coffee table.

Kane's eyes darkened. He cursed violently.

''Who?'' he demanded, his eyes promising retribution.

''My reelection campaign manager,'' Clayton said heavily. ''I went in to fire him this morning and he handed me that.'' He glared at the older man. ''I could kill you for doing this to Nikki.''

''I made love to Nikki,'' he returned solemnly. ''Please notice the wording. I didn't seduce her, have sex with her, or any number of less discreet euphemisms. I made love to her.''

Clayton relaxed a little. Not much. He was still furious. ''Did it have to be on the beach?''

''I couldn't make it to the house,'' came the rueful reply. The smile faded quickly though. ''Has Nikki seen this?'' he asked suddenly.

''No, Nikki heard about this,'' he said. ''She was warned not to go near you or these pictures would be smeared over the front page of every tabloid he could reach by the next morning.''

''So that was all it was. Thank God.'' Kane relaxed, looking as if he'd just won a state lottery. In another state, of course, South Carolina didn't have one.

''Haven't you talked to her?''

''I've tried to do nothing else,'' the other man said heavily. ''She said it was all a mistake, and I believed she meant it.'' His head lifted. ''But now I'm going to marry her. If you don't like it, that's tough,'' he added without blinking, his face hard and relentless.

''At least you're honorable enough to stand by her,'' Clayton said stiffly.

''Stand by her, hell. I love her! Do you think

I'd have touched her in the first place if I hadn't had honorable intentions?'' he demanded. ''She was a virgin, for God's sake!''

Clayton gaped at him. He hadn't expected that answer. ''A virgin?''

''You didn't know?''

''It's hardly the sort of thing a man can discuss with his sister.'' He hesitated. So many things were beginning to become clear. ''I thought Nikki knew it all. She doesn't really know anything...'' He looked up. ''You said you loved her.''

''I loved her the day I met her,'' came the grim reply. ''I couldn't stop. I tried, though.'' Kane took a sip of the scotch. His head lifted and he glared at the other man. ''You're a damned blackguard of a politician. You planted that waste at the dump site deliberately and led the media to it.''

''No, I didn't,'' Clayton said honestly. ''Haralson had one of his cronies find the dump and call in the media. I still don't know all of it. The one thing I'm sure of is why he did it. Your father apparently printed a story about his father that got him kicked off the president's cabinet some years ago and Haralson's mother committed suicide. It's you he's after, not Sam Hewett.''

Kane whistled. ''I wondered why the name sounded familiar. It's a wonder I didn't recognize it sooner, but I had other things on my mind.'' He looked up and frowned. ''But why are you here?''

Clayton didn't even blink as he replied. "Because I can't let him blackmail Nikki—or myself—for that matter. If I lose the election, I'll do it honestly. I don't need to use underhanded methods."

"Who else is he blackmailing?"

"My ex-brother-in-law."

"Torrance is gay, I take it?" Kane asked quietly.

"It's a little more complicated than that," he replied. "It's his secret, although he did tell me when they got divorced. I thought Nikki knew, but I don't suppose that she does now."

"I won't tell her. But I'm going to know."

Clayton hesitated, but only for a minute. He shrugged and quietly told the other man what he wanted to know.

Kane was silent for a long time. "You read about these things. You never quite believe them." He glanced at Clayton. "Haralson knows, I gather?"

"No. He suspects what you did," Clayton replied, smiling. "What he doesn't realize is that if Mosby were gay, he wouldn't be hiding it in the first place. He's not the sort. In fact, he has any number of gay friends."

"Which is probably where the rumors started."

"No doubt."

Kane stared at the photograph again. He grimaced. "Nikki isn't going to like this, but I only know of one way to stop a blackmailer short of killing him.'' He picked up the photo with a regretful smile. ''I think you know what has to be done.''

''That's why I came.'' He got to his feet. ''You'd better marry her soon. She lost her breakfast this morning.''

''And this is only the first week.'' Kane grinned like a Cheshire cat. ''My poor Nikki.''

Clayton glared at him. ''You ought to be ashamed of yourself!''

''For making a baby?'' he asked, eyebrows levering up. ''I lost mine,'' he said, his voice deepening. ''My son. I thought my life was over, that I'd never have the nerve to try again. But Nikki opened up the world for me. Ashamed? My God. I'm going to strut for the rest of the day, and then I'm going to drag Nikki up in front of the first minister I can find.'' He reached in a drawer and produced a document. ''That is a marriage license. You can come to the wedding, but after that, we will not expect you to be a regular visitor. Especially until after the election, which my candidate is going to win.''

Clayton found himself grinning. ''You bastard.''

Kane grinned back. ''It does take one to know one,'' he pointed out.

''You're going to print that?'' he nodded toward the photograph.

"Can you think of another way?"

"Not off the top of my head."

"Then the sooner, the better. Don't tell Nikki. I'll break it to her tonight."

Clayton glanced at him. "You'd better make her happy."

"That's a foregone conclusion. She loves me, you see," he added quietly. "She might not know it—or admit it—just yet, but she does."

"Does she know how you feel?"

Kane stuck his hands in his pockets. "I've been keeping that to myself." He looked up. "We always expect women to read minds. I guess sometimes they need telling."

"I guess." He went out the door. He looked back at Kane. "Like hell your candidate is going to win," he tossed over his shoulder. Deep laughter followed him into the yard.

Bett was lounging on her sofa with the phone to her ear. She started cursing and her face grew redder and redder. She sat up.

"But he can't do that! He can't fire you!"

Haralson laughed. "He isn't going to. I had his sister followed recently when she had a clandestine meeting with Kane Lombard. I got some photos that he isn't going to want to see printed."

Bett relaxed. "Thank God for that. What are we going to do?"

"I thought you were going to marry him."

"Are you out of your mind?" she shot back. "He's useful, but not that useful. I have no intention of living in Charleston, South Carolina."

"Snob."

She twisted the cord around her finger. "Mosby won't like it if you use that photo. He's still protective of Nikki."

"He won't know until it's too late. He won't bother me, either. I know something about him."

Bett smiled. "What?"

"That's for me to know and for you to find out."

"Be secretive. I'll make Clayton tell me."

"You'd better hurry, then, because he had a long tête-à-tête with his ex-secretary the other night and he's having lunch with her today."

"What?!"

"I didn't think you knew. If I were you, sweetie pie," he said sarcastically, "I'd spend a little time protecting my hunting preserve."

"Call Sam Hewett," she said shortly. "Tell him that his exec is out hobnobbing with the enemy camp!"

"I had that in mind," Haralson said.

"What will you do if Clayton comes up with something to use against you?" she asked after a minute.

"Mosby will save me. He'll have to."

"Then it will be all right, I guess."

Haralson laughed. "Of course it will."

Senator Mosby Torrance was fielding questions from reporters after a news conference. He'd supported the president on a vote to assist U.N. troops in the Serbia-Bosnian hostilities. His eyes lit on one particular female reporter for CNN, a beauty if there ever was one.

After the conference he paused to talk to her, his blue eyes appreciative on her exquisite skin. She had to be in her thirties, but she was a heavenly combination of beauty, brains and personality. She made his head spin....

A telephone call was waiting for him when he got back to the Senate Office Building. He motioned his secretary to put it through.

"Great timing!" Haralson laughed curtly when he heard Mosby's voice. "I caught you coming in the door, I guess?"

"I guess." Mosby was bitter and sounded it.

"Did I interrupt something? I hope not. Listen, I'm turning some photos of your ex-wife over to the press."

Mosby went silent. "What sort of photos?"

"Pictures of her with Kane Lombard in a, shall we say, compromising position." He laughed. "I don't expect you to say a word," he added coldly. "I know what you are. Unless you want the media all over you, closet queen, you'd better do as I say."

Mosby's eyes widened. "What did you call me?"

"Stop playing dumb! You've always known that I knew. You're gay."

Mosby's eyes twinkled. He felt liberated. He'd kept this barracuda on the payroll for years because he'd had the threat of exposure hanging over his head. And all along Haralson had thought he was gay?

He started laughing. He started and couldn't stop.

"I'll tell the whole damned world!" Haralson was threatening.

The laughter got worse. Vaguely, Mosby was aware of cursing and the slam of the telephone receiver. This was too good to be true.

But when he got hold of himself, he remembered what Haralson had said about some compromising photos of Nikki. He really couldn't allow her to be hurt by his own blackmailer. He owed her a warning.

He had his secretary dial Nikki. But the number he had wasn't the right one. It had been changed. He'd have to call Clay. He hoped there was enough time to save Nikki from whatever diabolical fate Haralson had planned for her.

The phone rang several times before it was answered. Finally a feminine voice replied, "Hello?"

Mosby recognized the voice. It was Bett. He almost spoke, but then he remembered that she and Haralson were thick as thieves. Had she been selling him down the river all along? He couldn't let her in on what he knew.

Slowly, he put down the receiver. He thought for a minute, then he buzzed his secretary. "Get me on the next flight to Charleston," he said.

"But, Senator, you've got a committee meeting..."

"Call and explain that I have an emergency in my district. Tell them," he added, "that it's a family emergency."

"Yes, sir."

He hung up and reached for his attache case. If he hurried, he might be in time to avert a disaster for Nikki—and, inadvertently, one for Clayton.

Chapter Seventeen

A tall, slender man wandered into the executive offices of Lombard, International. He was wearing jeans and boots with a long-sleeved red shirt and a denim jacket. His hair was in a ponytail and he wore dark glasses. He flashed his credentials and was immediately allowed into the big boss's office.

Kane Lombard was big and fierce-looking—not a man Cortez would have enjoyed tangling with.

"What can I do for you?" he asked Cortez after motioning him into a chair and offering him coffee.

"I want to talk to a man who works for you—a man named Jurkins."

Kane scowled. "Will Jurkins?"

"That's him." He hesitated. "There's something I'd better tell you up front. I do work for the government, but I have no jurisdiction here and no authority to question anyone in this particular circumstance.'' He leaned forward. ''But if you'll give Jurkins to me for about three minutes, I think I can help you extricate yourself from this damned mess that I helped Haralson mire you in.''

''You...?''

''Sit down,'' Cortez said wearily, motioning an infuriated Kane back into his executive chair. ''I'm a tenth degree black belt. Just take my word for it and don't ask for proof. I didn't know what I was doing. Haralson wanted a favor. I hate polluters. I've prosecuted any number of them over the years. But I'm on my first vacation in a decade and Haralson cost me any rest I might have gotten. Why don't you send for Jurkins and I'll let you in on a few closely guarded secrets about that toxic waste dump?''

Kane only hesitated for a minute. ''All right.'' He hit the intercom button. ''Get Jurkins back in here. Don't tell him I've got company.''

''I wouldn't dream of it,'' came the dry reply.

The last person in the world that Nikki expected to find on her doorstep was her ex-husband. Mosby Torrance looked tired, but he smiled as she stood aside to let him into the house.

''Sorry to show up like this, Nikki, but you and Clay changed your telephone number,'' he explained, when they were seated in the living room.

"We had to," she said. "Too many people had it." She studied his face with quiet affection. He was older, but still devastatingly handsome. Mosby, with his blond hair and blue eyes and perfectly chiseled patrician face. If it hadn't been for Kane, and the feelings he'd ignited in her, she might still be mourning Mosby.

"Haralson called me earlier," he told her. He leaned forward with his arms crossed over his knees. His eyes narrowed. "Nikki, he's got some photographs of you and Kane Lombard."

"Yes, I know," she said tightly. "But I've dealt with Haralson. He won't print them."

"Yes, he will," he said finally, watching her react. "Oh, not now, probably—but closer to the election, yes, he will. He's gone over the edge, Nikki. He wants to hit everybody. If he publishes those photographs, he can hurt a lot of people."

She looked at him with anguish in her face. "I didn't know I was being followed. I was so careful..."

"You have no idea what sort of people he conspires with," he told her quietly. "Nikki, they have cameras so tiny they can be fed under doors, through windows. They have cameras and sound equipment that can pick up actions and conversations from great distances. Haralson has connections at the FBI and even the CIA."

"He's angry at Clay because I wanted Clay to

fire him. He's angry at me, too. He'll cut us both down..."

"I'm not going to let him cut down anybody," he replied. "He thinks he's got me on a meathook. In fact, I know someone who can settle his hash for good."

"Why didn't you do something before?" she asked.

"Because he had something on me. Or thought he did." He searched her eyes sadly. "You never knew why I couldn't consummate our marriage."

"I found out," she said, averting her eyes. "You let me find out."

"I let you find me in bed with a man," he replied. "But I'm not gay."

She turned back toward him, her eyes wide as saucers.

"Ask Clay," he said wearily. "Tell him I said it was all right to tell you. I've come to the conclusion that he was right all along. If I'd admitted the problem in the beginning and had something done, who knows how it might have turned out. As it is, I'm going to have to do something, as distasteful as it seems to me. I can't go on like this, risking blackmail and pretending to be something I'm not just to spare myself embarrassment." He opened the attache case while a puzzled Nikki stared at him. He tossed a packet of papers onto the coffee table. "Think of it as counterblackmail,'' he said. ''Give those to Clay, with my blessing.''

''What are they?'' she asked, picking up the sealed envelope.

''Things you don't need to know, little one. Tell Clay that I've already set these wheels in motion. The material in there—'' he pointed to the envelope ''—is just for his information. He won't need to do a thing. Not one single thing. He thought he had an ally, you see.'' Mosby smiled slowly. ''But it was my ally.''

He got up and moved closer to Nikki. His fingers lightly stroked down her cheek and his regrets were all in his eyes. ''I was trying to save my political neck when I let your father force you into marrying me,'' he said quietly. ''I panicked. Because I did, we both suffered. We couldn't have a normal marriage and I thought too much of you to make a travesty of it, so I pretended to be something I wasn't.''

Her eyes searched his. ''I wouldn't have cared what was wrong,'' she said huskily. ''I loved you!''

He drew in a long, hard breath. ''I know.'' He smiled sadly. ''That's the cross I have to carry with me. I'm glad you found somebody, Nikki. I hope he can make you happy.''

''He could have,'' she said miserably. ''I love him very much. But Haralson has killed it all. He made me lie to Kane, and now Kane will hate me.''

''Oh, I doubt that.'' His fingers loosened and fell away from her face. ''You deserve a little happiness.''

''What about you, Mosby?''

He shrugged. ''I'll go overseas and have some discreet surgery,'' he said mysteriously. ''After that...I'll see.'' He laughed curtly. ''I'd rather not, but I seem to have very few choices left. There's always a Haralson around.''

''Everybody has skeletons, didn't you know?'' she asked.

''Most people are lucky enough not to have them disinterred, though.'' He smiled. ''Don't look so morose, Nikki. Dreams still come true.''

''Not in my life, they don't,'' she said.

He searched her sad eyes one last time and left the house as quickly as he'd entered it.

Nikki studied the envelope in her hand with a curious frown. What in the world could Mosby have in there that would save Clay from Haralson?

Jurkins entered the office for the second time in as many days. He was more nervous this time, though, especially when he saw the dark-haired man sitting across from Mr. Lombard.

He stopped just inside the closed door and stared from one man to the other.

‘‘This is Cortez,’’ Kane introduced. ‘‘Will Jurkins,’’ he indicated the other man.

They shook hands. Cortez noticed that Jurkins’s palms were sweaty and hot. The man was almost shaking with nerves.

He sat down heavily in the chair adjacent to Cortez’s. ‘‘Yes, sir, what did you want?’’ he asked Kane.

Kane leaned back in his chair and crossed one long leg over the other. ‘‘I want to know how you managed to pay off your daughter’s medical bill at the local clinic.’’

Jurkins’s caught breath was eloquent. He shivered.

‘‘Several thousand dollars in a lump sum,’’ Kane continued. ‘‘You paid cash.’’

Jurkins started to try to bluff it out, but these men weren’t going to fall for any bluff. He was unprepared, caught red-handed. Well, there was one thing he could try. He slumped and put his head in his hands. He let out a heavy, hard breath. ‘‘I knew it would come out,’’ he said huskily. ‘‘But I couldn’t turn him down. I was afraid they’d stop treating my baby if I didn’t have the money. It’s just me, we haven’t got anybody else. I couldn’t lose her.’’

He lifted tired eyes to Kane’s. ‘‘She’s all I got in the world. It didn’t sound so bad, when he explained it to me. All he wanted me to do was say that one company wasn't working out and hire another one to take its place. That's all. He never said I was to do something illegal, Mr. Lombard. He just said I was to tell you the other company didn't do its job right. He said I was to do that, and to hire Burke's to replace it. That's all."

"You didn't ask him why?" Kane asked coldly.

"My little girl's got leukemia!" Jurkins said miserably. "I had to get her bills caught up so they wouldn't let her die!"

Kane felt the man's pain, but Cortez showed no such reaction. He leaned toward the man. His dark eyes were steady, intimidating. "Your little girl goes to St. Jude's," he said quietly. "The only expense you have is at the clinic and it isn't several thousand dollars worth. Your daughter does have leukemia. She is also in remission, and has been for six months. However, Mr. Jurkins," he added very quietly, "you are a heroin addict. And the clinic you frequent is the province of one of the most notorious drug lords in the Carolinas. You took the money from Haralson to support a habit—not to secure your daughter's health."

Jurkins had jumped up, but Cortez had him in one lightning-fast motion, whipped around and shoved back down into the chair. Cortez stood over him, powerful and immovable, and Jurkins decided to cut his losses while he could.

"All right, I did it. But I couldn't help it," Jurkins groaned. "I couldn't, I couldn't...!"

"Would you telephone the local police, please," Cortez asked Kane. "I think we'd better have the assistant D.A. over here, too, and the Department of Health and Environmental Control field representative."

Kane shook his head as he studied the broken man before him. "Jurkins, didn't you have enough grief already?" he asked sadly.

"I had...too much," the man whispered, his head down. "Too much grief, too much pain, too much fear...and too little money and hope. It got to me so bad. At first it was just enough to make me sleep, when she was in the hospital, to make me forget how bad it was. But then, it took more and more..." He looked up at Kane. "It was just to hire another company to haul off your trash," he said, as if he couldn't understand what all the fuss was about. "What's so bad about that?"

Kane and Cortez exchanged glances. It was just too much trouble to try to explain it to him. He didn't understand at all.

After Jurkins was taken away Kane drank coffee with Cortez, trying to find the right way to thank him.

"It's my job," Cortez said with a lazy smile.

"Sometimes, though, I don't enjoy doing it. Jurkins's little girl is the one who'll suffer the most."

"No, she won't," Kane promised tersely. "I'll make sure of that. He'll get treatment and I'll try to have the charges against him reduced. I'll get him a damned good lawyer."

Cortez smiled quizzically. "He nearly closed you down."

"So he did. But a miss is as good as a mile."

Cortez finished his coffee and got to his feet. "I'm glad it worked out for you."

"It hasn't yet. But maybe it will." He shook hands with the other man and scowled curiously. "Listen, how did you get onto Jurkins?"

"Through Haralson. He's been watched for several months," came the surprising reply. "He was supplying the clinic where Jurkins got his stuff—part of his money-making operation."

"I saw him with Clayton Seymour one day. I did wonder how a senate aide was able to afford a BMW," Kane had to admit.

"Through selling drugs," Cortez replied. "I let Haralson think I was here on vacation. I didn't know he was after you, but I was hoping for a link to that clinic. And there it was."

"Luckily for me," Kane said.

"Indeed. Fingering the clinic was only one part. I had to have corroboration from a witness who would testify. Until now, I couldn't get one. Haralson played right into my hands. I traced the dump site back here and found your man Jurkins at the end of it. He tied up all my loose ends at once."

"What happens now?"

Cortez lifted an eyebrow. "I have Haralson arrested for drug trafficking and merge back into the woodwork in Washington." He lowered his voice. "I'm not supposed to be working in this area."

"You're government," Kane pointed out.

"I was FBI. At another time I was CIA. But now I'm not so visible, or in quite the same sort of work. A friend of mine died of an overdose earlier in the year," he added surprisingly. "Haralson was involved. I had a score to settle, and the timing was right."

"If you're no longer in law enforcement, what sort of work do you do?" Kane asked, curious.

Cortez chuckled, but he didn't answer the question. He held out his hand. "Good luck with the media. I hope they give you the same coverage now that they gave you when you were supposed to be a bad guy."

"Are you kidding?" Kane asked cynically. "They'll apologize on the classified page. But my family will attack them on the front page." He grinned wistfully. "There are times, mind you, when I don't mind having a father who publishes a tabloid."

"I can understand why."

"Who are you?" Kane asked with an amused smile.

"Can you keep a secret?"

"Sure."

Cortez reached in his pocket and handed him a small battery. "I'm the Energizer Bunny." He grinned and walked out, leaving Kane no wiser than before.

Derrie was sitting in the outer office of Sam Hewett's headquarters when Nikki walked in the door.

"A spy, a spy!" Derrie exclaimed dramatically, pointing a finger at the newcomer.

"Oh, shut up," Nikki said pleasantly. "As one campaign manager to another, let bygones be bygones. The voters will pick the best man."

"Thank you," Sam Hewett said with a grin as he joined Derrie and Nikki, with the other campaign workers chuckling before they went eagerly back to work.

"You haven't won yet, Mr. Hewett," Nikki said, smiling as she shook hands with him. "But you're a nice man to fight. You're a clean hitter. No low blows."

"I wish I could say the same for your brother," Sam replied quietly. "But I haven't forgotten the way he attacked Norman's brother Kane."

"I can tell you truthfully that you've seen the

last of the sneak attacks,'' she said, noticing that Curt Morgan was paying a lot of covert attention to the conversation.

''I do hope so.''

''Can you spare Derrie for lunch?'' Nikki asked. ''I really need to talk to her.''

''Certainly. Go ahead.''

''Thanks.''

The two women left. Curt was frowning, but he made no attempt to follow them.

''Curt is up to something,'' Nikki said.

''Oh, I know that,'' Derrie replied. ''He's Senator Torrance's man. But he isn't spying on us to hurt Clay. In fact,'' she added with a grin, ''I'm pretty sure that he's found a way to help.''

''I know he has. Mosby came to see me. He left me some documents for Clay.''

Derrie stopped walking. ''Did you give them to Clay?''

''Yes, about ten minutes ago. He looked at them and gave a whoop and took off out the door.''

''Good for him. I hope he nails Haralson to the wall.''

''What's going on?'' Nikki asked pointedly.

''I'm not quite sure,'' Derrie said, ''except that Mr. Haralson has made a lot of people very angry. Fred Lombard went racing out of here early this morning, grinning from ear to ear. Whatever it is, I think most people know except us.''

"Mushrooms. We're mushrooms."

"Why?" Derrie asked curiously.

"Because they keep us in the dark and feed us...."

"...don't say it!"

Nikki chuckled. She linked her arm through Derrie's. "Let's have lunch. Then I want to ask you to supper tomorrow night."

"I won't come and eat with Clayton and Bett," Derrie said firmly.

"My dear, Bett is on her way to becoming yesterday's news."

"I don't understand."

"You will, sooner than you think. How about Chez Louie?"

"That's fine," Derrie said. She stared at Nikki, but the other woman wasn't saying another word.

Bett glared at Clayton from across the desk. "What do you mean, I'm fired?"

"Just what I said," he told her. "I fired Haralson. Now I'm firing you."

She smiled coolly. "You can't fire me, dear man. What Haralson knows, I know. If you try to remove me, I'll tell everybody about Nikki and Kane. I'll tell everybody about Mosby, too."

Clayton moved around the desk and sat down, propping his legs across it. "Do go ahead," he invited. "I'm sure it will make great reading."

"Well, I will," she said, shaken. "I mean, it will damage you. It will certainly damage Nikki. And it will probably destroy Mosby's entire career. He might even commit suicide."

He shook his head. "Mosby's far too fastidious. He wouldn't want to get blood over a suit he paid several hundred dollars for."

"Several thousand," she stated.

"I never said he was cheap."

She hesitated. She wasn't used to having anyone call her bluff. "Clay, you're overwrought. Let's go out to eat and just relax for a while."

"I don't need to relax. And Derrie's coming over for supper. It will be just like old times."

"You promised to marry me," Bett said coldly.

"Did I? When?"

"In bed!"

"No. You said you were going to marry me," he corrected. "I didn't agree that I would."

"You'll be sorry if you go through with this," she said very quietly.

"I'll be sorrier if I don't." He picked up the telephone. "Don't let me keep you, Bett. I'm sure some of the groups you lobby for would love to discuss strategy with you."

Her hands clenched by her sides. "I had to force myself to sleep with you," she said with a cold smile. "I hated every minute of it!"

He smiled. "Yes, I know. I'm sorry you had to sacrifice yourself in such a distasteful way."

She turned, picked up her purse and jacket and walked out without looking back. Clayton watched her, but only for a minute. His mind was on Nikki.

The telephone rang over and over, but there was no answer at the house. He hung up, and his face was troubled. That photograph he'd given Kane was going to be in print and on the stands by early afternoon. He didn't want Nikki to see it before he'd warned her what was coming. The shock might harm her or the child.

The child. He smiled. It was early; probably too early to tell if Kane was right and she really was pregnant. But he thought what a wonderful mother Nikki would make. If she loved Lombard, he supposed he could force himself to be civil to the man. He wouldn't admit for all the world that he saw something in Kane Lombard to admire.

As for Bett, that was a lucky escape. No doubt she'd go running to Haralson and that set of photos he had would be offered to the highest bidder. But timing was everything, and with any luck, Lombard's tabloid would hit the stands this afternoon with enough impact to knock Haralson's eyes out. Clayton hoped with all his heart that he'd done the right thing.

Chapter Eighteen

The front page of the Lombard tabloid was shocking. It showed two people making feverish love against a tree; but only from the waist up. The headline above it was even more shocking. It read, "Romeo And Juliet For The Modern Age; Adversaries Become Lovers."

The young woman staring at it on the shelf had gone a pasty shade of white. Her companion was tugging at her arm, even as one of the women in line belatedly recognized the face on the cover and equated it with the white face leaving the drugstore.

"He printed it!" Nikki gasped. "Haralson printed it, did you see? Oh, my God...!"

"Nikki, that was the Lombard tabloid," Derrie

pointed out uneasily, helping her friend into the car.

"I hate him," Nikki whispered, sobbing with rage. "I hate him! How could he do that to me, to Clay?"

"Calm down, now," Derrie coaxed. "You'll make yourself sick. I'm going to drive you home, Nikki. It will be all right. You have to stop crying."

"I can't. I want you to drive me to Lombard International. I will not go home in tears. I'm going to break his jaw for him!"

"No, you aren't." Derrie kept driving toward the Battery, ignoring Nikki's outbursts that lasted all the way there.

"Thank God, Clay's home," Derrie mused as she pulled into the driveway.

Clayton came out onto the porch and she motioned furiously for him to come. He ran to help Nikki into the house.

"I'll make some coffee," Derrie said, leaving Clay to watch his sister.

"The animal. The swine. The filthy pig!" Nikki choked. "I'll break his neck. Have you seen it? His family tabloid, and they printed that...that disgusting photograph! They're in league with Haralson, I knew they were...!"

"Calm down," Clay said, holding her wet face against his chest. "Calm down, now, and listen to me. I tried to fire Haralson and he showed me the photos, Nikki."

"Wh...what?"

"That's right. He tried to blackmail me." He grinned. "Nobody blackmails me. I took them to Kane Lombard."

She stared at him, heartbroken. Her own brother had sold out to his worst enemy.

"We compared notes about Haralson," he told her. "And then I made the comment that I'd like to skewer his liver for what he did to you. That's when he explained things to me. It seems that you're marrying him very soon because you're pregnant."

There was a crash as Derrie dropped two cups of coffee on the spotless lacquered wood floor.

"I hope you enjoy mopping," Clayton told her calmly. "And I'd like mine in a cup, please."

"You know what you can do with the cup," she replied, smiling nicely as she turned to go back into the kitchen.

"I'd like to hear you repeat that flat on your back on the kitchen table!" he shouted.

"Clayton!" Nikki gasped.

He grinned at her. "Don't worry. We're not going to fight. Two things, Nikki. Are you pregnant, and are you going to marry Kane Lombard?"

"I am not pregnant," she said violently.

"You're losing your breakfast."

"I hate breakfast!"

"He loves you, he says," he added.

Her face softened magically. "He does?" The softening went into eclipse. "That's a lie! He does not, or how could he have let his venomous relatives print that ghastly photograph of us and distribute it all over Charleston? Oh, Clayton, people stared at me as if I were some hussy!" she wept.

"We know you're not a hussy. But if you're pregnant, I don't really think Kane is going to let you remain single for long. He seems pretty intent on dynasty building."

"He lost his son."

"I know. He told me. But that isn't why he wants to marry you, if the way he looks when he talks about you is anything to go on."

"I don't want you to think I was meeting him behind your back deliberately," she began.

"I know that."

"I only wanted to tell him about the waste dump," she continued. "I know he didn't do it. He isn't that kind of man. But Haralson is, and he hates the Lombards."

"So I found out. Derrie and I put our heads together. She has a friend who found out a few things I missed. Now Lombard has the whole picture, and Derrie's friend went to see Kane with enough evidence to get his neck out of the noose.

Added to what Mosby sent me, it's more than enough to send Haralson to prison.''

''What was in that envelope that Mosby gave me for you?'' she asked.

''You're better off not knowing.'' He searched her green eyes. ''You aren't carrying a torch for Mosby?''

She smiled. ''I think I'm carrying one for Kane.'' She touched her stomach with a wry grimace. ''Although how he can know before I do...''

''Maybe it's like that when you love someone,'' Clayton said quietly. ''I don't know.''

''Maybe you will someday,'' she replied.

He leaned over and kissed her cheek. ''Ready to go and buy a trousseau? Kane Lombard doesn't strike me as a waiting sort of man.''

''I haven't said I'll marry him,'' she pointed out.

''And you'd better put the announcement in the paper pretty soon,'' Clayton added, ignoring her protests. ''After what came out in that tabloid today, there'll be a scandal if you don't.''

''Say, did you see the afternoon paper?'' Derrie asked, scanning it as she came in with a tray of cups and saucers and a pot of coffee. ''There's an announcement of Nikki's engagement to Kane Lombard.''

''He didn't! He wouldn't!'' Nikki burst out.

Derrie chuckled. ''He did.''

Nikki glowered at both of them. "Well, I won't marry him."

They both looked at her stomach. She put her hands over it protectively. "I won't," she repeated.

"Have some coffee," Derrie invited, handing a cup of it to Clayton.

"Don't mind if I do."

"I'd like some, too," Nikki began.

Derrie handed her a glass of milk, smiling.

"I hate milk!"

"It makes babies big and strong," Derrie coaxed.

"How did you...?"

"Eavesdropping," Derrie nodded. "I learned from him." She pointed toward Clayton. "He was always standing outside conference room doors with his ear to them."

"I was not." He glowered at her.

"How do you think he knew how to vote while he was in the state legislature?"

"I read the issues and made up my own mind," he reminded her.

"After I explained them to you." She polished her nails on her skirt and looked at them. "God knows how many mistakes you'd have made without me."

He started to speak, stopped, and shrugged carelessly. "Well, I'm not making any new ones. Why don't you come back and run my campaign for me?''

''Because I'm running it,'' Nikki replied.

''You're pregnant.''

''So?''

''Sam would never forgive me if I left him now,'' Derrie told him. ''But we can be friends. Until after the election.''

He lifted one eyebrow and smiled slowly. ''Just friends?''

She laughed softly. ''Well, anything's possible,'' she said demurely.

The phone rang and Nikki reached beside her to answer it. It was a well-wisher. She hung up. It rang again. Within ten minutes, it seemed that everyone in Charleston and North Charleston had recognized her in one paper or the other and wanted to comment on the Romeo and Juliet story. Nikki was fuming by the end of the day, and not at all in the sort of mood to answer the phone one last time and find a smug Kane Lombard on the other end of it.

''You!'' she exclaimed. ''Listen here, you snake in the grass…!''

''What time tomorrow do you want to be married?'' he asked. ''One o'clock would suit me very well, but if that isn't convenient, we can try another time.''

"How about another century? I am not marrying you!"

There was a pause. "My father would love that."

"Excuse me?"

"He's got the next headline set in type already. Want to hear it?" He began to read, "Mother Of Romeo And Juliet Baby Refuses To Marry Heart-broken Father Of Child."

"Oh, my God!"

"Yes, sad, isn't it? I expect people will call and write and accost you on the street, you heartless Jezebel."

"Kane, how could you?"

"Well, you did help, after all," he reminded her. "In fact, you remarked that it felt very good." He paused. "I wonder how that would look in print?"

"You blackmailer!"

"I did the only thing I could, you know," he relented, his voice soft and quiet. "He would have published the photographs."

"I suppose he would have."

"As it is, I've cut the ground from under him. He now has photos that have no intrinsic value to shock or humiliate. And you and I have some unfinished business."

"This isn't the way it should happen," she pointed out.

''Probably not,'' he agreed quietly. ''All right. We'll do it the right way. By the book, my dear.''

''By the what? Kane? Kane!''

But the line was dead. She glared at the receiver. ''You're a horrible man and I will not marry you!''

''Oh, I'll bet you will,'' Clayton said. He held out a glass. ''Drink your milk.''

John Haralson had finished his third glass of scotch whiskey. He heard his motel room door open but it didn't really register until he saw Cortez and a uniformed man standing in front of him.

''Cortez!'' he greeted. ''Have a drink!''

''No, thanks. You'll need to come with us.''

He blinked. ''Why?'' he asked with a pleasant smile.

''It's a pretty long list.'' Cortez read the warrant. ''Violation of the controlled substances act, possession with intent to distribute, attempted extortion, bribery...you can read the rest for yourself.''

Haralson frowned and moved a little unsteadily to his feet. ''You're arresting me?''

''No. He is. You're being arrested right now for violation of South Carolina state law. You'll be arraigned on federal charges a bit later.''

''You're on vacation.''

Cortez smiled coldly. ''I haven't been on vacation since I engineered the first meeting with you at FBI headquarters where you were trying to dig information out of one of your cohorts,'' came the quiet reply. ''And by the way, you'd better have this back.'' He handed the startled man the two-dollar-and-fifty-cent gold piece.

''You bought it.''

''Not really. I don't collect coins. But it was helpful to let you think I was obsessed with that particular one, after I saw you buy it.''

''Of all the underhanded things!'' Haralson roared.

''You wrote the book on that.'' Cortez slid his sunglasses back on. ''He's all yours,'' he told the police officer. ''Take good care of him for us. We'll be in touch.''

Haralson yelled after him. ''You don't have any jurisdiction down here or in this case! You work for the FBI!''

Cortez lifted an eyebrow. ''Do I?'' he asked with amusement, and kept walking.

The same evening, the front door at the Seymour home opened to admit a gift-laden Kane Lombard. He walked past Clayton into the living room, where he dumped his burdens on the sofa next to a startled Nikki.

''Roses,'' he said, pointing to three large bouquets, one of each color, ''chocolates, CDs of romantic music, two books of poetry, and perfume. Chanel, of course,'' he added with a grin.

Nikki gaped at him. "What is all this?" she asked dully.

"The accoutrements of courtship," he explained. He sat down beside her, ignoring Clayton. "The ring is in my pocket, somewhere. It's only an engagement ring, of course. You have to come with me to pick out the wedding band."

"But I haven't said I'll marry you..." she stammered.

"Of course you'll marry me," he said, extricating the ring in its velvet box from his jacket pocket.

"I hate diamonds," she began contrarily as he opened the box.

"So do I," he agreed. "That's why I bought you an emerald."

He had, too. It was faceted like a diamond, with incredible clarity and beauty. Nikki stared at it, entranced. She knew that a flawless emerald commanded the same price as a quality diamond; in fact, some were even more expensive. And this stone had to be two carats.

She looked up, her eyes full of delighted surprise.

He smiled at her. "Never expect the obvious from me, Nikki," he said gently. "I'm not conventional."

She studied his broad, leonine face, reading the sorrows and joys of a lifetime there. Her hand lifted to touch it, to trace its hard contours. She did love him so.

"Marry me, Nikki," he said softly.

"All right."

He smiled, holding her hand to his cheek. "My father will cry, you know," he said.

"He can always find another headline." She nuzzled her face into his chest. "Perhaps Haralson's arrest will make a good one."

"Oh, no," he told her, glancing at Clayton, who was just coming into the room with a tray of coffee and milk. "Haralson's going to be top secret until the Justice Department is through with him. I understand that their chief prosecutor is taking a special interest in the case."

"He could plead insanity and get out of it," Clayton remarked as he set out cups of steaming coffee for Kane and himself and a cold glass of milk for Nikki.

"I told you, I hate milk," she muttered at her brother.

"And I told you, it's good for the baby," he replied with a knowing look.

Kane didn't even look embarrassed. He was beaming.

"You needn't look so smug, either of you," she told them, sitting up to drink her milk. "I haven't had any tests. It's too early to tell, anyway."

Clayton leaned forward. "Nikki, how about some scrambled eggs?"

She paled and began to swallow noticeably.

"She loves them," Clayton told Kane. "But just lately, the mention of them makes her sick. Interesting, isn't it?"

"It was potatoes when my mother was carrying my youngest brother," Kane told Clayton. "She couldn't eat them until he was born."

"How many of you are there?" Clayton asked curiously.

"Four. Three boys and one girl. Our sister is married and lives in France. My mother is dead now, but my father already thinks there's nobody like Nikki. He knows the Blairs, too," he added, chuckling. "Claude has been singing your praises to my father ever since he realized that we knew each other." He hesitated. "He's also arranging a wedding present."

"A cat," Nikki said without pause.

"How did you guess?" he chuckled.

"She's missed Puff," Clayton remarked. "It will be nice for her to have another cat." He studied Kane. "You knew that Haralson had been arrested. How?"

"Haralson's so-called friend Cortez came to see me," he replied. "That gentleman would make one bad enemy, so I'm glad he's on my side."

"Mosby thought he was helping me by sending

Haralson down here,'' Clayton said heavily. ''Neither of us knew that he was playing right into Haralson's hands. And none of us had any inkling that the Justice Department was already watching Haralson for another reason entirely.''

''Who is Cortez?'' Nikki asked curiously.

They both looked at her. ''FBI,'' Clayton said. At the same time, Kane said, ''DEA.'' They both stared at each other.

''Which?'' she persisted.

They laughed sheepishly. ''It seems that he has some uncoordinated credentials. Perhaps he's a stray KGB agent looking for work,'' Clayton replied.

Kane put down his cup. ''Whoever he is, he's saved my neck. I'll have to pay a fine to help with the cleanup, but they found toxic waste from a number of other companies in that dump. Burke is in trouble up to his neck and faces a jail sentence, along with my errant employee.''

''I won't be getting any more mileage out of your situation, either,'' Clayton promised the older man. ''However,'' he added meaningfully, ''if you were still polluting, and doing it deliberately, the fact that you're going to be my brother-in-law wouldn't help you.''

Kane chuckled. ''I'm glad to hear it. Integrity is a rare asset these days. Nice to know it runs in the family.''

Clayton nodded, acknowledging the compliment, and sipped his coffee.

The small café in downtown Charleston was busy. Phoebe didn't really understand why she'd bothered to go back there every day, sitting and waiting for someone who was surely already back at his job in Washington, D.C., and out of the state. It must be some mental aberration resulting from too much time spent digging up old pieces of pottery, she told herself.

She was halfway through her second cup of coffee and it was time to leave. She had shopping to do. She started to get up, just as a tall man in sunglasses came in the door.

His hair was loose, hanging down his back in clean black strands. He was wearing jeans and boots and a denim shirt with pearl snaps. A couple of people gave him a frankly curious stare. He ignored them, making a beeline for Phoebe. He took off the sunglasses and hooked the earpiece into the pocket of his denim shirt. He held out his hand.

She took it, ignoring the covert looks of other customers, and let him lead her out the door.

He put her into the rental car without a word, climbed in beside her, hooked his sunglasses back on his nose and drove off.

Neither of them spoke. He drove to the coast and parked on a dirt road overlooking the ocean, in a spot lined with live oaks. He got out and so did she. They walked down to the deserted beach.

The wind blew his hair as he looked out over the ocean, and her blue eyes studied the bronzed smoothness of his face, its straight-nosed, high-cheekboned profile adding to the subtle mystery of him.

"You're leaving," she said perceptibly.

He nodded. "I have a backlog of work waiting. Two new cases will be coming up pretty soon, too, from here—a discrimination suit and a drug trafficking charge."

"You'll have to testify, you mean," she said.

He took off the sunglasses and turned. His dark eyes slid over her face quietly. "To try the cases," he said. "I'm a federal prosecutor—an attorney for the U.S. Department of Justice."

She was impressed, and it showed. "You said you were FBI."

"Oh, I was," he agreed readily. "And I worked for the Drug Enforcement Administration and the CIA just briefly, too. But law was always my first love. It still is." He smiled slowly. "I was a fairly decent lawman. But I'm a hell of a prosecutor."

She didn't doubt it for a minute. He had the look of a man who could intimidate anyone on a witness stand.

"You must like your work."

"For now," he agreed. "I was offered a job as

a defense attorney for a Native American rights group. I almost took it, too. Maybe someday. The best way to fight for any group is in the courts, Phoebe. Fighting in the streets only gets you arrested.''

''I suppose so.'' She searched his dark face. ''I'm sorry I didn't get to know you,'' she said. ''You're not like anyone I've ever met—and not just because you're Comanche.''

He smiled sadly. ''The years are wrong,'' he said gently. ''You're barely twenty-two. I'll be thirty-six my next birthday. I grew up in rural Oklahoma in a town populated by Comanche people. I practice my native religion, I live according to my cultural heritage. If you've ever heard of cultural pluralism—and being an anthropology student, you should have—I'm a prime example of it.''

''I know what it is—living in the mainstream while clinging to one's own ethnic identity.''

He nodded. His lean hand touched her soft face and his thumb drew very lightly over her mouth. ''But I'd like to keep in touch with you, just the same,'' he said. ''I don't have so many friends that I can turn down the chance of adding one to my life.''

She smiled back. ''You can come to my graduation in the spring.''

''Send me an invitation.''

She pursed her lips. ‘‘Don’t come in a loincloth carrying a rattle and a feather,’’ she murmured with a feeble attempt at humor.

He didn’t take offense. He smiled quizzically. ‘‘Medicine men carry feathers and rattles. Why would you connect them with me, I wonder, instead of a bow and arrow?’’

Her pale brows drew together briefly. ‘‘Why...I don’t know,’’ she said with a self-conscious laugh.

‘‘My people have been medicine men for five generations,’’ he said surprisingly. ‘‘The old people still go to my father for charms and cures.’’

Her face brightened. ‘‘But, you never mentioned that.’’

‘‘I know.’’ He smiled. ‘‘Uncanny, isn’t it?’’

She nodded. Her eyes slid over his long hair with curiosity and pleasure. He had wonderful hair, thick and silky and long. She wanted to bury her hands in it.

‘‘Go ahead,’’ he said with a long-suffering sigh. She looked puzzled. He shrugged, answering the question she didn’t ask. ‘‘You aren’t going to rest until you know how it feels, so go ahead. I’ll pretend not to notice.’’

Her eyebrows lifted. ‘‘What?’’

‘‘You can’t stand it, can you?’’ He caught her hands and lifted them to his hair. The action brought her very close. She felt weak-kneed at the proximity, and tried to disguise the uneasy breathing that he was sure to notice.

His hair was as silky as it looked, cool and thick and very sexy. She was fascinated with it.

He endured her exploring hands with stoic pleasure, enjoying the expressions that passed over her face as she looked at him close-up.

"I feel like a museum exhibit," he remarked.

She looked up into his eyes, thrilling at the expression in them. "Why?"

"I can see the wheels turning in your mind," he replied. "You're equating my bone structure with what you know of Mongolian physiology and you're dying for a look at my dentition to see those shovel-shaped incisors."

"Actually," she corrected, searching his eyes, "I was thinking how sexy your hair is to touch."

"You shouldn't think of me in those terms," he said, his voice deep and very slow.

"Because you're Comanche and I'm white?" she queried breathlessly.

He nodded. "And because I'm more than a decade older than you."

"You said that we could be friends," she reminded him.

"We can. But you can't notice that I'm sexy."

"Oh. All right."

Her hands went to his face, to trace its elegant lines. His eyes closed, so that she could touch the ridge where his thick eyebrows lay, and the long, thick lashes of his closed eyelids.

His nose was broad and straight, and below it, he had a wide, chiseled, very sexy mouth. His teeth were white and straight. She'd read somewhere that Native Americans had very few cavities compared to white people.

While she was exploring him, his body was reacting to the closeness of hers. He moved back a few inches and his eyes opened. His lips were parted, and his breath came too quickly through them.

His lean hands caught her waist and lingered there, without pulling or pushing, while they looked at each other.

"You smell of spring flowers," he said.

"And you of wind and fir and open land."

His dark eyes wandered slowly over her face, capturing expressions, texture of skin, eye color, hair texture. "Take your hair down."

She only hesitated for a minute. "Why?" she asked as her hands went to the bun. "Do you want to compare length?"

"Perhaps."

She took the pins out and shook her head, letting waves of platinum blond hair fall around her shoulders. His hands lifted to it, testing its baby softness, its fine silky texture.

"It isn't quite as long as mine," he remarked.

"Or as thick," she added. Shyly, her hands slid back up and into the cool strands of his own hair, clutching handfuls of it as she moved imperceptibly closer. Dimly aware that she was being provocative, but unable to stop herself, she tilted her face up to his.

His eyes fell to her parted lips and lingered there while he touched and lifted the silky strands of her hair and fought to maintain his reason.

"The only thing I ever really liked about white culture," he said huskily, and his head dipped closer, "is the way you kiss each other."

Her lips parted in breathless anticipation, and she felt his hand contract in her hair. "Careful," she whispered unsteadily. "I may be addictive."

"So may I."

His hand tilted her face at a closer angle and his mouth brushed in tender, brief strokes across her lips. The touch was arousing, especially when it was complicated by the gentle nip of his teeth on her lower lip and the nuzzling contact of his face with hers.

Her nails bit into his upper arm as he tormented her mouth. "That isn't fair," she managed shakily. "You didn't say...you were going to do that."

"Now you know." He nudged her lips a little roughly. "Open your mouth for me," he whispered. "And I'll show you how hot a kiss can get."

She felt the sun on her face through the trees as she complied, felt his arms suddenly swallow her up and lift her against the length of his powerful body. Then she felt his mouth grinding down into hers, his tongue penetrating the soft darkness behind her lips. She heard a high-pitched gasp echoing in the madness of the passion he was kindling, and realized with wonder that it had been torn from her own throat.

The slamming of a car door barely registered. Cortez heard it, though, and pulled his head up. He didn't look at Phoebe's face, because he knew the temptation it was going to represent. She was trembling in his arms. He let go of her, steadying her, just as a family of tourists descended on the beach.

"Don't you kids go too close to that water!" the man yelled. "You'll get sucked under!"

"That's right, you wait for us!" the woman called.

The normality of it brought a faint smile to Cortez's face. He did look at Phoebe then and he grimaced. She looked devastated.

"I knew it was a bad idea," he said.

She felt shaky inside. She touched her tongue to her swollen lips and tasted him on them. "So did I."

He caught her hand in his and led her back to

the car. He hesitated as he started to open the passenger door for her.

"Look at me."

She lifted her eyes to the storms in his.

He searched them intently, with an unblinking scrutiny that made the shaky feeling much worse. She could barely breathe at all, and it showed. He wanted nothing more in the world at that moment than to invite her back to his motel room and spend the rest of the day making unbridled love to her. But it would mean nothing. It would lead to nothing.

"I'll drive you home," he said, turning away to open the door.

"I would…go with you, if you asked me," she said tautly, not looking at him.

"Yes, I know. And I want to ask you to," he returned honestly. "But we've already agreed that addictions are unwise and that this is a relationship without a future. We kissed and it was very good," he added, looking down at her with a wistful smile. "Leave it at that."

Her soft eyes held his. "I'll bet you're the Fourth of July in bed," she said.

"Christmas and New Year's Eve, too," he returned with a smile. "Eat your heart out."

"I probably will," she sighed. "It would have been the high point of my life."

"The world is full of men," he said cynically. "Most of them make love well enough."

"I wouldn't know."

His eyes cut back to hers and searched them. They narrowed with intense feeling.

"I was waiting for someone explosive and mysterious," she explained. She smiled demurely. "If you come to my graduation, who knows what might happen?"

He didn't smile. He wasn't sure he was still breathing. "The years are wrong. You need someone your own age."

She lifted an eyebrow. "If you really thought that, you'd never have kissed me at all."

His jaw clenched. Damn women with logical minds, he thought. He opened the door for her without another word and drove her back to the café where she'd left her vehicle.

"I don't know that I'll be able to get down for your graduation," he said stiffly when he was ready to leave.

She looked in the driver's window at his expressionless face, and knew without words that he was finding it difficult to say goodbye. So was she.

She smiled at him, her blue eyes twinkling. "You'll hate yourself for the rest of your life if you miss it," she told him. "I promise you will."

He grimaced and glowered at her. She couldn't see his eyes through the dark glasses. "Maybe."

She stood up, away from the car. ''Drive carefully. I have proprietorial rights now.''

''Because of one kiss? Dream on!'' he said curtly.

''Cultural appropriation,'' she told him. ''Primary group assimilation. I'm gong to assimilate you.'' She licked her lips slowly. ''Just thinking about it should keep you sleepless for the next seven months.''

He was going to break out in a cold sweat if he didn't leave. He put the car in gear. ''Hold your breath,'' he invited, and pressed down on the accelerator.

Phoebe chuckled softly to herself, watching him run for it. He'd be back, all right. She smiled all the way home.

Chapter Nineteen

Nikki was knee-deep in invitations for her wedding to Kane, with the phone at her ear while she addressed envelopes, trying to get a stubborn government agency to give her permission to hold a political rally in their building.

"I have certain inalienable rights," she quoted, frowning as she crossed a "t" on an address. "One of them is the right to public assembly at a place of my choosing. You only own the building, not the street in front of it. Is that so?" She chuckled. "All right, have us arrested. That should make a very tidy headline for the morning editions. You wouldn't like that? I didn't think you would. Yes, I thought you might see things my way. I'll look forward to meeting you. Thanks. Goodbye."

She hung up, her mind more on the addresses than her *savoir faire* at manipulation.

Kane, watching her, was laughing to himself. She had a keen brain and she exercised a form of diplomacy that might have come out of his own book. He adored her.

She felt eyes on her downbent head and lifted her own to meet Kane's. She beamed.

"I'm on the last one hundred invitations," she said. "I wish we could coordinate the wedding to coincide with the election, though," she pondered. "It would give us such an advantage at the polls..."

"Your candidate, not mine," he chided.

"Your future brother-in-law," she corrected pertly.

He bent over her, his eyes acquisitive and warm. "Did I mention that I loved you this morning?"

"Only five times," she replied. "A few more never hurts."

"Say it back."

"I do, every time I look at you. Kiss me, you mad fool!" She draped her arms around his neck and jerked him down onto the sofa with her in a tangle of arms and legs.

While he was trying to keep them from tumbling onto the coffee table and into her cup of cooling coffee, a throat was loudly cleared at the doorway.

They looked up. Clayton glowered at them.

"Can't you stop that?" he muttered. "For God's sake, we haven't even had breakfast yet!"

They looked at each other. "Are you sure he's your brother?" Kane asked.

"He must be adopted," she murmured, smiling against his lips. "Otherwise he wouldn't be such a wet blanket after all I've done for his campaign. Something must have upset him."

Clayton took that as an invitation. He moved right to the huge coffee table, moved the coffee cup and invitations aside, and linked his hands on his knees, ignoring the fact that he was interrupting a very private conversation.

"Derrie's on that soapbox about the owl again," he began with a long sigh. "Now, listen, Nikki, we've got to get this owl off my back. I know we can't...Nikki, will you stop nibbling on your fiancé long enough to pay attention to what I'm saying. This is important!"

Nikki sighed. She arranged Kane into a sitting position, curled herself into his lap, and gave her brother her undivided attention in a bit of physical diplomacy that left both men speechless.

Kane lifted an eyebrow at her. "It will be a pity if he loses the election," he said, nodding toward Clayton. "You're a natural at politics!"

"I'm going to be a natural at motherhood, too," Nikki pointed out, smoothing a loving hand over her belly. "Besides, I'm going above and beyond the call of duty on my brother's behalf, already."

"You mean with the campaign?" Clayton asked.

"I mean that I'm producing a new voter for you. The thing is I'm not going to be a lot of help to you after I finish this latest bit of organization. You see," she added with a loving glance at Kane, "I had to go to the doctor this morning for a checkup and he listened to the baby's heartbeat."

"Are you all right?" Kane asked at once. "You didn't tell me you were going to the doctor!"

"I was saving it for a surprise. I'm all right!" she said, exasperated by the terrified looks in two pair of eyes. "It's just that things are a little more complicated than we thought."

"Complicated, how?" Kane asked tautly.

She curled up in his arms with a loving sigh. "The doctor heard two heartbeats."

"Two…" Kane began.

"…heartbeats!" Clayton finished.

The men exchanged complicated looks and Kane's was positively arrogant.

"Twins!" Kane burst out, beaming down at her as he wrapped her up closer in his arms.

Nikki chuckled. "Yes. How's that for family loyalty, brother mine?" she added, smiling at her brother across Kane's broad chest. "I'm not just producing one brand-new voter for you—I'm producing two!"